Beach
Mysteries

Rehoboth Beach Reads

Short Stories by Local Writers

D1239925

Edited by Nancy Sakaduski

A Playful Publisher

Cat & Mouse Press
Lewes, DE 19958
www.catandmousepress.com

© 2020 Cat & Mouse Press, Lewes, DE, 19958

All rights reserved. Published 2020.

ISBN: 978-1-7323842-7-9

Cover illustration/book design by Emory Au. © 2020 Emory Au.

PERMISSIONS

REPRINTED WITH PERMISSION:

"A Killer White Paint," Rich Barnett. © 2020 Rich Barnett.

"A Stitch in Time," Chris Jacobsen. © 2020 Christiana D. Jacobsen.

"A Whole New World," Jennifer Walker. © 2020 Jennifer Walker.

"Baba's Flying," Paul Geiger. © 2020 Paul Marion Geiger.

"Bus to the Beach," Kathaleen and Terrence McCormick. © 2020 Kathaleen L. McCormick and Terrence J. McCormick.

"Catching Up," Susan Towers. © 2020 Susan Louise Towers.

"Circles," Tara A. Elliott. © 2020 Tara A. Elliott.

"Clubhouse Showers and Sleepless Hours," Doretta Warnock. © 2020 Doretta Warnock.

"Hiawatha's Smile," Doug Harrell. © 2020 Douglas Gaines Harrell.

"Incident at Canary Creek," Justin Stoeckel. © 2020 Lyle Justin Stoeckel.

"Murder at The Sea Wall," Pat Valdata. © 2020 Patricia Valdata.

"Mystery at the Lilac of the Sea," Caren Pauling. © 2020 Caren Pauling.

"Not Your Ordinary Thanksgiving," Sarah Barnett. © 2020 Sarah Barnett.

"Teething Toddlers Tell No Tales," Rachael Tipperman. © 2020 Rachael Tipperman.

"Thaddeus Zoon—Mayhem on the Ferry," Teresa Berry. © 2020 Teresa V. Berry.

"Thalassotherapy," Carolyn Eichhorn. © 2020 Carolyn Eichhorn.

"The Dripping Man," Will Eichler. © 2020 William Eichler.

"The Ship to the Grey Havens," Linda Chambers. © 2020 Linda Huntly Chambers.

"The Sound of Lightning," Kim Biasotto. © 2020 Kim Biasotto.

"Tiny Solves the Case," James Gallahan. © 2020 James Kenneth Gallahan.

"Treasured Time," Michele Connelly. © 2020 Michele A. Connelly.

"What Lies Within Us," Sarah Beth Harris. © 2020 Sarah Beth Harris.

Table of Contents

PREFACE

These are the winning stories from the 2020 Rehoboth Beach Reads Short Story Contest, sponsored by Browseabout Books. Writers were asked to create a story—fiction or nonfiction—that fit the theme "Beach Mysteries" and had a connection to Rehoboth Beach. A panel of judges chose the stories they thought were best and those selections have been printed here for your enjoyment. Like *The Beach House*, *The Boardwalk*, *Beach Days*, *Beach Nights*, *Beach Life*, *Beach Fun*, and *Beach Dreams* (other books in this series), this book contains more than just "they went down to the beach and had a picnic" stories. The quality and diversity of the stories is simply amazing.

Most of the stories in this book are works of fiction. While some historical or public figures and actual locations have been used to give the reader a richer experience, the characters and situations in these works are fictitious. Any resemblance to real persons, living or dead, is purely coincidental.

For contact information or other Cat & Mouse Press publications, go to: www.catandmousepress.com

Most of the stories in this book are works of fiction. While some historical or public figures and actual locations have been used to give the reader a richer experience, the characters and situations in these works are fictitious. Any resemblance to real persons, living or dead, is purely coincidental.

For contact information or other Cat & Mouse Press publications, go to: www.catandmousepress.com.

ACKNOWLEDGEMENTS

Thanks to Browseabout Books for their continued outstanding support. We are so lucky to have this great store in the heart of our community. They have supported the Rehoboth Beach Reads Short Story Contest from day one and continue to be the go-to place for books, gifts, and other fun stuff.

I thank both the Rehoboth Beach Writers' Guild and the Eastern Shore Writers Association for their support and service to the writing community. These two organizations provide an amazing array of educational programming, and many of the writers whose stories appear in this book benefitted from their classes, meetings, and events.

I thank this year's judges, Tyler Antoine, Dennis Lawson, Rebecca Lowe, Laurel Marshfield, Mary Pauer, and Ron Sauder, who gave generously of their valuable time.

Special thanks to Emory Au, who captured the theme so well in the cover illustration and who designed and laid out the interior of this book as well.

I also thank Cindy Myers, queen of the mermaids, for her continued loyalty and support.

An extra-special thank-you to my husband, Joe, who helps on many levels and puts up with a great deal.

I would also like to thank the writers—those whose work is in this book and those whose work was not chosen. Putting a piece of writing up for judging takes courage. Thank you for being brave. Keep writing and submitting your work!

—*Nancy Sakaduski*

Mystery at
The Lilac of the Sea

By Caren Pauling

The hours between noon and four are like purgatory for us bed and breakfast owners. That crazy time between checkout and check-in, when all the turnaround magic happens. I'm pretty sure my blood pressure is always elevated at crunch time, especially before a busy weekend.

I was plugging in the vacuum in the Anna Hazzard room—all our bedrooms are named after early settlers to Rehoboth Beach—when I heard the *ding* of Mrs. Tomlinson's text.

"Turnpike is a mess but we're still aiming for four o'clock."

"Great. See ya soon!" I added a quick heart emoji.

The Tomlinsons had been regulars at the inn for years. I'd put a bottle of cabernet in each bedroom as a special touch to honor their daughter Cynthia's wedding weekend. In the morning, we'd do Belgian waffles and mimosas before they headed out to the spa for pre-ceremony pampering.

I'd been running The Lilac of the Sea for three years now, ever since my parents retired to Florida and my brother began working for a Philadelphia law firm, with a family of his own in the suburbs and no interest in the family business.

My folks inherited the 1899 Victorian house from my Dad's Aunt Marie. They were teachers and turned it into a summer bed and breakfast when I was nine years old. I grew up plucking blooms from our Hyde Park roses and arranging them "just so" into crystal vases in each room. "Our Julia—floral arranger to the stars," my Mom would gush. My brother and I were used to emptying trash and refilling salt and pepper shakers, among other chores. And when our parents needed to greet new guests, we spent afternoons boogie boarding, filling up on Dolle's saltwater taffy and playing arcade games until dinner. We never ventured out of the house without loose change weighing us down. Summers in Rehoboth were the best, and we were the envy of our friends back home in Bucks County, Pennsylvania, where school break meant lawn mowing and maybe a swim at the town pool.

I figured I'd get a head start on setting the sunroom tables for tomorrow's wedding brunch and had begun arranging place settings when I heard a car door slam. *Shoot! Did I forget to hang the* No Vacancy *sign?* Glancing out the window, I saw a woman I didn't recognize coming up the walk.

I leaned halfway out the door. "Can I help you?"

"Uh, yes. Do you have a minute to chat?"

I'd put the woman in her late seventies. She was dressed in white linen pants and a nautical-print silk blouse.

"Are you looking for accommodation? I'm booked up for the weekend, but the Rehoboth Arms might have vacan—"

"I'm not looking for a room. I, uh, was hoping to speak to the owner."

"Well, that would be me. But I'm a bit pressed for time."

The woman seemed to consider her words carefully. "I'm afraid something's been left here that's very precious to me … but I can see you're busy." She turned to leave.

"Wait! If you tell me what it is, I'll look in our lost and found. Were you a guest with us recently? I'm sorry, but I don't remember you."

She turned to face me, cleared her throat awkwardly, and clutched her pearls. "Well, you see, it's … it's been a great while since I've been here. Years." Her eyes filled with tears. "I just … I need more than a few minutes to explain."

C'mon Julia. You're in the hospitality business, after all. Give her time. "Why don't you come in, and we'll chat."

* * * * *

I led her to the sunroom and gestured for her to sit down, as I furtively glanced at the clock.

She looked around nervously. "So where to even begin … My parents once owned this place."

"What? So you're—"

"I'm Eva Gradwell. My parents were Thomas and Anna Smith."

I'd remembered those names from my parents' ongoing narrative of Lilac of the Sea history. "So, my great aunt Marie bought the inn from them in 1962?"

"Yes, if memory serves me right. That's about when we would have moved to North Carolina. Of course, it wasn't an inn then. It was our family home." She looked around, taking in the many changes.

"What brings you back today? You said you left something?" *You left something decades ago?*

"You see that's where things get a little tricky. I, uh, need to give you a bit of backstory."

I glanced at the clock again and wondered if I appeared as time crunched as I felt.

"My mother, well, she had a bit of a past. As a teenager, she dated a young man named Rory Lynch. They were deeply in love. Rory went off to war in 1942. Shortly after he left, she found out she was … with child."

I did the mental math. "With you?"

"Yes. Back then, you see, this was a big problem. My mother was quite scared. She was eighteen, pregnant, and unmarried."

At this point I could either offer her tea with the inevitability of her staying even longer or remind her that I was busy. "So, you said you left something here? I really hate to rush you, but I'm getting ready for a busy weekend."

"Oh dear. I'm sorry. How about this? I'm staying this week with my son and his family in Bethany. Perhaps I could come back tomorrow?"

Somehow, I felt the weight of what Eva needed to share and understood it couldn't be rushed. "Tomorrow would be good. Is noon OK?"

"Yes. I'd like that very much. Thank you …?"

"Julia. My name's Julia."

"Thank you, Julia. Thank you for your kindness and your time."

* * * * *

I didn't feel kind and hoped I hadn't visibly lacked patience with Eva. I grabbed the sheets out of the dryer and turned the rooms over with new linens, freshened the bedside flowers, and replaced the mini soaps in each of the bathrooms.

As I went from room to room, I found myself looking under beds and behind dressers. Silly, really, as it had been ages since Eva was last here. Whatever it was she was missing, wouldn't we have found it by now?

Throughout the years we had found various things left behind by guests—earrings on side tables, the odd sock here and there. We even found an expensive sapphire ring once. But I couldn't imagine what she was looking for that we might still have.

I guess I'd have to wait until tomorrow to find out.

* * * * *

"So, she left something? What do you think it could be?" Liam asked, as we waited for our second round of Yuenglings.

"I'm honestly stumped. Who leaves something in a house and comes back for it, like, sixty years later?" I tore into a cheesy nacho after scraping the olives off.

"Maybe she wanted an excuse to look around the place. Sometimes older people just want to reminisce." Liam was looking over my head and seemed distracted.

"Hey, what's going on with work? Any news?" I was happy to change the subject.

Liam trailed a finger through the condensation on his beer bottle.

"I'm not sure. Ron was a little hush-hush today. They know I want the manager gig. I don't want to push it and come off desperate." He locked his eyes on the band setting up.

Liam and I had met two years ago, when I was out for girls' night at Dogfish Head. He was an assistant manager, going table to table, greeting guests. I hadn't dated much since moving to Rehoboth to run the inn, and he absolutely caught my eye. As we were settling the check, Liam had slipped me his phone number. The next night, we met for ice cream and walked the boards, swapping stories of our lives. Being in our forties, we skipped the small talk and dug deeper, faster. Liam was established and had his life in order, with no cobwebs from his past. My mother always questioned why he was still single, and I'd responded that it was for the same reason I was single—because we didn't want to settle for the wrong person. And while we bantered constantly that we were too old to settle down, I was confident Liam *was* the right person.

* * * * *

"Oh, Julia, you have outdone yourself." Mrs. Tomlinson came downstairs, carrying an enormous garment bag containing Cynthia's wedding gown, which she hung in the foyer. She admired the buffet covered with trays of Belgian waffles, fresh fruit, and yogurt parfaits, along with glasses of mimosas.

After brunch, the Tomlinsons headed to the Sea Spa for pre-wedding pampering and then on to the beach ceremony, followed by an

Atlantic Sands reception. I cleaned their rooms quickly as I awaited Eva Gradwell's visit and the rest of her story.

* * * * *

"So, where did I leave off?" Eva dipped her tea bag in and out of her mug.

"Your mother had just found out she was expecting you, and her boyfriend was off to war."

"Oh dear. Thank you. As you age, details get a little muddy." She laughed nervously. "Unsurprisingly, my grandparents were upset. Pregnant out of wedlock in 1942. Well, today it's not the biggest deal in the world but back then …"

I could only imagine.

"No one knew how long the war would last. My grandparents kept my mother pretty secluded, especially when she started showing." Eva warmed her hands on her teacup. "My mother gave birth to me on September 25, 1942. She and my father exchanged frequent letters. She sent him my baby picture. While it was unconventional, certainly, he was ecstatic to hear he had a daughter and couldn't wait to come home so they could marry and be a family."

It was a bittersweet story, but I was eager to hear what any of this had to do with me and my inn. *What are you not telling me, Eva?*

"Only, they would never marry. My father was killed in action in 1944."

* * * * *

As Liam and I walked the beach later that evening, I thought about all I'd taken for granted in my forty-three years of life. I hadn't lived through a war or experienced real loss. Eva's story hit me hard. We stopped to gaze at the setting sun, foamy waves teasing our bare feet. Liam stood behind me and wrapped his arms around my shoulders as we looked out to sea together.

Even though she had visited twice, Eva had still not shared the whole story. I had been interrupted by a reservation call right after she recounted her father's death, and then she needed to get back to watch her grandchildren. The story was a puzzle I was eager to piece together.

"I still think she's just lonely and wants your company." Liam brushed my hair behind my ears, and we joined hands as we continued walking.

"I feel like she wants to tell me something big but can't find the words. Honestly, I kind of like her nostalgia. You know me, I'm a hopeless romantic."

We stopped to gaze up at the Atlantic Sands, where Cynthia, her new husband, and their family and friends were probably dancing the night away. I snuck a glance at Liam, who grabbed my hand tighter, leading me toward the boardwalk.

"C'mon. I want funnel cake."

* * * * *

The Tomlinsons were in and out, loading their car to leave while I made the morning coffee.

"I need a vacation from all this wedding stuff." Mr. Tomlinson laughed as he plopped down for breakfast.

"*You* need a vacation?" Mrs. Tomlinson lovingly punched his shoulder. "You, my dear, don't know the meaning of wedding stress until you're the mother of the bride." She looked at me and winked.

"But seriously, Julia, thank you for hosting us," Mr. Tomlinson said. "We couldn't imagine celebrating Cynthia's big day without being in our home away from home. Your folks did right by giving you the keys." Mr. Tomlinson raised his coffee cup to toast me.

"Now, Julia, speaking of weddings, might you have good news any time soon about you and that young man Liam?" Mrs. Tomlinson gave me a sly look and coyly took a sip of coffee.

"Oh, you'll be the first to know." My usual answer for anyone who brought up the marriage question. I headed back to the kitchen to cook their omelets. As I took the egg carton out of the fridge and placed it on the counter, I paused and felt the sting of tears. Maybe I was just tired, but all this wedding talk was draining.

* * * * *

Eva arrived as I was gathering lemonade and cookies to enjoy on the front porch for what I hoped would be some answers.

"Hello, my dear." She gave me a quick hug and took a seat in the wicker rocker.

I set the tray down between us. Although I'd only known Eva for a few days, I felt a kindred spirit with this woman who had lived in my home so long ago.

"I know I've been taking up a lot of your time." Eva looked into my eyes. "I promise I'll … oh what do my grandkids call it? *Get to the point.*" She laughed and took a sip of lemonade.

"So, when my mother heard Rory was dead, she was devastated. My grandparents were worried. She was grieving a very difficult loss. And they were concerned for her reputation and theirs too. They wanted my mother to marry, but they knew no one would marry a woman who was …"

"It was tricky." I saved her from searching for the right word.

"Yes. That's a good way to put it. So, after I was born, my mother went to work as a nurse while my grandmother watched me. She made a good living, and as the years went on, people just assumed my mother was a war widow. She eventually met the man I would call Dad."

"Thomas Smith?" I grabbed a cookie.

"Yes. Thomas became the father any child would dream of having. We'd spend hours, just the two of us, right here on this porch. He'd read to me and we'd play checkers. He was a good man who accepted me as his own. Oh, I loved him so." Eva looked at me through eyes the shade of blue sea glass, dampened with the beginning of tears.

"Oh, Eva, I'm so glad your mother found happiness with Thomas." My heart ached for this woman.

"They had a good long marriage, and he died about a year ago. My mother is quite lost without him." Eva dabbed her eyes with her napkin. "When one is older and loses a spouse, life has a way of … halting. My mother is in her nineties and doesn't feel she has much to live for. Well, until …"

Tell me, Eva. Tell me.

"Last month, my mother received a package. Oh, Julia, you'll never believe this." Eva's sweet face brightened with excitement. "The package was from Rory's sister."

"Wait … what?" I almost spilled my lemonade.

"Yes! You see, after Rory died, his family moved to Illinois to be closer to their relatives, and my mother lost contact with them. Well, Rory's sister sent this package to Mother, along with a note explaining she had received a call from a man in Lewes who discovered an old cigar box at his antique store. Turns out the box was full of letters from my mother to Rory. We'd assumed Rory's belongings were long gone, but it turns out they were sent years later to his address in Delaware after his family had left the state. They weren't able to locate the family, and of course they couldn't find my mother because the letters had her maiden name. Eventually, the letters ended up in a local shop. The store changed hands recently and the new owner became curious about the letters. He was able to track down Rory's sister and somehow Rory's sister was able to find my mother. Oh Julia, the beauty of the internet."

"Wow, that's amazing!"

"My mother just cried. Receiving these letters more than seventy years later healed her broken heart and gave her peace. And … there's something else."

Here we go …

"Julia, you're going to think I'm crazy for suggesting this, but, well, while these letters would appear to be my mother's last connection to Rory, there's one more thing. And it's here, in this house."

"Yes, Eva?"

"My mother dreamed of being Rory's bride, so much so that, while she waited desperately for him to come home from war, she made her own wedding dress. And I think it's still here, in your attic, where she left it."

"But—"

"When my mother agreed to marry Thomas, she felt it inappropriate to wear the dress that was meant for Rory, so she hid it, as a way of keeping it where it belonged. In the past."

"Surely someone in my family would have found it, though. We've kept so many things in the attic over the years."

"My mother stowed it in an old wooden box underneath some loose floorboards. Julia, if you are willing, I'd like to see if it's still there, and if it is, return it to her to cherish for the rest of her years."

* * * * *

I led Eva to the attic and we checked for loose floor boards. We were about to give up when I spotted a board that seemed uneven. It took a bit of effort, but I was able to lift it. Underneath was a box. I got it out and we carried it downstairs to the front porch.

"You do the honors, Eva."

Eva's aged hands worked the clasp, slowly lifting the lid to reveal a perfectly preserved wedding dress. Off white, Chantilly lace. It took my breath away.

* * * * *

Liam reached over to try my trout amandine in the candlelight of La Fable. We raised our glasses to toast the past, to treasured secrets of The Lilac of the Sea. We toasted the present, to Liam's promotion and my newfound friendship with Eva. Then, after Liam knelt before me with an open velvet box, we toasted our future. And while we did, I couldn't help but realize that I already had my something borrowed—the perfect dress.

CAREN PAULING GREW UP IN THE PHILADELPHIA AREA AND HAS BEEN ENJOYING SUMMERS AT THE BEACH IN DELAWARE FOR TWENTY YEARS. NOW RESIDING IN AVON, CONNECTICUT, CAREN LOVES NEW ENGLAND (EXCEPT FOR THE COLD WINTERS), TIME SPENT WITH FAMILY AND FRIENDS, RUNNING AND EXERCISING, AND HER NEWFOUND PASSION FOR MYSTERY WRITING. SHE IS A PROUD ALUMNA OF WEST CHESTER UNIVERSITY AND A COLLABORATING AUTHOR OF THE RECENTLY RELEASED BOOK, *THE GREAT PAUSE: BLESSINGS AND WISDOM FROM COVID-19*. CAREN'S INSPIRATION FOR "MYSTERY AT THE LILAC OF THE SEA" WAS BORN FROM HER LOVE OF TRAVELING AND SPENDING TIME IN MANY BED AND BREAKFASTS, AND HER LONGTIME PONDERING OF SOMEDAY OWNING ONE.

The Ship to the Grey Havens

By Linda Chambers

College, if you go, is the place you're most likely to find the friends that last longest and run deepest. The journey is just beginning; the world is yours. We're shiny and new and everything is possible. These are the friends who jump in the car with you; they ride shotgun, and whoop and holler, and give the finger when necessary. I'd felt this way about Jools.

1980

Late June. I was stretched out, face down on crossed arms, skin sparkling with droplets and tingling from the last quick run into the ocean, a fine sheen of sand on my ankles and feet from the dash back to the towel. The sun was hot, already drying my two-piece suit. I could fall asleep.

I felt several taps on my arm. "Ems, Ems." Another tap.

"What?"

"See that?"

"*What?*"

"*That.* Look."

I twisted around on my towel. Jools was sitting up, casually elegant, as she stared out to sea. When I didn't answer, she poked me again without breaking her gaze.

"What?"

"Look." Her voice was urgent.

I heaved a sigh and dragged myself up on my elbows. It was late afternoon. There were still quite a few people in the water, and nearby, a family with beach chairs circled like a wagon train passed snacks and soda over their bags and coolers.

"Where am I looking?"

"There." She swept off her sunglasses and shoved them up on top of her head. She gestured toward the ocean, shading her eyes.

I squinted. Far out on the horizon, an enormous tanker was silhouetted against the sky.

"Tanker?" I asked.

"No, to the left, to the left." She gestured again.

I squinted harder. Something shimmered in front of the tanker, something midway between it and the shore. I blinked, and it came into focus. It was a boat, long and riding low in the water. It looked like a schooner, although I wasn't all that sure what a schooner looked like. It had three large sails, tips pointed upwards, a tiny flag streaming from the last tip. Behind, the tanker gleamed in black, bright yellows, and reds; the sky was Maxfield Parrish pale pink and blue, and the ship itself rested in a warm turquoise ocean. The scene was shot through with color, except for that boat. It was gray. Varying degrees of gray, yes, but definitely gray. It was as though a black-and-white photograph had been cut out and laid onto a color shot.

"You mean the gray boat?"

"Is that what you see? A boat?"

"Well, what else would—"

"It isn't moving, Ems," she said flatly.

She was right. This required my attention. I sat up, dusting some of the sand off my legs.

"Wait, wait," I said. "It's a *kite*."

"Again," Jools said, "not moving."

She was right. Kites bounce up and down and twirl in circles, according to the wind; this one was perfectly still. The sails were rippling, but the ship itself wasn't moving. That didn't make sense.

Jools turned to me. "Right?" She looked anxious. "It's just sitting there, I mean, it's not doing anything, it's not …" As she spoke, she was turning back to the horizon.

I followed her gaze.

Whatever it was—boat, kite, illusion—it was gone.

"OK," I said, "say it was a boat, and it … vanished? In the mist?"

We looked at each other, then looked back at the horizon.

The tanker was still visible, its colors sharp and vibrant against the blue sky.

"So, tell me what you saw," Jools said.

I paused. We were new at our friendship and still in the discovery process. Rehoboth was part of that process. During our sophomore year in college, which is when we started our friendship, we'd discovered that our families had spent vacations there throughout our childhoods. Midway through the spring semester of our junior year, Jools suggested, casually, that she'd be heading to the Delaware beach for a few days when school finished. Would I like to come? I said, sure.

This was our very first trip together. I didn't want to say the wrong thing. So, I took the easy way out. "Tell me what *you* saw."

There was another pause, this time on her end. She studied me, expressionless. Two seconds, three seconds, four, then—

"Whoa! *That* was an easy way out!" She laughed and gave me a light shove.

I shoved her back and joined in the laughter. "Fine!" I said. "What do *you* think it is, then? Wait. Don't tell me, don't tell me. *Oooo,* ghost ship! Ghost ship!"

"Hey, *you* said 'kite.'"

"I did, yes, for a minute."

Jools nodded. Her laughter slowly ebbed, and her face smoothed. "So did I," she said. "The *first* time I saw it." She reached for her beach bag and pulled out her T-shirt.

It took a few seconds for that to sink in. "The … what?"

She scrambled to her feet, brushing off the sand, packing up her stuff. "Come on. I'm starving."

We chattered about nonsense on the way back to the Sandcastle Motel for a quick shower and change of clothes. When we were dressed, we headed back to the boardwalk and dinner at Grotto Pizza.

"Two slices of cheese and a birch beer," I said to the waitress.

"Same," Jools said.

We high-fived, thrilled that we shared the same order. Afterward, we sat on a bench on the boardwalk, facing the ocean. We each had a bucket of Dolle's popcorn in our lap.

"OK," I said, "let's hear it. When was the first time you saw that ship?"

A handful of popcorn was on its way to her mouth. She paused, her gaze shifting to the horizon.

"What have I told you about my Aunt Winnie?"

"Not much." I ticked off what I knew. "I know she was your father's aunt, so she was your great aunt. She was your favorite relative. She lived in … Philadelphia? I know she died a few years ago."

"You know how you have some relatives who are quirky? Winnie was quirky. My dad told me his whole family went to Atlantic City for vacations until Winnie started going to Rehoboth. She's the one who convinced them they should go to Rehoboth too. That's how the tradition started. Every summer, she'd come down from Philly and spend at least a couple of days with us. One of those visits was right before she died."

"I'm sorry," I said. "How old were you?"

"Twelve. No, thirteen. Winnie and I walked to the boardwalk, *here,* and sat down. She said she was sick; she said she was dying. She was very matter of fact about it. I started to cry. She put her arm around me and said it was just another journey, and we sat like that, quiet. Then I felt her straighten up. She told me to look out at the ocean. I shook my head. I didn't want to. I was … angry. She told me it was very important that I look, so I did, finally. I saw the ship."

"*That* ship? The one we saw?"

She nodded and popped a handful of kernels in her mouth. I waited for her to stop chewing.

"And?" I prodded.

"She told me to watch for that ship. That's how she would be traveling. She said one day I would be here, at the ocean, and I'd look up, and there it would be. I'd see her on the ship and we'd wave to each other. 'I'll be waiting for you,' she told me, 'on the other side.' So, I did. I looked."

Silence. I was holding my breath, perched on the edge of the bench.

"*Well? Did* you? See her?" I asked, tugging her arm. "Tell me what you saw!"

There was a pause. She was looking out over the ocean. The sun was beginning to set. I wondered if she were waiting for the ship to reappear. I turned and stared in the same direction.

"Nothing," she said, finally. She popped another kernel in her mouth and chewed.

We meandered down Rehoboth Avenue and wandered into the bookstore. I told Jools how excited my mom had been when it opened a few years ago. It became the first stop she'd make upon arrival. Dad could unpack and organize us kids; Mom needed to stock up on books. "Browseabout?" Dad had said, when he first heard the name. "More like pack a lunch and move in." That's how she spent days at the beach, sitting in her chair, reading. Dad was in the water; Mom was buried in a book.

When we left the bookstore, we saw that the lights had grown brighter on the boardwalk as the sky had darkened. The sounds were louder—music and rides and laughter and shouts. We wandered back up, directionless, each uncertain of what the other wanted to do next.

"Funland?" I suggested, keeping my fingers crossed that this was something she liked too.

"Yes!"

When we entered the midway, I made a beeline for The Haunted Mansion ride, which was new.

Jools demurred. "I don't like scary rides, and I particularly don't like enclosed ones. But you go."

By the time I emerged from one of the best dark rides I'd ever experienced, Jools was racking up an amazing number of points at Skee-Ball. The tickets spewing out of the slot were forming a small Mount Everest on the floor. She saw me, waved, and began gathering them up. I figured she was heading for the checkout to exchange her tickets for one of the cheap prizes. She wasn't. She stopped beside a sad little kid, who was fruitlessly throwing a ball up the Skee-Ball lane, a pitiful number of tickets dangling from the machine. The kid's weary mom was beside him, with a "time to go" look on her face.

"Here," Jools said, holding out her enormous bundle of tickets. The kid's eyes grew wide and he took them gratefully.

Jools turned back toward me. She didn't see the kid's face split into an enormous grin; she didn't see the mom's grateful expression. She just handed off the tickets.

When we got outside, I said, "That was exceptionally cool."

Jools grinned. "That was Winnie's idea. First time she took me to Funland. 'Give them to someone who needs them,' she said. Shamed me out of ever getting gaudy trinkets and cheap toys I don't really want."

* * * * *

Time passes. Things change. Some friends drop out of our orbit. It might be marriage; it might be kids; it might be career; it might be all or none. Others do not. Distance and time don't matter with those friends. When you register the year, you realize you've known them half your life.

2003

I don't remember the ship coming up again until 2003, when Jools dragged me to see *Return of the King*, the final installment of *The Lord of the Rings*. I was not a big fantasy fan, but she was, so I went. In the final moments, the hobbits arrive at the landing; some will board the ship that will take them to the Grey Havens. When the ship came into view, sails billowing, I gasped. I couldn't help myself.

Jools's hand clasped mine. It jogged her memory too. When we talked over dinner after the film, we came to the conclusion that it wasn't the ship that made the impact. It was the particularly poignant moment—good friends saying goodbye to each other, knowing they'd never see each other again, boarding a ship to take them to a better place. Good grief. Even *I* was sobbing at the end.

We were in our forties by then. We were busy with our own lives. That was the last time we spoke of it, and the last time I thought of it … until now.

* * * * *

More time passes. More things change; rearrange. We know the triumphs and the failures; we know the meaning of the calls that come late at night; we've sat with each other in hospital waiting rooms and held each other's hands in the rooms themselves; we've been there at the worst of times so we truly, honestly, can measure the best of times. Now you register the year when you've known them longer than anyone else. Finally, we reach that point in time when that friend is the one who holds all of our memories, and we hold all of theirs.

NOW

My best and oldest friend and I sit on a bench outside Grotto Pizza. We just finished our fortieth "yay, we're at the beach" meal—two slices of cheese pizza and a birch beer. We're in Rehoboth earlier than usual, two weeks prior to Memorial Day, and it's late afternoon, so the beach is almost deserted.

She'd called a few days ago and said, "Let's not wait. Let's go now. Can you do it, Ems?"

Back in the day, we'd jump in her car or mine and make the drive from Baltimore together. Time passes; things change. We don't live in the same town anymore; we're driving on our own.

"Sure," I said immediately, even though it was going to be difficult. I'm retired but not flush, and a few of my freelance projects were coming due. Still, there was something in her voice. And, obviously, she sensed something in mine.

"It's my treat this time," she said. "No argument. I mean it."

She knows things haven't gone so well the last few years. When I see her, I'm thinking things aren't going so well for her either. There are deep shadows beneath her eyes; she looks frail.

It's late afternoon, but there are still a few folks in the water. Far out on the horizon, an enormous tanker is silhouetted against the sky. Kites are soaring through the air.

One kite appears suddenly and catches my eye. It unfolds, shimmers in front of the tanker. It's big, with three large sails, and is long and rides low in the water. It's distinctive among the other kites because it's *gray*. Not colorless; shades of gray. I notice something else about it. The other kites—triangles and sharks and streaming birds—bounce up and down and twirl in circles, while this one stays still.

Something jogs my memory, which is none too good these days. I'm turning to Jools as I speak: "Do you see …"

But she's transfixed. Her hand is clutching my wrist; her eyes are locked on the horizon. My voice breaks her trance and she turns to me, eyes wide.

"Do you see it?" she asks breathlessly. "Ems, do *you* see it too?"

I look back at the horizon. The ship waits, sails billowing.

Something's forming in my mind, but it isn't quite there yet.

"You do see it," she whispers. Her eyes are luminous. She's waiting for my reply.

I hesitate because I'm still not sure why this matters so much. Her fingers tighten; I wince. She releases my wrist.

"Tell me what you see," she says finally. Her voice is flat. Some of the eagerness is gone and some of the light has faded from her eyes.

But that's what does it. *Tell me what you see.*

The memories shimmer back, much like the ship itself. It was our first trip to Rehoboth. Our first baby steps into a lifelong friendship. Forty years ago, I'd taken the easy out, throwing the same query back to her. "Tell me what *you* saw," I'd said.

Not this time.

"I see a gray ship," I say, my voice firm, my eyes meeting hers. "Three sails that billow. I thought it was a kite—"

"You did the first time, too, but..."she begins.

"... there was no string." I complete her sentence.

The light is coming back into her eyes.

"No movement," she says.

"No mist," I reply.

Wordlessly, she turns toward the water and points. The tanker is still visible, far out on the horizon, clear as day.

The ship remains, as though waiting for us to catch up to it, waiting for the rest of the story.

And then I do. I catch up. I know what she'd done so many years ago.

She'd lied. If *I'd* taken the easy out way back when, then so had she. I know the answer before she gives it; I know why we're here.

My question forty years ago: "Did you? See her? Tell me what you saw."

Her answer forty years ago: "Nothing."

Now, I ask again. "Tell me what you saw."

"I saw my aunt on the deck of the ship."

Jools covers both my hands with hers and holds them tightly. I know it's going to be hard. I steel myself and look into her eyes.

"And one day—soon, I think—you'll see me."

I'm not aware that I'm crying until she reaches out and brushes away my tears. We smile at each other. We sit back on the bench, hands clasped. In front of us, out in the ocean, the gray ship slowly shimmers away into the sunset.

LINDA CHAMBERS IS A BALTIMOREAN WHO VISITS THE DELAWARE BEACHES EVERY CHANCE SHE GETS. "THE SHIP TO THE GREY HAVENS" IS THE FOURTH OF HER SHORT STORIES INCLUDED IN CAT & MOUSE PRESS COLLECTIONS. THE FIRST THREE PARTS OF HER FANTASY NOVEL, *THE SWORDS OF IALMORGIA,* ARE NOW AVAILABLE ON AMAZON KINDLE, WITH MORE ADVENTURES TO COME, AND SHE IS WORKING ON AN ADAPTATION OF "THE EMPEROR'S NEW CLOTHES" FOR CHILDREN'S THEATER. SHE IS A PLAYWRIGHT AND STAGE DIRECTOR, IN THE PROCESS OF ADJUSTING TO THE NEW THEATRICAL NORMAL AND LOOKING FORWARD TO A POST-PANDEMIC WORLD.

Clubhouse Showers and Sleepless Hours

By Doretta Warnock

"Are you sure this is the right address?" asked the Uber driver.

Paul shuffled through his travel papers. "Yeah, this is it—263 Seashell Lane, Rehoboth Beach. Why do you ask?"

"I've never seen anyone at this house; some lady died there and now it's supposed to be haunted."

"That's ridiculous." Disgusted with the driver's rudeness, Paul gave him a smaller than usual tip before hoisting his wife's suitcase and then his own from the trunk of the car. They paused to admire the handsome home as they walked through the wrought-iron gate at its entrance.

"Wow, this house is way nicer than ours. Remind me again what Jim did for a living before he left your company," Susan said.

"Jim made enough money to retire from his accounting position at forty-five. He relocated to Delaware to become a self-made millionaire, or so he says. I haven't seen him in over twenty years."

Together they wheeled their suitcases to the front door. Susan rang the doorbell.

Jim's sister, Karen, opened the door. Her bleached-blond, shoulder-length hair, short shorts, and spaghetti-strapped blouse were too young for her sixty-three-year-old body. "Jim, Jim, they're here."

Jim appeared and hugged his old friend. Jim's thin physique and thick blond hair were attributes overshadowed by his eyeglasses, which were held together with a piece of black electrical tape.

"You shaved your mustache and dyed your hair," Paul said.

"Well, I had to do something to look younger. Come, let me give you the tour."

The quartet walked through the great room with its tray ceiling, columned pillars, and stone fireplace. Off to the right was the master suite with a king-size bed, a bathroom, and a second bedroom that Karen used as her she cave. Two more bedrooms branched off to the left from the great room. One was Jim's bedroom, furnished with the twin bed and dresser from his youth. The last bedroom doubled as an office with a rolltop desk, computer, and wall-to-wall bookcases stuffed with accounting books. Susan scanned the photo array on the wall and noticed a picture of her husband in his younger days. "I recognize Paul," said Susan, "but who are these people in the other pictures?"

"This is a picture of our parents," said Jim. "This is our cousin Linda. Unfortunately, she drowned one day when we were swimming at Rehoboth Beach after the lifeguards had left."

"That's awful. I'm so sorry."

"Thank you. And this is my high school friend Carol. Here is where you will be sleeping. You are our first overnight guests in the four years we have lived here, so we got an inflatable bed for you." Susan was shocked. Karen and Jim had a four-bedroom house for the two of them but no guestroom?

"And this is your bathroom. We wanted to make you feel like you're still on your cruise, so we gave you little shampoo and conditioner bottles. But they are just for show. We don't shower here; we'll shower at the clubhouse tomorrow. I'll leave you to unpack, and then you can join us in the kitchen for lunch."

After Karen and Jim left, Susan asked, "Did you see Jim's glasses?"

"I couldn't miss them."

"Why is there a picture of you on the wall? I didn't think you were that close."

"We're not."

"It's like you're his only friend. This is creepy. Can we please get out of this house?"

"Come on, Susan. I haven't seen Jim in twenty years. Be a trooper for me. It's only going to be a few days." Susan nodded as they left to join Karen and Jim in the kitchen for lunch.

"Hey, do you want to hear a funny story?" asked Paul. "The Uber driver told us nobody lives here because the house is haunted."

"That's what we tell all the neighbors to keep them away," said Jim. "It was easy after Carol's accident."

"What accident?" asked Susan.

"She tripped on the porch, hit her head, and lapsed into a coma. She died three days later. Oh, and before I forget to tell you, all the neighbors think we're married. We like it that way; no questions to answer."

Paul sneezed.

"Did you get sick on your cruise?" asked Karen. "Don't give it to me. Here, sit down at the table; I'll give you something for it."

Paul watched her spin the two-tiered pharmaceutical lazy Susan taking up half the table. She passed by all the prescription pill bottles and vitamin supplements, stopping at the vitamin C. "Here take this." As Paul reached to grab the pill, his watch glinted in the sunlight. "Wow, is that a Rolex?"

"Yes. Do you like it? I got a nice buy on it in St. Thomas."

"And I got this," Susan said, fingering her necklace.

"Is that 14-karat gold?" asked Karen.

Susan nodded.

"Wow, I'm jealous. Anyway, I thought you would enjoy a light lunch today. I'm sure you two are stuffed from all the food you ate on your cruise." She handed an apple to each of them.

Paul and Susan exchanged glances, each knowing what the other was thinking. The boys discussed old times at work. Karen explained how she had had a great job as an executive chef at Harrington's until a car accident left her with nerve damage in her fingers and she became permanently disabled. Susan felt sorry for her. She explained how lonely she was living in Michigan with Paul, leaving all her family and college friends behind in California when they got married.

By dinnertime Susan and Paul were famished. Susan offered to help Karen with the cooking, but she declined. Susan wondered how disabled she really was if she could still cook.

After bragging about a sale at BJ's, Karen mustered up dinner—one thin slice of ham each, served with a small serving of instant potatoes and a small helping of green beans. She topped it off with one scoop of vanilla ice cream each for dessert.

Susan knew Paul must still be hungry. The dinner would have fed the two of them but had been divided into four small portions. If Karen cooked like this every night, it might explain why Jim was so slim.

Sleeping on the air mattress that night was a challenge. Every time one of them turned over, the bed shook, waking up the other one, and the overhead fan did nothing to break the oppressive heat.

When morning came, Paul said, "Why don't they use the air conditioner? I can't stand it anymore. I have to open the window and let some air in here." He opened the window and tried to grab another hour of sleep.

"Paul, wake up. The police are in the driveway." Susan turned from the window at the sound of pounding coming from the front door. She opened their bedroom door a crack to see what was going on. Paul joined her in time to see Jim answer the door in his plaid pajamas.

"Is everyone all right? We got a silent alarm from this address." A police officer handed Jim a piece of paper.

Jim was wearing neither glasses nor hair on his head; he was balder than Paul.

"Oh my god, he wears a toupee," Susan said, laughing softly.

"And where are his glasses?" asked Paul.

"He's wearing contacts."

"How can you tell?"

"He's not bumping into furniture and he's reading the police report. Plus, there's that telltale eye blinking."

"But how come he wasn't wearing them yesterday instead of those hideous glasses?"

"Who knows. Maybe he's just weird."

"Why were the police here?" Paul asked later at breakfast.

"You opened your window and it set off my alarm. I forgot to tell you, you can't open outside doors or windows without shutting off the alarm first," Jim said.

"I'm sorry; we didn't know. We were so hot, and the air conditioner wasn't working," Susan said.

"Oh, it's working. We just keep it on low. I hope we don't get fined for a false alarm," Jim said.

"If you do, just let us know. We'll pay the fine. After all, it was our fault. Let's eat. I'm hungry. What's for breakfast?" Paul asked.

Susan spotted four packs of instant oatmeal lying on the counter. Apparently, they were to have one package apiece. At home, they would have had two each. This was going to do nothing for their empty stomachs. Maybe it was a good thing. Susan thought they might be the first people in history to come home from a cruise without gaining weight.

"Do you have any coffee or tea to wash it down?"

Jim opened a cabinet above the sink. It was lined from top to bottom with every type of herbal tea imaginable, but no coffee. Susan settled on peach tea. "Do you have any coffee for Paul?"

"We don't drink coffee."

"Jim, why don't you go to the clubhouse and get some," said Karen.

Jim was back in no time with a thermos full of hot coffee, but Susan wondered why he didn't buy coffee from the store for his guests instead of taking it from the clubhouse.

After breakfast, the foursome played several games of pickleball, swam laps in the outdoor pool, and relaxed in the hot tub. They took a shower at the clubhouse and came back to the house for lunch. Karen served them half a peanut butter sandwich and half an apple each. Still hungry, they spent the afternoon playing corn hole and mah-jongg. For dinner, Karen again served one slice of ham and skimpy portions of instant potatoes and green beans.

It wasn't until bedtime that evening that Susan got a chance to let loose her feelings. "I don't understand it. I thought you told me Jim and Karen were rich."

"They are."

"You could've fooled me. Clearly, they don't spend their money on food or furniture. Jim doesn't even have a full-size bed. If they shower at the clubhouse every day, I'm sure they don't have much of a water bill either. Or an electricity bill, and how cheap can you be to steal coffee from the clubhouse?"

"It's a mystery to me. Maybe tomorrow will be a whole different ballgame."

But the next day for breakfast, Jim went to the clubhouse for coffee. Karen served one package of oatmeal each. They played pickleball and showered at the clubhouse. For lunch they ate half a peanut butter sandwich and half an apple. They played mah-jongg and corn hole in the afternoon and had one slice of ham, a handful of green beans, and a minuscule serving of instant potatoes for dinner. Karen felt as if she were trapped in the movie *Groundhog Day*.

In bed that night, Susan massaged her stiff neck while she waited for Paul to come out of the bathroom so she could discuss Jim and Karen. He opened the door.

"Hey, Susan. We're out of toilet paper."

"Did you look under the sink for another roll?"

"Of course. There's none. You'll have to ask Karen for another roll."

"Me? Why me? They're your friends."

"It's a girl thing."

Susan rolled her eyes, put on her robe, and walked barefoot through the great room to the other side of the house. She timidly knocked on Karen's door. Karen answered the door with a paperback novel in her hand.

"I'm sorry to bother you, but we're out of toilet paper. Can we have another roll?" The shocked look on Karen's face told Susan all she needed to know; this was an imposition. Boy, how different Susan did things in her own house. She always left five rolls in the bathroom for her houseguests, to save them the embarrassment of asking. Karen disappeared into her bathroom and reemerged with a roll of toilet paper, which she handed to Susan.

"Thank you."

"You're welcome. Good night."

The words started spilling out of Susan's mouth as soon as she reached her bedroom. "Oh my god. I got the toilet paper, but you would have thought I asked for the moon. Paul, no one is that cheap. I think they're poor. And I forgot to bring it up last night, but didn't you think it was odd that they want the neighbors to think the house is haunted and that they are a married couple? They clearly sleep in separate bedrooms. Who would care?"

"Maybe they're rich because they don't spend their money."

"But why don't they spend it? Neither one of them is married; there are no children to leave it to."

"It's a mystery that we aren't going to solve tonight. Go to sleep. Tomorrow we'll be spending the day at the beach and you can finally try Thrasher's fries."

The next day, Paul offered to buy lunch. They stopped at a liquor store for beer and then at Casapulla's for some Italian subs and potato chips.

When Paul pulled a wad of bills from his wallet to pay, he couldn't help but notice the spark in Jim's eyes.

"Wow, you carry a lot of cash."

"You know how it is. I always bring too much money with me when I travel. I worry my credit card will get stolen or not work. But since this is my last day, I figure I can spend some of it."

As Karen drove the group toward the beach, she asked Susan, "How are your kids?"

"They're great. Two are nurses and one is a stay-at-home mom with our two grandkids."

"Do they know you extended your vacation to stay with us?"

Susan thought this was a strange question but answered honestly. "No, we didn't mention it. They don't know who you are, anyway."

Paul saw a sign for Rehoboth Beach to the left, but the car veered to the right. "Where are we going? I think you missed the turn for Rehoboth Beach."

"Oh, we're not going to Rehoboth Beach. Too many people playing music and throwing sand. We're going to a secluded fishing beach, where we won't be bothered."

Susan tried not to show her disappointment. She and Paul were not strong swimmers, and neither would swim without lifeguards; they didn't want to end up like cousin Linda. Karen and Jim had no beach chairs, so they ended up spending the day sitting on their towels, watching a lone fisherman, who caught nothing.

On their last morning in "paradise," Susan woke stiffer and hotter than ever. She grabbed the leftover cruise documents and began fanning herself. "Paul, can you check the air conditioner vent? Maybe it's not open all the way."

He held his hand in front of the vent but felt no breeze. Using his car key as a screwdriver, he removed the vent plate. "It's blocked. No wonder it's so hot in here."

"Here, let me see; my hand is smaller than yours. Maybe I can reach whatever is blocking it." Susan used her iPhone flashlight to see into the shaft. She gasped. "It looks like a roll of money."

"Can you get it?"

"I'm not touching it. They'll think we took some of it. What kind of friends do you have? Do you think they stole it?"

Instinctively, Jim checked his wallet; his money was still there. "Let's do a little research on the internet. I'll ask Jim for the Wi-Fi password. Besides, we need to print our boarding passes anyway."

After another breakfast of instant oatmeal and stolen clubhouse coffee, Paul asked Jim for the password. "That's only for us; we don't give that out."

Why not? Susan thought this was strange. "That's OK, Jim. We're going to visit my old college roommate today before we leave. We can use her internet."

Later, in the Uber, Paul said, "I didn't know you had a roommate that lives around here."

"I don't. It just gave us an excuse to get out of there. We can go to the library to print our boarding passes and look up any interesting news stories involving Jim and Karen."

"Good thinkin', Lincoln."

At the Rehoboth Beach Public Library, Paul went to print their boarding passes while Susan solicited the help of the librarian to find a newspaper database on the computer. She was deeply absorbed in a story when Paul came up behind her.

"Did you find anything?"

"There's only one story about them from 2000. They were living with their parents in Wilmington."

"That's twenty years ago."

"Apparently their parents, Sheila and George Stafford, died suddenly. The police suspected foul play, but the deaths were attributed to food poisoning. Wasn't 2000 when Jim retired?"

Paul nodded. "I bet they killed their parents and took their money."

Outside, Susan continued, "Think about it. It all makes sense. They moved about one hundred miles from Wilmington to Rehoboth Beach, where no one would know them. Jim changed his appearance, and they are posing as husband and wife. If the police were looking for them, they would be looking for a brother and sister. They keep people away by saying their house is haunted and go to private beaches where they won't be recognized. And Karen was an executive chef, so she might know how to poison someone."

"Do you hear yourself? That is nothing more than a conspiracy theory. These are my friends you're talking about, not some criminals. Besides, that doesn't explain why they're so cheap or why they're hiding money in the wall. I'm sure there is a rational explanation. Let's go ask them and clear this up."

"You don't just walk up to people and ask them why they're cheap or whether they killed their parents. Or … why did you steal my necklace? Oh Paul. It's gone."

"Calm down. You probably left it in the bedroom in one of your senior moments."

"I hope you're right. Let's just tell them we found the money and see what they say."

"Alright but promise me you won't accuse them of being cheap or killing their parents."

"You got it."

Susan and Paul returned to 263 Seashell Lane and a less-than-cordial couple greeted them.

"Where did you two go?" asked Karen, with Susan's necklace boldly displayed on her wrinkled neck.

"We told you," said Susan. "We went to visit my college roommate."

"No, you didn't. You told me you had no family or friends that lived near here. Try again."

"Alright. We went to the library. We found some money hidden in the duct in our bedroom. We were trying to figure out where it came from. We thought maybe the previous owner stole it and hid it there for some reason."

Karen laughed. "Is that all? Why didn't you just ask? That's our money. I know Jim told you he was a self-made millionaire. That's not quite true. We inherited money from our parents when they died. With me working, we thought it would be enough to last us until we died, so Jim retired. But then our income went way down after I had my accident. It's getting harder to make the money last."

"Why don't you keep it in the bank?" asked Paul.

"Because we don't trust banks," said Karen. They charge fees and the government makes you pay taxes. We can't afford to share any of our money with them."

That explained why they were so cheap, but did they murder their parents? Karen wanted to get safely out of the house. Her life wasn't worth a necklace. "If you'll excuse us, we need to pack. We found an earlier flight."

Paul and Susan packed quickly, haphazardly throwing their belongings into their suitcases. "We'll call the police once we're safely in the Uber." They wheeled their luggage into the hallway.

"How about a piece of chocolate cream pie before you leave? I just made it."

It wasn't oatmeal, peanut butter, apples, ham, instant potatoes, green beans, or ice cream. This was something new and it sure was tempting.

Susan looked at Paul. Together they said, "No thank you." They waited on the front porch for their Uber, leaving the clubhouse showers and sleepless hours behind.

"Well that didn't go as planned," Jim said, taking Paul's picture from the wall.

"So, who can we invite next?" Karen said, closing the plantation shutters on the front door and throwing the chocolate pie into the trash.

DORETTA WARNOCK IS A RETIRED ELEMENTARY SCHOOL TEACHER WHO SPENT YEARS TRYING TO INSTILL HER LOVE OF WRITING IN HER STUDENTS. TO GET THE IDEAS FLOWING, SHE STRESSED WRITING ABOUT WHAT YOU KNOW. "CLUBHOUSE SHOWERS AND SLEEPLESS HOURS" IS BASED ON WHAT SHE KNOWS—SPENDING AN AWFUL VACATION WITH OLD FRIENDS. HOWEVER, THE STEALING OF MONEY AND MURDER ARE PURE FICTION. THIS IS DORETTA'S FOURTH PUBLICATION AND SECOND STORY WITH CAT & MOUSE PRESS.

Circles

By Tara A. Elliott

The sun dangled low over the ocean and the moonflowers were just unfurling as Sabrina rubbed the spot where her wedding ring used to be.

I can't blame Sean. He's only five, she thought. *He didn't know.* Her finger felt nothing but skin where the gold band usually pressed into her flesh. She poured herself another glass of wine and stretched back on the wrought-iron chair in the garden, enjoying the silence, her son now washed and sandless, tucked fast into the guestroom bed of the house they'd rented for the week. Her husband, John, was snoozing on the couch and half-listening to the Orioles game on the television—they were on a winning streak. He was exhausted after the long day of searching the broken bits of rock and shell for what had been lost.

For months, until her husband bought her a replacement, Sabrina would feel the ghost of the ring around her finger.

* * * * *

Deputy police chief Dale Messick was chewing the end of a straw. His wife wanted him to quit smoking, but try as he could, he couldn't seem to shake the need to have something in his mouth. Straws were hard to come by these days, ever since the Save Our Lakes Alliance 3 and the Rehoboth Beach Homeowners Association had asked Mayor Kuhns to start banning single-use plastic. The ban wouldn't officially go into effect until 2021, but many restaurants and bars had already switched to paper straws. Paper never lasted, and Messick had tried toothpicks, but they were too small to be satisfying. The only place he could get them (and *only* if requested) was at Doggie Style, and his wife hated him going into a restaurant with that name. To her, it was almost as bad as Ocean City's The Bearded Clam. Not to mention it was a small hike off the boards just to get there. Messick was shaking his head when the man approached him.

"Officer? I was hoping you could help me."

Messick sized up the man as he'd been trained to do. He was middle aged, overweight, and probably about six two. His white belly hung over his green swim trunks, and both his chest and belly hair were matted with sunscreen and sweat. The man ran a hand through his thinning hairline, a widow's peak of gray, streaked with remnants of brown.

"Yes," said Messick. "What can I do you for?" He pulled the straw out of his mouth.

"My wife. My wife found this on the beach, and I wanted to, well, she wanted me to … I mean, I wanted to turn it in to you."

"What is it?"

"This." The man handed the ring to the deputy, first holding it up to the light so the policeman could see it. The diamond sparkled.

"Where'd you find it?" Messick noticed he was standing near the off-beach smoking station and returned the straw to his mouth. The sweet smell of cigar smoke from an old man on a bench who was smoking a Black & Mild almost pushed him over the edge.

"We were straight out from Grotto's, down by the water." The man kept nervously shifting his flip-flopped feet. "My wife went to cool off in the waves. She found it with her toes. "She's really good like that—she can pick up anything with her feet. The man rubbed his belly. "It's good 'cause it keeps me from bending over—"

"Where's your wife?" Messick didn't give a rat's ass if this woman could drink a beer with her feet. All he wanted was a goddamn cigarette. Messick made a mental note that Grotto's wasn't too far from Whiskey Jack's, and from what he noticed, the man just might have made a pit stop.

"She's um, back at the blanket. She worships the sun. I can't but take so much of it. I don't tan—I burn—and sitting around with nothing to do, well, I'd rather be watching the Orioles lose."

"Where? Show me." Messick followed the man as he teetered and wove up the beach to where his wife was sunning herself. The straw in his mouth was getting more and more frayed.

"'Brina?" asked the man. His wife was face down, her large frame taking up much of the blanket. "This nice officer—"

"Deputy," Messick cut in.

"Deputy. Well, um, he's the one I gave, um, the ring you found to, like you asked me to do, and he's got … he's got some questions."

The woman woke, brushed a bit of sand from the side of her face, and pulled oversized sunglasses from her straw bag. Her blond hair had peacock-blue tips.

"Ma'am," said Messick, tipping his hat. *No doubt,* he thought, *one of those Baltimore suburban housewives who wishes she were years younger.*

The woman pawed at her hair, gathered it, and put it up in a clip. "Yes, officer? What is it you need?" She pulled a cigarette from her bag and rummaged for a lighter.

"Ma'am, you're not allowed to smoke on the beach." Messick repositioned the straw.

The woman put her cigarette back in the pack and sighed. "It's completely ridiculous, the rules around here anymore." She uncapped a bottle of Honest Tea and took a swig.

"Glass …" started Messick, but then he shut his mouth. He was way too keyed up in need of nicotine to pick a fight with this woman. "Where'd you find this ring?" He held it up so she could see it.

"Oh, I was down by the waitress over there." She gestured toward the boardwalk with the wave of hand, nails painted purple with silver glitter sparkles.

"You mean the water, sweetheart. The water. Over there." And the man pointed to the ocean.

"What time was it?" Messick asked.

"How the hell am I supposed to know? What time is it now?" She reached for her cell phone, touched the screen a few times, frowned, then tried to unlock it again.

"It's just after three," the deputy prodded.

"Well, I don't know, probably about two hours ago? John, where the hell have you been? It's three o'clock. I sent you up there with the ring—"

John interrupted her. "I couldn't find an officer—sorry, a deputy—on the boards, darling."

"I bet," said his wife. "And I bet that's not alcohol I smell on your damn breath either."

Deputy Messick knew better than to get involved in a family squabble. He had found out what he needed to know. He walked down to the water's edge, tucked the ring into his breast pocket, looked around, then turned back and walked up the beach toward Whiskey Jack's. He grimaced as loose sand seeped into his shoes, knowing he'd have to dump them. As he entered the bar, he patted his pocket to see how many straws he had left for the day. A straw was halfway poking through the pocket of his shirt, sticking out of a rip he'd been meaning to fix. *Oh shit.* The ring was gone.

* * * * *

Scott was walking behind her again. Ja'nell knew it. He didn't want to be seen with her. She was fine to sleep with but not to hold hands with on the boardwalk. Well, he had another thing coming. She was tired of being his "Black girlfriend," and she was going to let him have it. *To hell with him,* she thought, as she adjusted her bikini top. There was a time when people of her color weren't even allowed on this beach. She knew it because her grandfather told her all about Rosedale and seeing Louis Armstrong play there when he was a child, and her great aunt often spoke about visiting Highland Beach across the bay. Well, she'd be damned if she was going to let Scott get the best of her. *There are plenty of men who would be proud to be seen with me—white, Black, or whatever color.* Men's heads turned as she walked past—some married, holding the hands of wives or toddlers, others too young to know to avert their eyes. Ja'nell's long braids fell halfway down her back, and her waist was tiny, emphasizing the hourglass of her body. She knew how to do makeup too, having watched hours of tutorials on YouTube. She knew how to highlight her features as well. But she'd be damned if she was going to let this white boy get the best of her. She turned to give Scott a piece of her mind.

Scott didn't know why Ja'nell was mad at him; all he knew was that she was. They passed Dolle's and Beach Treats and kept on going. He wondered when she would stop. The way she was walking, she had to be angry. She was practically stomping on the boardwalk. He kept his distance because he hoped her anger would burn out as she walked. Just outside Whisky Jack's, Scott caught a glimpse of something gleaming. He stooped to see what it was. A gold ring was wedged between two boards. He quickly pried it out of the crevice. A diamond glinted in the bright afternoon sunlight. He whistled low and long. Ja'nell turned around at just that moment. Scott knew this was bad, but he didn't realize how bad.

The anger running through Ja'nell's mind vanished. Seeing Scott down on one knee was almost more than she could take. Tears sprung at the corners of her eyes.

"Scott?"

"Ja'nell, no. It's not what you think …"

"You want to marry me?" Ja'nell asked, an almost proud tone to her voice. Maybe she was wrong. Maybe Scott loved her after all.

"Ja'nell—"

"Scott!" She took the ring and placed it on her left ring finger. She flew to him, wrapping both arms around his neck.

"Ja'nell," Scott whispered almost inaudibly. "That's not for you. I … I … I just found it."

"Yes, Scott, oh my god, yes!"

The crowd that had begun to gather clapped wildly. Scott was still down on one knee.

Scott stood, put his arm around Ja'nell, and pulled her away from the bystanders, who were now chanting, "Kiss, kiss, kiss!"

"I *found* this ring." Scott whispered in her ear, conscious of the crowd, and scared to tell her but more frightened not to. "I'm sorry, Ja'nell. I'm not proposing."

"WHAT? What do you mean you're not proposing? You just did!"

"I found that ring on the boardwalk. I was just picking it up when you turned around."

"I have been with you for six goddamn years, and you're NOT proposing?"

The crowd started to back away, realizing this was an uncomfortable situation and yet not wanting to leave. The drama of the situation was clear, and they wanted to enjoy this fight from a distance.

"No," said Scott. "Ja'nell, I found the ring on the boards."

"Just like my mother told me. Why buy the cow when you can get the milk for free. *I'm done.* I'm *so* done at this point, Scott. I wasted six years of my life waiting for you. Six years of my goddamn life. My sisters warned me. A Pisces and a Scorpio never mix." At that, Ja'nell took the ring off her finger and threw it at Scott. She threw it so hard it bounced off his chest, and then she stomped up the boardwalk.

Scott went after her, not stopping to pick up the ring, which had fallen into another space between the planks, beyond the eyes of the now-thinning crowd. Not seeing any of the argument, but noticing quite a few people lingering, Deputy Messick helped move them along, straw tucked firmly into his cheek.

A few seagulls flapped above North Avenue near Thrasher's, where the pickings were good. Every once and a while, a kid would drop a fry or two, and the gulls would puff up and fight for their claim. One found a fry, large and salty, coated in malt vinegar. Another found a ring. Both finds were swallowed whole.

* * * * *

For the first time since his wife died in a tragic car accident, Sean was feeling brave enough to take his young son, Ben, to the beach by himself. He had been dealt a bad hand, losing Sarah the way he had, then having his mother drift away entirely, lost to primary progressive aphasia. It was an awful disease, and only Sarah had been able to quiet his mom. Sarah's theory had been that if they went along with the delusions, eventually his mother would forget she had them. Sarah was special that way—she had a tenderness for children, animals, the sick. After Sarah's death, his mother started hiding her clothes around the house, because "they" were coming to steal them. Sean never found out who "they" were, but after finding his mother's underwear and bathing suits behind books on shelves and in the trash can, he couldn't bring himself to go along with the delusions.

His mother had never gotten over losing the ring. And as she lost her mind more and more, she'd call for the lost ring over and over while wandering through the house in circles, rubbing the spot on her hand where the ring had been.

His dad had stashed a newer ring he'd gotten her as she grew more and more forgetful. "She'll just lose it," was his response.

She looked old to Sean now, and the blue was long gone from her hair, the polish gone from her nails. She never even called his dad by name anymore. And his dad stopped calling her "honey" and "sweetheart" because she would forget who he was and think he was out to hurt her.

So, she roamed and rubbed her hand, ranting, "Where's my ring?" It completely unnerved Sean, who always felt guilty—he couldn't forgive himself—even though he really couldn't remember what had happened and could only recall bits and pieces from the story his parents told him year after year until it became his history.

"'Brina," his dad would say, "the ring is gone. Sean threw it in the ocean when he was five, remember? We looked for hours. He wanted to catch himself a mermaid. Now, how 'bout them O's?" And he'd put an arm around his wife and lead her back to the special chair he bought for her so she could stand and be gently lifted into a sitting position. He'd turn on the game, because even though she'd never liked baseball, what the hell did it matter at this point?

The thought of Thrasher's fries and saltwater taffy ran through Sean's mind, and introducing Ben to the thrill of the waves, finding seashells, and the taste of soft-serve ice cream was what drove him on as they slowly crawled up Route 1 through the traffic toward the ocean.

* * * * *

Back in Rehoboth for the first time in many years, Ja'nell was having a reunion with her sorority sisters following a long, drawn-out divorce. Needing a break, she went for a swim. She let the cool ocean water sweep over her. *Body surfing, that's what I liked best when I was a kid.* She waited for a tall green wave to build up behind her and let the propulsion of it push against her back and carry her in, disregarding the sand that washed into her suit.

When she reached the shallows where the water was knee high, she stopped to laugh, then started walking toward the beach. She felt as she never had before. No man in her life, and none on the horizon. She felt entirely free and one with the sea. When the next wave threw her a bit off balance, she laughed again, and felt something twirl with the current against her foot.

Collecting bits of purple shell was an obsession for her—it reminded her that even the ocean, as big as it was, always smoothed whatever was broken. She often carried a small piece in her pocket or glove, to remind her that there was something bigger in this world than herself. She used her toes to scoop up whatever it was into her hand. Beneath a half-smoothed clam shell, she was shocked to find a diamond ring. *It can't be.* The diamond caught the sunlight and cast a rainbow against her skin. Knee deep in the waves, she smiled.

She came out of the water, her long dark braids dripping, to find a handsome man under a teal umbrella with his young son who was busily building a sandcastle. He was looking straight at her.

"Did you lose this?" She laughed, holding it out to Sean in the open palm of her hand.

"Mermaid!" Ben giggled.

Sean looked up into her warm eyes and smiled. The waves continued their endless break along the edge of the shore.

Tara A. Elliott's poems have appeared in *TAOS Journal of International Poetry & Art*, *The American Journal of Poetry*, and *Stirring* among others. She is the founder and director of Salisbury, Maryland's Poetry Week, the co-chair of the Bay to Ocean Writers Conference, and the president-elect of Eastern Shore Writers' Association. She has appeared as poet-in-residence for Freeman Stage and was awarded a fellowship to the Virginia Center for the Creative Arts (VCCA). "Circles" is her first short story, which she was dared to write by her ten-year-old son. For more information about Tara, visit www. taraaelliott.com.

Thaddeus Zoon—Mayhem on the Ferry

By Teresa Berry

"Thaddeus! Mrs. Pinsky can't find her good silver cake knife!"

Ma's voice sure carried. "OK, Ma, I'm going."

That's how it usually started. People lost things, and I helped find them.

I've had this knack since I was a kid and my dad lost his glasses. He taught high school math, and if there was ever an absent-minded professor, Dad fit the bill. I can't even explain how I did it. I pictured the glasses in my mind and could see them on a shelf in the refrigerator. Turns out, Dad had just made himself a sandwich and put his glasses in the fridge by mistake.

Dad lost a lot of things, and I found them. A couple of questions and *boom*, I could see them clearly. Ma was amazed by my talent, and she told Mrs. Lacey next door. Before you knew it, I was finding things all around the neighborhood. Usually, I didn't mind, but sometimes I found things that didn't want to be found. Like in 1965 when I was twelve. That's when everything changed.

My dad was a cook in the navy during World War II. After that, he taught math during the school year but when summer came, we headed to Rehoboth Beach, Delaware. Dad had a little restaurant called The Bluefish right off the beach. We lived upstairs and for three months, I smelled like bacon.

Ma didn't like the beach that much—or maybe she didn't want to smell like bacon—so she stayed home in Pennsylvania with my little sister, Maureen. Could be that's how my parents stayed married for so long.

I asked Dad not to tell anybody at the restaurant about me being a finder, because people lost a lot of stuff at the beach and I wouldn't have any time for fun. That worked out OK for a few years, until the Cape May-Lewes Ferry started up in 1964. Dad spent two years on a big destroyer in the war, but he got seasick on anything smaller. Luckily, by then I was old enough to run errands by myself, so Dad would send me to Cape May on the ferry if he needed something special.

One Saturday morning, I rode my bike to the ferry launch to take the hour-and-a-half ride from Lewes to Cape May. Mrs. Applegate and her lady friends were coming to the restaurant for their book club meeting, and Dad always sent me to get fancy tea and a nice selection of baked goods for them.

The bay was calm, and the sky was full of seagulls. They are finders too, so I always brought scraps from the kitchen for them. I liked to toss a piece up and watch one of them swoop down and catch it in midair. Sometimes a whole group would hover overhead and practically take it right out of my hand.

While I waited on a bench, the SS New Jersey pulled up to the dock. It was low and sleek, and the line of cars jockeyed for position as they filed into its cavernous mouth. Just before the ramp was lifted, I rode in and stashed my bike along the side. The echo of slamming car doors and the fog of exhaust filled the lower deck, as people made their way up the tinny metal stairway to the fresh air above.

As soon as I stepped aboard I felt the vibration and heard the guttural hum of the pulsing engines. It made me think of a hundred horses, just chomping at the bit to get started. And when we finally cast off, the massive iron beast lurched into action and the murky water lapped at the sides as we made our way across the Delaware Bay.

The passengers were mostly the same every trip—parents holding their kids tight, teenagers tempting fate by leaning over the rail, and truck drivers and workmen happy for a break. Ladies held their hats against the breeze, and men stood tall and inhaled the sea air. The pace of life slowed down, and the lullaby of the bobbing ship had a calming effect on everyone's mood.

After a while, I went into the large passenger cabin with its metal seats and tables bolted to the corrugated steel floor. I don't know why the hot dogs tasted so much better on the ferry, but I always bought two at the small concession stand.

Once we made it to Cape May, I hopped on my bike and went to the café behind the Emlen Physick House on Washington Street. Mrs. Becker offered tea and sandwiches to visitors touring the old Victorian house. She baked fresh scones every day and had a package ready for me when I arrived.

"Hello, Thad," she said. "I have a tasty white peony tea for you today." I hated it when she called me Thad, but she made the best muffins and always had one of her "uglies" for me. "This one just didn't rise right, so I can't sell it. I thought you would enjoy it." And I always did.

I stashed the scones and tea in the saddle bags on my bike and hurried back to the landing for the return ferry. The cars were all loaded when I arrived, and I had just enough time to ride over the threshold of the SS *Delaware* before the ramp went up. A couple of stragglers were heading up the stairway, and I noticed a woman sitting in her car, holding onto the steering wheel. Some people were scared to ride the ferry and would rather stay in their car.

I knew Captain Sam Jennings commanded the *Delaware,* so I went up to the pilot house. He let me stand on the bridge because my dad was a navy man and all. He showed me the controls and pointed out the buoys he used to navigate. We were about halfway across when a woman came in saying she couldn't find her husband. She was afraid he had gone overboard. It was the same woman I had seen sitting in her car.

Now yelling "man overboard" is about as bad as shouting "fire" in a crowded theater. All hell broke loose. The engines powered down. Deck hands ran around in a panic, looking over the sides of the ship. The captain made a plea on the loudspeaker for everyone to look for anything in the water.

Luckily, a New Jersey Port Authority cop was on board, so he was summoned to the bridge. The lady really started bawling when he came through the door. They all ignored me, so I just stood and listened.

"Ma'am, I'm Officer Porter. Where was your husband when you last saw him?"

"He wasn't feeling well," she said through her handkerchief. "Neither one of us likes boats. We get seasick. Howard thought some fresh air would help, so he was by the rail. Maybe he got sick and fell when he leaned over to …" her voice trailed off in tears, but we all got the picture.

Officer Porter took down the details—his name, what he was wearing, whether he often felt faint. Captain Sam started a slow, wide circle to get back to where poor Howard may have gone into the water.

I listened to all this and watched the expression on the woman's face. I didn't want to go against my rule of no finding at the beach, but the lady looked so distraught that I had to ask.

"Do you have a picture of your husband, ma'am?" The interruption only succeeded in getting Officer Porter's swift attention.

"What's your name, kid?"

"Thaddeus Zoon."

"And what, exactly, do you have to do with this?"

"Uh, I help people find things."

"Oh you do, huh? Well, I was just gonna ask about a picture, so butt out." Officer Porter turned back to the woman.

"Mrs. Grimaldi, do you have a recent photo of your husband?"

Mrs. Grimaldi pulled out a picture that looked as if it had been torn in half. There was Howard, with a big smile on his face, holding a bowling ball. He was wearing a blue bowling shirt with *Heavy Rollers* embroidered over his heart. Judging from his hefty girth, the name fit perfectly.

As soon as I saw the picture, my mind flashed, but all I saw was darkness. Could that mean Howard was already dead and underwater? I felt hot all over and sensed a tightness as if he might be in a small space. That wouldn't be the water. He must still be on the ferry. But where? Then his bowling shirt sparked my brain again.

I remembered that the stragglers I had seen earlier had shiny windbreakers the same color. Could they be bowling jackets? I looked down onto the passenger deck and saw the two men standing by themselves, while everyone else was frantically looking out to sea. When they thought no one was watching, they headed for the stairway down to the car deck.

Those stairs led to the back of the ferry, where Mrs. Grimaldi's car was parked. Hers was the last car loaded, so it was just inches from the edge of the boat. Only a security chain across the opening would keep someone from "falling" overboard. I had the feeling Howard was still alive but was in trouble. Everyone else was focused on Mrs. Grimaldi. I had to hurry.

"Officer Porter, I think I know what happened. We have to get down to the car deck, quick!"

I went ahead, out of the pilot house and down to where the two men had been standing. I looked up to see Officer Porter looking at me over the railing above.

"Come on, I think those two guys are going to toss Mr. Grimaldi out the back!"

I didn't know if Officer Porter followed me or not, but I had to get to the car. Whether Mr. Grimaldi was alive or dead, those two guys could throw him out the back of the ferry and that would be it.

I saw the two men standing behind the car next to the Grimaldis'.

Their trunk lid was open, and they were struggling with something inside. The trunk. That's it! Mr. Grimaldi must be tied up in the trunk. I ran toward the men.

"Hey! What are you doing?"

The men looked up, then dropped whatever they were holding back into the trunk and closed the lid. The shorter one came around the car toward me and I stopped short.

"We thought we saw something in the water and were looking for a rope to throw out."

At that moment, I heard footsteps and turned to see Officer Porter bounding down the stairs. Thank goodness, the calvary had arrived.

"Over here!" I waved. "I found him! They were going to throw him overboard!"

The men froze. Officer Porter pointed to the trunk and ordered the men to open it.

The bigger man's hands were shaking as he tried to get his key in the lock, but finally the lid flew open and the men backed away. Officer Porter cautiously approached, but I rushed over, anxious to rescue Mr. Grimaldi from his watery fate.

There was nothing in the trunk but some fishing reels and a tangle of frayed rope. How could that be? I looked back at the two men, who now seemed more frightened than threatening. I saw that the windbreakers they were wearing had a fish on the chest, not the *Heavy Rollers* logo. Were these guys just fishermen trying to do a good deed?

Officer Porter once again turned his attention to me. "What was this all about?" he said through his teeth. "I must be stupid to listen to a skinny kid that helps people find things. Get outa here." He dismissed me with an angry wave. "I'm calling the coast guard."

I should have stuck to my rule of no finding while at the beach. Deflated, I went back up to the passenger cabin. Mrs. Grimaldi stood by the concession stand. One of the deck mates was getting her a cup of coffee. I walked over to make my apology.

"Mrs. Grimaldi, I'm real sorry about your husband. I was just trying to help." She appeared more nervous than worried, but when she saw me, she got downright angry.

"Why don't you mind your own business, you little Sherlock Holmes. Not everybody wants to be found, you know."

That seemed like a strange thing to say. Our eyes met and my mind flashed again. The image was still dark, but I felt even hotter this time and could hardly breathe. The engine noise was loud, yet the ferry was almost at a complete stop.

Not everybody wants to be found.

She took the coffee from the deck hand, nodding meekly at his comforting words, but her eyes held a warning for me.

Officer Porter was entering the cabin, so I turned quickly and went out the other side. I couldn't depend on his help; I was on my own. I leaned against the rail and looked out over the bay. The images had passed, and the cool air helped me think. If I were Mr. Grimaldi and didn't want to be found, where could I hide on a ferry? Where was it hot and loud? Just one place—the engine room.

I figured the door that led below deck would be locked, but to my surprise it opened right up, and I snuck down the stairs. My eyes slowly adjusted to the dim glow of the auxiliary lights on the wall.

The temperature increased as I descended, and the steamy room was tight and claustrophobic. Huge diesel engines groaned, gauges clicked, and valves opened. I looked around and tried to concentrate on the image I could vaguely see in my head. That's when I came across a door.

I opened it and the light rushed in to reveal a rotund figure on the floor. His head rested on a large duffle bag and his face glistened with sweat, but he wasn't moving. I could see he was breathing lightly but was in big trouble. I rushed over and shook him.

"Mr. Grimaldi! Howard! Are you OK?"

Mr. Grimaldi blubbered into consciousness, and his first reaction was to struggle. I nearly got clocked but ducked just in time.

I grabbed him by the shoulders. "What are you doing here? Everyone is looking for you."

His response was incoherent. I didn't know what to do. He was way too heavy for me to move, and if I told Officer Porter, he wouldn't believe me.

I heard squeaky footsteps coming my way. The people who put Mr. Grimaldi here must be coming back to finish him off. What could I do? Even if I would leave him, there was nowhere for me to go. They'll kill me too and throw us both overboard.

"Kid, are you down here?" It was Officer Porter. I was almost in tears.

"Yes! Over here. It's Mr. Grimaldi. He's in awful shape."

Porter's footsteps got closer and he appeared in the doorway.

"How did you find me?"

Porter pushed me aside to check on Mr. Grimaldi.

"You're not the only one that can find people, ya know. I saw you sneak out when I showed up. Figured you were up to no good again, so I followed you. That's what real detectives do."

I should have felt good that I had found Mr. Grimaldi, but I didn't. Porter's words really hurt. I quietly went back upstairs and watched as he and a few of the deck hands struggled to get Mr. Grimaldi out of the engine room. They roped off part of the passenger cabin and laid him down on one of the tables. Mrs. Grimaldi was confined up on the pilot deck and the captain got the ferry back on course for Lewes.

When we got to the landing, the state troopers were there. No one was allowed to get off until they put Mr. Grimaldi in an ambulance and his wife in a police car. Officer Porter gave one of the troopers the big duffle bag and turned around to come back on board. He saw me watching from the rail and pointed at me with a stay-there look. Now he was after *me*.

He found me slumped down outside the passenger cabin, wondering what my dad would think of me being arrested. Before I could plead my innocence, Officer Porter pulled me up onto my feet. I held my breath.

"You did OK for a kid. You got good instincts. You might get little pictures spinnin' in your head, but remember, I got experience. I could tell that Mrs. Grimaldi was hiding something. Her story smelled like rotten fish. She finally admitted that her husband robbed a bank in Atlantic City and they were trying to escape on the ferry."

"There was money in that duffle bag?"

"Yeah, she had the bright idea of fakin' her old man's death and claimin' he went overboard with the cash if the cops ever caught up to her. Her nephew worked at the concession stand, so he unlocked the door to the engine room."

"Tommy, the hot dog guy?"

Officer Porter nodded.

"Howard went down and hid in the electrical room. Mrs. Grimaldi thought he could sneak back and get in the trunk of their car after the search was called off. Drive right off the ferry to who knows where. But they didn't count on you being on board."

"Me?"

"You put a monkey wrench in their plan when you went runnin' down to where their car was parked. Tommy couldn't give Howard the all-clear signal and the big galoot passed out from the heat. He could've died down there if you hadn't found him."

"So, I'm not in trouble?" For the first time I saw him smile.

"Nah, you could actually be a detective someday." He slapped me on the back. "Just don't rush off because you see something in your mind. Think about what those pictures are tellin' you and you'll make a great cop."

Cop? Officer Porter thinks I could be a cop?

The passengers were finally allowed to leave, and I saw Tommy taken off in handcuffs. The ferry was ready to go back to New Jersey with Officer Porter and a lot of impatient passengers. I was over two hours late getting the scones to the restaurant, so I rode home as fast as I could. Dad had heard about the big heist and figured I was involved, but there was no time to talk. Mrs. Applegate and her friends were arriving, and they all wanted to hear my story. I told them all about it and how Officer Porter thought I'd make a good cop and that Mrs. Grimaldi called me a little Sherlock Holmes. The ladies decided their next book would be a Holmes mystery, and invited me to join them for their monthly meeting.

I read a lot of Sherlock Holmes books that summer and saw Officer Porter a couple times on the ferry. The days went fast, and although I hated to leave, I was happy to go home and get back to finding things for the neighbors. It was different now, though. I had a plan for where my talent would take me, and I gained experience with each new case.

"Thaddeus!"

Yeah, Ma's voice sure carries.

TERESA BERRY GREW UP IN SUBURBAN PHILADELPHIA WHEN TRIPS TO THE JERSEY SHORE OR THE DELAWARE BEACHES INVOLVED A RIDE ON THE FERRY. "THADDEUS ZOON: MAYHEM ON THE FERRY" IS HER FIRST PUBLISHED SHORT STORY AND SHE HOPES THE CHARACTER WILL APPEAR IN A SERIES OF LIGHT MYSTERIES SET IN THE TRISTATE AREA (PA-NJ-DE) DURING SIMPLER TIMES. LEARN MORE ABOUT THADDEUS AND HIS FAMILY AT WWW.THADDEUSZOON.COM.

TERESA NOW LIVES IN HOCKESSIN, DELAWARE, WITH HER HUSBAND, ALAN. WRITING HAS ALWAYS BEEN PART OF HER LIFE, AND AFTER A LONG CORPORATE CAREER, SHE IS FOCUSING ON WRITING FICTION. SHE HAS SEVERAL LONGER PIECES UNDER CONSTRUCTION AND LOOKS FORWARD TO SEEING WHERE THEY TAKE HER.

JUDGE'S COMMENT

Tight beginning, an interesting setting, and a strong narrative arc. Dialogue moved both plot and characters forward. Overall a well-constructed and executed short story, enjoyable as a mystery beach read!

A Killer White Paint

By Rich Barnett

Who in the hell steals paint? That's the question Barry Bayard mulls as he searches his house for three missing cans of white paint. Last night he'd arranged them carefully on newspapers on the floor of the butler's pantry just off the kitchen. This morning, only the newspaper remained. He's certain he locked all the doors before going to bed, and there's no evidence of a forced entry. Nobody else should have a key.

He pours himself a large cup of coffee and makes one final pass through the first floor of the rambling cedar-shingle house that until recently had belonged to his Uncle Henry and Aunt Kathryn. Barry hadn't been keen to buy the place until Henry and Kathryn offered it to him at a bargain price. It had been decades since he'd spent any time in Rehoboth Beach. A New Yorker now, Barry preferred the posh Hamptons social scene. But, as an investor in tech start-ups, he had a talent for identifying a good investment and moved quickly to seize the multi-million-dollar real estate opportunity before his aged relatives changed their minds.

Of course, the house needed some work to bring it up to his exacting standards—granite countertops in the kitchen, double sinks in the bathrooms, and a swimming pool was a must. The very first thing he had to do, however, was paint the inside of the house the right shade of white. He runs his hand over the dark wood paneling in the library; it doesn't suit him at all.

Later that day, after a trip to the paint store, Barry gets to work. He strips down to his boxer shorts and white Nittany Lions T-shirt. He syncs his iPhone to his favorite painting music—the Rolling Stones—

and sets out hog-bristle brushes and lambswool rollers. He opens a new can of paint, leans over, and takes a big whiff. *Perfection.* The smell of VOC fumes is to Barry what the madeleine was to Proust, an explosion of summer and youth.

Barry hadn't been born into wealth. His parents had grown peaches and strawberries on the old family farm in western Delaware. Barry was motivated, though, and he worked as a house painter in Rehoboth Beach every summer from age sixteen until he graduated with a finance degree from Penn State. He relished the quiet that came with painting, as well as the physical repetitiveness of the task. Painting allowed him to disconnect. And he took great satisfaction in seeing the transformation wrought by his efforts. Even now, thirty years removed from those halcyon days of youth and with a fat bank account, he still did all his own painting.

Just as Barry is about to dip a brush, he's interrupted by the chirping sound of his iPhone. He recognizes the New York number showing on the display screen—an investor he can't ignore.

Ten minutes later he returns to his task. A slick of black coffee grounds floats on top of the white paint.

He sucks in his breath and stomps over to the Krups coffee maker in the kitchen. Sure enough, the coffee grounds are gone. *What the hell?*

He dials up his older sister, Susan, a decorator in New Orleans, but gets only her voicemail. "Something weird is going on in the Rehoboth house. Call me."

I'll keep an eye on the remaining can of paint, he thinks, reaching for one of the hog-bristle brushes. *Damn it. Now* they're *gone!*

A few minutes later, his iPhone chirps and he picks it up. *Susan.*

"Darling, I got your message. What's the problem?"

Barry explains.

"I see … Oh, dear … Sounds to me like you've gone and bought yourself a house with a poltergeist. What you need is a 'Come to Jesus' meeting with your surly spirit. Simply invite him to join you for a cocktail to discuss these incidents in a civilized manner."

"Do spirits drink?"

"Doesn't everyone? Listen, darling, someone is trying to make a connection. Down here they say spirits cause a commotion when they need to get something off their chests. Address the problem and it should go away."

Barry takes his older sister's advice and writes out a formal invitation asking the spirit to join him for cocktails and conversation at 6:30 p.m. and leaves it on the English bamboo table in the library. Then he goes off to his makeshift office in the kitchen to study some IPO documents.

When the appointed time arrives, so does the spirit, poltergeist, or ghost (Barry isn't sure what to call it), emerging from thin air like a hologram. The handsome, older-looking gentleman is seated in a green silk wingchair in the library, with his leg crossed, nattily attired in a pair of gray linen pants, white shirt, royal-blue sweater, and black loafers, sans socks. Barry is surprised and intrigued, but not afraid.

The two men eye each other before Barry sticks out his hand. "Hello, I'm Barry Bayard; pleased to meet you."

The spirit sits, unmoving, ignoring the outstretched hand, before finally responding to Barry's overtures. "I'd like to say the same, but I'm afraid I cannot, given the circumstances."

Hmm, Barry thinks, *no handshake, no pleasantries. Game on.* In his world of high finance, Barry is used to difficult men. He stands and walks over to the wet bar where he has set out liquor, wine, ice, and glasses. Pouring himself a healthy vodka and tonic, he addresses the spirit. "What can I bring you?"

The spirit finally answers. "A gin and tonic would be lovely."

Barry mixes the drink and sets it on a table beside the spirit. He is tempted to touch the spirit but he doesn't. "It appears," Barry says, "that we have a little problem. You seem determined to make it difficult for me to paint."

"That is correct."

"May I ask why?"

"Because I do not approve of you painting my house."

"*Your* house? I paid $1.7 million for this place and I have the right to do with my property as I wish."

"You may be the legal owner, Mr. Bayard, but I am the *rightful* owner. Permit me to introduce myself. My name is Jim Thompson."

The spirit looks at Barry as if he expects Barry to recognize him, which Barry does not. "Why are you haunting my house?"

"Mr. Bayard, I am not haunting anything. Have you heard moans and groans or the shaking of chains? I am merely protecting myself from the philistines."

"I beg your pardon. I'll have you know I live in Manhattan and have a fine appreciation for the arts," Barry replies tartly.

"But you have no taste, or you would never consider turning a classic seaside cottage into some sort of monochromatic modern art gallery with your white paint.

"For your information, Mr. Thompson, it isn't just any white paint. I've selected Oxford white, a shade that changes with the light but creates a logic and continuity that effortlessly relates rooms to one another."

"Pooh."

"Against the right white backdrop, art and life can take center stage."

"Rubbish."

"And besides, all this dark wood is depressing," Barry declares, waving his hand around. "I don't like it."

"This wood, Mr. Bayard, is of *significance*. It is Delaware cypress, harvested from what was once a great cypress swamp in the southwestern part of the state. I personally selected the trees and had them milled specifically for this house. What remains of the swamp is now protected, which means this wood is *irreplaceable*. Just like the brick fireplace in the living room. Do you know, Mr. Bayard, these bricks came from the old Cape Henlopen lighthouse? They were salvaged when it toppled into the Atlantic Ocean in 1926. The Cape lighthouse was first lit in 1769."

At this, Jim Thompson stands. Shaking his fist, he declares in a deafening voice: "Precious wood and old brick should never be painted!"

Barry calmly takes a sip from his vodka tonic before answering. "This house is an investment, and as such it must be managed so as to increase its worth. Would you rather I just knock it down? Because if I don't take care of it and update it, then the next owner will almost certainly tear it down."

"I could stop it."

"Coffee grounds, Mr. Thompson, cannot stop a bulldozer."

The spirit smiles and leans forward. "But coffee grounds can give pause, as they have done to you. Coffee grounds can frighten. Fear of the unknown will stop a bulldozer."

"But progress, Mr. Thompson, will not be slowed. And we both know money always wins out."

"You are a cynical man, Mr. Bayard."

"I am a practical man. And I shall do with my property what I wish."

The man and the spirit stare at each other. After a few minutes, the spirit speaks: "Thank you, Mr. Bayard, for your hospitality, but it appears we have nothing more to discuss. Therefore, I shall be going." And he vanishes.

Barry sits there for about a half hour, thinking about what has just transpired. Or what he thinks has transpired. Has he been arguing with a ghost? He isn't really sure. The cocktail on the bamboo table beside the wing chair where the ghost had been sitting sits untouched. When he takes the glasses into the kitchen, he notices the four remaining unopened cans of paint he'd bought earlier in the day are gone.

A month later, Barry returns to Rehoboth Beach, this time accompanied by his sister Susan. They arrive early on a Saturday morning with bags of gourmet groceries, lots of vodka, and four new gallons of Oxford white paint.

"I still cannot believe your house is haunted by Jim Thompson," Susan squeals. "I'm dying to meet him."

For the entire five-hour drive from Manhattan, Susan regaled Barry with the legend of Jim Thompson, the son of a prominent Delaware family who gained fame and fortune for reviving Thailand's silk industry before vanishing without a trace on Easter Sunday, 1967, while hiking in Malaysia. His body was never found, but the fabric company he founded lives on today. Barry was intrigued with the story and impressed that such a persona had designed the house. That didn't negate the fact that Thompson had become a major irritant.

With Susan guarding the cans, Barry methodically paints the butler's pantry. Both siblings are surprised as the first coat, then the second, go on without incident. The next day, the two of them paint the kitchen white.

"It's a killer shade of white," Barry says, stepping back to admire the color. "I suppose Mr. Thompson has given up," he boasts, as he stands at the sink, cleaning his brushes and rollers.

Perhaps, but not likely, Susan thinks. She'd never heard of a ghost giving up a fight so easily. At that moment, she hears a yelp and a thud and spins around. Barry has taken a tumble. The antique, cream-colored Ben Ourain rug lies crumpled along the wall, as if it has been pulled from under him.

"Perhaps," Susan suggests, "it's time for another chat with Mr. Thompson."

Barry pens another invitation on a card and leaves it on the bamboo table in the library as he did the first time.

Just as before, the ghost of Jim Thompson magically appears, dressed the same as the first time Barry encountered him.

"Good evening, Mr. Thompson."

"Good evening, Mr. Bayard."

"Permit me to introduce my sister, Susan Parasol, a decorator from New Orleans."

Jim Thompson silently stares at the bejeweled and bespangled redhead before finally responding, "Charmed."

"It is certainly a pleasure to meet you," Susan gushes. "I'm a big fan of your work and I absolutely love, love, love your butterfly house fabric! That it was inspired by a decoration found on an eighteenth-century Chinese snuffbox, why, that is absolutely brilliant."

Barry takes a deep breath and dives back into the issue at hand. "Susan tells me you built this house for your mother, but you neither owned it nor lived in it."

"Technically, you are correct; however, this is very much my house. I designed it. I oversaw its construction. I even named it *Mon Plaisir*."

"We both know that wouldn't constitute ownership in a court of law, Mr. Thompson, especially not in Delaware."

"I am not a lawyer."

"Surely you must agree that the kitchen and the butler's pantry look splendid in Oxford white. The vintage kitchen cabinets and built-in shelving now look stylish but timeless."

"Yes, I suppose."

"Then may I proceed?"

"No. I strongly disapprove of your vision for *Mon Plaisir*. And I have heard you talking about painting this library. A library should be dark and quiet. A white library would lack gravitas. Are you a reader, Mr. Bayard?"

"Unfortunately, no. I spend more time reading contracts."

"Tsk, tsk. Well, you should know I designed my library with the reader in mind. It is a reflective space, where one can get lost in a story and where time can misbehave."

Susan interjects herself into the conversation. "But a library's purpose is also to house and showcase books. Imagine how the colors and textures of books would look when contrasted against the white. It will draw you to the books. The effect will emphasize rather than hide them."

Mr. Thompson gives her a wave of the hand and stares directly at Barry. "Books are not décor. Let me make myself perfectly clear. I forbid you from painting my library."

Barry flares his nostrils at the direct challenge, but he keeps his calm. He'd learned that under such circumstances it was better to say little and let your opponent reveal his hand. Besides, he has no experience dealing with supernatural beings.

"What if I pay you to leave. I'll write you a check tonight for $100,000."

"I don't need money, Mr. Bayard. And besides, where would I go?"

"Go back to your beloved Bangkok."

"That city is ruined. My house there is now a museum full of tourists. Besides, I like it here, especially in the winter when the town goes to sleep. Speaking of which, I bid you a good night." At that, he vanishes, leaving Barry and Susan sitting alone in the library.

Later that night, Barry lies in bed, reading old newspaper and magazine articles about Jim Thompson, known as the Thai Silk King and one of the most important and powerful Americans living in Southeast Asia during the 1950s and 1960s. Stories about his disappearance had been front-page news for the *Wall Street Journal* and the *New York Times.* Because a body had never been found, many believed he had been eaten by tigers or kidnapped and killed by the CIA.

Most of the men Barry dealt with were motivated by money. Jim

Thompson seemed to have been motivated by romance, as seen in his work to revive the dying Thai silk industry and his love for traditional Thai architecture and culture. Romanticism was also behind his support of Vietnamese, Laotian, and Cambodian national independence movements, positions that put him at odds with the US government and which many believed played a role in his disappearance.

As the sleeping pill he took begins to do its magic, Barry realizes he might have uncovered the solution to his problem.

The next day, Barry leaves a written invitation in the library requesting Jim Thompson to join him alone that evening in the library to continue their conversation. He isn't sure Thompson will come, but he is betting on Thompson's good manners.

Again, the ghost appears. "And to what do I owe this conversation tonight, Mr. Bayard? Are you going to try and convince me to like your white walls by pointing out, perhaps, that the ancient Roman libraries tended to be built from white stone and marble?"

"Would that argument have worked?"

Jim Thompson remains silent.

"I didn't think so. Mr. Thompson, I'm not going to try and convince you of anything because I see how useless that would be. I've asked you here to tell you I have decided not to paint the library or the rest of the house."

"And why is that?"

"You've told me things about this house I never knew. It is special, and its pedigree, I believe, will enhance its value."

"Well, I must say, I'm pleased. Surprised, but pleased."

At that moment, Barry pulls out a two-foot-tall, wooden threshold from beneath his chair, kneels, and quickly wedges it into the doorjamb. He'd hired a local carpenter to build it for him earlier in the day. A raised threshold, according to Thai folklore, deters unwanted spirits.

Barry had read how Jim Thompson had installed them all over his own home in Bangkok. Barry reasoned that if a raised threshold could keep a spirit from entering a room, then it should also keep a spirit from leaving a room. He had, in effect, imprisoned the ghost of Jim Thompson in the library.

"You should have seen the look on the old boy's face," Barry says to Susan afterward. "When he realized what had happened, he wasn't too happy. But, hey, he's the one who made such a fuss about his damn library. He better love it as much as he says he does, because he's gonna be stuck in there until he comes around to seeing things my way." Barry and Susan clink their wineglasses in celebration.

The next morning while Susan sleeps in, Barry removes the draperies from the living room windows and pushes the furniture into the middle of the room. He covers everything with a white canvas tarp. Down on all fours, Barry sets out his hogs-hair paintbrushes, lambswool rollers, and paint tray and sets his iPhone's Rolling Stones playlist to shuffle. He never sees the bottle of red wine come crashing down onto the back of his skull.

Jim Thompson puts down the broken bottle, a California old vine zinfandel, and carefully pushes Barry's face into the paint tray, making sure to submerge the unconscious man's mouth and nose in the Oxford white paint in order to cut off the oxygen. Within a few minutes, Barry Bayard is dead.

He rubs his hand down the dead man's neck to the muscular shoulders. *Tsk, tsk. If only the handsome man hadn't been so stubborn.* But what choice did he have after such a ridiculous stunt the night before? He had used the threshold myth to manipulate his Bangkok house servants. Who believed such folklore? He picks up the jagged neck of the bottle of wine. Now for that annoying decorator sister …

Rich Barnett's humor column in the magazine *LETTERS from Camp Rehoboth* just celebrated fifteen years, and his most recent book, *Fun with Dick and James,* was published in 2016. Rich's short stories have recently appeared in *Saints and Sinners: New Fiction from the Festival 2020* and *Best Gay Stories 2017.* Rich resides in Rehoboth Beach, just around the corner from the house in his story "A Killer White Paint." It is one of his favorite houses in Rehoboth, and Jim Thompson did indeed design it as his mother's summer home. As far as Rich knows, the house isn't haunted.

Judges' Comments

A brilliant send-up of gentrification at the beach, "A Killer White Paint" seems, at first, a quaint story of the supernatural, tinged with esoterica. But then it bares its teeth in the final act.

Bus to the Beach

By Kathaleen and Terrence McCormick

"Now that 'Three Dog Night' and 'Brogues and Black Powder' are wrapped up, what are you going to write?" Terry sipped from the DD coffee he had just bought from the drive-through on Route 1, and pointed the car south.

"Dunno." Kathy was fiddling with Facebook on her phone.

"Well, you should write something!"

"Alright, if it's so easy, give me an idea. And don't forget to stop at The Wooden Indian gift shop, so we can get something original for a wedding gift. I am really happy for Angie and Belle. You know, this will be our first Mrs. and Mrs. wedding, and—"

"Bus to the Beach." Terry took another swig of his coffee. "There's a good title, right there on that bus pulling out."

Kathy put her phone down and looked up. A bus clearly labeled "Bus to the Beach" belched and pulled away from the intersection. "Hey, that's a great idea! You are getting into this." She turned to look at him, amazed at his newfound creativity. "Maybe you have a writer inside you and I never knew it." She needed to probe. "How would you play it out?"

Terry thought for a minute. "Well, there are people on the bus."

"Who?"

"A man and a woman."

"Tell me about them."

"Maybe he's Italian and his wife is Irish."

Kathy, feeling that Terry was onto something, pushed him further. "Why are they on the bus?"

Terry sipped his coffee, one hand on the cup, the other on the steering wheel, as he mulled this over. "They met at the beach. Rehoboth. It's the anniversary of when they met."

"Hmm. Name him. Tony? Joey?" The pedal was down and Kathy was not about to let it up.

"Too common." Terry took another gulp of coffee. "Sal." Terry seemed surprised to suddenly see Sal in his mind's eye. "Sal. A bricklayer." There it was.

Kathy smiled. "Sal. Salvatore Cataldi. I like it. Sal and Moira. That's it!" Kathy dug through her bag, pushed her yarn aside, and pulled out her black-marbled composition tablet. Then, with pen in hand, she began …

* * * * *

Salvatore and Moira Cataldi settled into their seats on the bus to the beach as it pulled away from the Biden Train Station in Wilmington.

"Did you bring my Kindle?"

"Yes, Sal."

"Did we pack water?"

"Yes, Sal."

"Did you ask Scott to feed and walk Duke?"

"Yes, Sal."

"For Pete's sake, Moira, stop saying 'yes, Sal'!"

"Yes, Sal." Moira laughed at her joke.

Tell me again, why aren't we driving our own car to Rehoboth?"

"You have cataracts and can't drive at night, and I don't want to drive that far."

"Then why didn't we just stay home?"

"Because fifty years ago we met at Dolle's in Rehoboth and I want to celebrate that moment."

Sal reached over and kissed Moira. She fussed with her wedding ring. "Sal, it has been a good fifty years." She leaned her head on his shoulder and smelled his Old Spice cologne. It had not changed in all those years. Her cologne evolved—Tigress, then Chanel No. 5, now Obsession—but she used it only on special occasions. Nothing could improve on the clean smell of Ivory soap.

The bus glided over the Roth Bridge and rolled past fields filled with tasseled green ears of corn. Sal nodded off and Moira reached into her big quilted bag and pulled out a needlepoint project. She nodded at the girl seated across the aisle from her. "Have you ever tried needlepoint?"

"No, ma'am."

"It's a great time passer." Moira appraised the girl's purple mullet. "I like the purple. Do you think I could pull off something like that?"

The girl stared at her. "Maybe, but why would you want to?"

"I don't know. Why did you?"

The girl cracked her first smile. "Because I knew it would piss off my parents."

Moira passed her a bottle of water. "What's your name?"

"Pippa."

"Well, Pippa, did they get mad?"

"At the hair? Hard to tell. They're always mad about something—my friends, me, Leah."

The bus changed lanes and hit the noisy rumble strips. Sal opened his eyes. Noting the new friendship, he nodded. "Who have we here?"

"Sal, this is Pippa."

"Going to Rehoboth are you?" Sal asked.

"I am. I thought maybe I'd find a job there, you know, Funland or something. If I get a job, Leah will come down." She gnawed on a fingernail.

Tying off a thread, Moira glanced up. "Where are you staying?"

Simultaneously, Sal queried, "Is Leah your sister?"

"Girlfriend." Pippa ran her abused fingertips through her hair and raised her intense blue eyes to meet Moira's.

Moira, a retired teacher, caught her breath. *Oh Sal, don't say anything.* Sal had a heart of gold, but he had a habit of putting his foot in his mouth. To him, "gay" meant happy, and pride was what you felt when you hit a home run.

Instead of answering Moira's question, Pippa asked, "What are you guys going to do at the beach?"

Moira took Sal's hands in hers and smiled. She loved his rugged hands, hands that worked with bricks and cuddled babies, hands the size of baseball mitts. "We met in Rehoboth. It was one of the best days of my life."

"It was that two-piece, pink-checked, bathing suit that caught my eye. Sal laughed. "There she was, sunburned nose and cotton candy stuck in her hair, laughing with her friends. I winked. When she smiled back at me, I walked over, bowed, and offered to rescue her from the cotton candy that was attacking her hair. She curtsied, and I took her by the hand and walked her to the fountain and washed the cotton candy out of her hair."

Moira picked up the story. "Oh, he was a gallant knight! Slayer of cotton candy! Only then did he introduce himself. 'Sal. I'm Sal,' he said. 'Marry me.' I thought he was daft! *Marry you*, says I? And why would I do that? He answered, 'Because I spent two years in 'nam and I'm not going to waste another second of my life. Marry me.'"

Sal jumped back in. "She didn't say no, but she didn't say yes either. She did ask me to wait for five minutes. She strutted off the boardwalk and went down on the beach to a blanket that was spread over the sand. I stood right there, planted on the boards. Hopeful. Her friends followed her to the blanket, but she waved them off. She put a gray Kappa Alpha tee shirt given to her by one of the campus football jocks over her bathing suit, stuffed a towel and a transistor radio into a straw bag, plopped on a big hat, and came back across the beach. She wove her way between umbrellas, then up the steps. When she reached the boardwalk, she took gladiator sandals out of the bag and laced them around her ankles. Never looked back. She walked right up to me, put her hand in mine, and said, 'I'm Moira. Where are we going?'" Sal smiled. "If she only knew!"

The bus passed the new sports complex at Milford. There were now more car dealerships than corn.

"Just like that?" asked Pippa. "It was love?"

Sal laughed. "Just like that. She was hungry, so we went to Grotto. Sat there for two and a half hours just talking. Then we went down to Funland and I won her a stuffed dog. It was on the carousel that I stole a kiss. Our first. Only then did I ask her what was with the Kappa Alpha shirt. She looked right into my eyes said, "It is from a friend and he is yesterday."

Pippa sat silently. Tears welled up in her eyes. "It sounds so easy."

Sal summed it all up. "Fifty years, three kids, six grands, thirteen dogs, one hamster, a teaching career for her and a construction job for me. Not always easy, but always perfect."

Moira took in Pippa's tears and passed her a tissue. "Everybody deserves to love and be loved, Pippa. In a way, it's a mystery. It doesn't have to be solved though, only lived."

"Yep," laughed Sal. "Go stand in front of Dolle's and maybe your prince charming will find you today."

Moira rolled her eyes. So did Pippa.

"Or Princess Charming," Moira quipped.

Sal scrooched up his face, puzzled. "Nope. The princess always gets rescued by Prince Charming."

Pippa and Moira shook their heads.

* * * * *

Back at the house, Terry put down the printed pages Kathy had handed him to read. "I like it. You had a pink-checked bathing suit, didn't you?"

"I did. But the day we met I was wearing the black one with the netting, remember?"

"I'll never forget. And those gladiator sandals!"

"So, the story. What do you think?"

"I like Sal. He commits quick. But the kid. How is this going to work out?"

"Hmm. Not sure, but it will. It's an enigma how this works. At a given point, the story takes over and writes itself. I'll be back in the office. Yell if you need me."

* * * * *

The bus dropped off the trio and many more at the Rehoboth

bandstand. Pippa disappeared into the Thrasher's-vinegar-fries-munching, Dolle's-saltwater-taffy-chewing, suntanned and sandy summer crowd. Sal put on his Phillies baseball hat and Moira took his picture with her iPhone. Hand in hand, they posed in front of the iconic Dolle's sign. Moira awkwardly and unsuccessfully tried for a selfie, so a young teenager offered to take their picture. Sal, still strong at seventy-three, scooped Moira up in his arms and carried her to the water fountain. There, they kissed while others looked on with curiosity and smiles.

"We fell in love here," Sal boomed. "Right here. Fifty years ago. It happened in a heartbeat."

There was laughter and applause, the calls of gulls, and the crash of waves. From a white bench on the boardwalk, a thin girl with purple hair looked on. Moira noticed Pippa and whispered to Sal. "Honey, she looks hungry. So thin."

"Come on." Sal motioned to Pippa. "Get on over here before I have to come dunk you in the fountain. Let's go. My little lady is hungry."

Pippa looked confused.

"Join us, Pippa. Sal wants you to join us for lunch."

The three of them walked to Grotto Pizza. They ate and talked and talked and ate, triangles of orange, bite by bite, more parmesan, a few flakes of red pepper, more bites. Pippa matched big Sal slice for slice.

"Tell me 'bout your kids," Pippa said through a mouthful of pizza.

Moira smiled the smile of special memory. "Well, Scott is the oldest. He has three girls. Then there's Todd. He has two boys and a girl."

"That's only two. Sal said you have three."

"We do have three, but now Jenny is our angel. She was in a car accident and she didn't make it. She was only eighteen."

"My age." Tears welled up in Pippa's eyes. "I am so sorry. I think she was lucky to have two such great parents."

"We are the lucky ones, Pippa. We have a happy family and on every occasion we set a place at the table for Jenny. I know I will see her on the other side."

"She was lucky. My parents put me out. They don't even want to see me on this side."

"Hey, hey, hey!" Sal interrupted. "This is a celebration. Let's go get our feet wet, then ride that carousel."

"Geez, I wish Leah could meet you guys."

"Have you and Leah been friends long?" Moira asked.

"Seems like forever, but just two years. I can't imagine life without her."

"Then she must be very special. Maybe someday we can meet her. Right, Sal?"

"Yeah, I'd like that. Good friend, huh?"

Just then two men rushed into the surf, hand in hand. Sal shook his head. "It's just not right. It was Adam and Eve, not Adam and Arnie."

"Love is love," said Moira.

Pippa turned her face to Sal. "Well, I love Leah and the God I know is the God of love." She dropped her backpack, kicked off her flip-flops, and raced into the surf.

"Sal! How can you be so cold. Pippa is entitled to love wherever she finds it."

* * * * *

Terry, with one big hand on the head of his golden lab, pointed with the other at the word *cold*. He was proofing the fourth draft. "I would change this word. Sal isn't cold. He has a big, big heart. He's just dense."

"You're right." Moira scratched through "cold" and wrote "dense."

* * * * *

"Sal! How can you be so dense. Pippa is entitled to love wherever she finds it."

"What are you talking about?"

Moira looked Sal in the eye. "Pippa. Pippa loves Leah. They are more than friends. They are a couple. C-o-u-p-l-e."

"Well, uh, I don't buy it."

"Sal, love is love. You need to get over this. You like Robert and Ted in the house across the street from us."

"But they're brothers."

"No, Sal. Lovers. And married."

"Hmmmph." Sal's thinker face was chiseled like Rodin's statue.

"Yes, Sal. They're just like us. An old married couple." Moira gave Sal her teacher look, one eyebrow raised, mouth set in a rosebud. Sal stroked his chin, still thinking. Moira continued, "Sal, you just—"

Moira was cut off by screams as a surge of sunbathers rushed to the edge of the surf. "Riptide," said one to no one in particular. The lifeguard was already swimming out to the ever-more-distant purple head.

* * * * *

A limp body. CPR. An ambulance siren. Screaming.

"Mary, Mother of God!" Moira was half lifted by Sal out of the taxi, rosary beads in her hand.

Sal spoke through the glass window in the Emergency Department. "Sal Cataldi for Pippa Barclay."

"Have a seat. We'll call you when we can."

Moira moved the beads through her hand, muttering the prayer for each bead. Sal watched the clock. Tick. Pause. Tock. Pause. Tick. Pause An eternity.

"What is going on in there?" Sal sat, head in his hands. "I can't do this, Moira. It's like Jenny all over again."

"I know, Sal. Pippa is just a kid with her whole beautiful life ahead of her. I'm so scared." Sal enveloped Moira in his arms as tears ran down their faces.

When a nurse finally came out the double doors and approached them, Sal stood, then stumbled.

"Mr. Calaldi? Sit down. Put your head down. There. Some orange juice?"

Moira faced the nurse. "Pippa. How is Pippa?"

"She'll be fine. It was close, but the ocean didn't win this time. You can come back to see her."

The smell of alcohol and the sounds of pulsing and beeping machines replaced the ticking of the clock. The nurse led Moira and Sal to a treatment area in the ER. Sal pushed ahead, needing to verify for himself that Pippa was OK. The purple-crowned princess lay propped on pillows, with an intravenous line hooked to her left arm. Pippa opened her eyes, lashes casting a shadow on her pale cheeks.

"Who are you to Pippa?" the nurse asked, picking up her clipboard. "She's given permission for us to release information to you, but apparently she is homeless—"

"What's this homeless shit?" barked Sal.

"She could leave tonight if she had a place to go, but since she hasn't, we will keep her here and release her to a women's shelter tomorrow."

"She has a place. She'll go home with us."

Moira spun to look at Sal.

Pippa looked at Sal and Moira. "It's OK. Don't worry about me."

Moira was still focused on Sal, her eyes wet with tears, her lower lip between her teeth, one hand at her neck.

"Hush." Sal took full command. "You need a safe place until you get back on your feet. You can stay with us."

Moira clasped her hands and smiled broadly. "Oh, Pippa, you can have Jenny's room."

Pippa's lips fluttered into a smile, which then flitted away. Tears trickled down her cheek. "I can't. I really want to see Leah."

"Well, we can't wait to meet her. She can come over anytime, and you'll both have a chance to find work and get a game plan." Sal was firm.

Moira hugged Pippa and her tears were now tears of joy. Just like that. She turned to bring Sal into the hug, but he was gone. "Sal?" Moira moved to the curtain and peeked into the corridor. No Sal. She didn't want to leave Pippa for even a second, but Sal ... where was he?

And then Sal walked back into the room, calm as a winter morning, holding his black flip phone in his hand. "I just called our neighbor Robert. He'll pick us up." Looking softly at Moira, he nodded, "You're right. Love is a mystery. It comes in all shapes and sizes and colors. Love is love and tonight it is purple. I'm taking my two ladies home."

Denouement

Time passed quickly. Pippa Barclay earned a certificate in welding from Delaware Technical and Community College the following spring. Two years later, Pippa and Leah married in a civil ceremony held in the Cataldi backyard. Leah, employed at Happy Vines Flower Shop, prepared all the flower arrangements, purple of course. One year after the wedding, at the age of seventy-six, Sal died of a massive coronary. He never did get to meet Pippa and Leah's son, his namesake.

Since then, in remembrance of Sal, on the third Sunday of every August, Moira, Pippa, Leah, and 'little Sal' spend the day in Rehoboth Beach eating Grotto pizza, wading in the surf, and riding the carousel. Their laughter and love is purple.

* * * * *

Terry put the story back in the folder. He sipped his coffee and looked at Kathy accusingly. "I still don't know why Sal had to die. You could make him live."

Kathy flipped her hair back. "Sorry. It reached the point where the story took over. Sal died. I'm not God. I can't change the story."

KATHY AND COACH TERRY MCCORMICK, BORN AND RAISED DELAWAREANS, ARE BOTH RETIRED FROM THE EDUCATIONAL FIELD. THREE CHILDREN AND SIX GRANDCHILDREN KEEP LIFE VERY INTERESTING. "BUS TO THE BEACH" IS THEIR FIRST CO-AUTHORED WORK, AND YES, THE WRITING PROCESS DID HAPPEN AS THE STORY DEPICTS! THE STORY ITSELF IS FICTIONAL. KATHY HAS BEEN PUBLISHED LOCALLY AND INTERNATIONALLY. SHE IS HAPPY TO HAVE TERRY CAUGHT UP IN THIS FREE FALL CALLED WRITING.

A Stitch in Time

By Chris Jacobsen

Three blocks up Park Avenue from Front Street, Tilly waddled over to the steps of her church and grabbed the railing to help haul her large frame up and through the door, the wind whipping her long, colorful caftan. Once inside, she headed for the social room where weekly she met with a group of elderly women.

The calendar of the St. George African Methodist Episcopal Church listed the Friday morning gathering as the sewing group. Some knitted bed shawls for those in the hospital as others crocheted afghans for shut-ins. Tilly was a quilter.

Recently, Tilly arrived early to get a seat facing the ocean, although it could not be seen from the church. After greeting the other women, she put on her glasses and reached into her bag to pull out the final quilt square, which she hoped to finish that day. With her thick brown fingers, she tucked up wisps of gray hair into her headscarf and deftly began to appliqué a small square onto the background fabric, her needle creeping from right to left, making tiny precise stitches.

* * * * *

On the outskirts of Lewes proper, the breeze snapped the bed sheets that hung on the clothesline behind an old farmhouse. Meredith was busy creating a vegetable garden in the far corner of the property. Her hoe struck a rock. Leaning over, she grabbed it and tossed it onto the growing pile of rocks she had unearthed. Her auburn ponytail flipped back and forth with her movements. Her five-year-old son, Sawyer, flew in circles on his tire swing.

The anticipation of peas, beans, lettuce, and tomatoes motivated Meredith to continue her activity, although her back was beginning to ache. Soon, her hoe pinged against another stone. Unable to grab it easily, she used her small pickax to search for an edge. Despite several attempts to lift it, the stone did not budge. Standing up, she removed her gardening gloves and rubbed her lower back.

Suddenly, Sawyer shouted, "Mommy, I have a new friend!"

Meredith looked up in surprise, which swiftly turned to concern when she saw that her son was alone. With their house being somewhat remote, there were no nearby children for Sawyer to play with. She had suggested inviting a classmate over, but he seemed to prefer coming up with ways to entertain himself.

"You do?" his mother responded with a weak smile. "Tell me about him."

"It's a girl, and her name is Callie Rebecca."

Meredith slowly let out a deep breath. Dropping her gloves to the ground, she said, "Hey, let's head inside for lunch. Go wash your hands."

"Come on, Callie!" Sawyer threw open the back door, letting it slam behind him.

Meredith made her son's favorite grilled cheese sandwich and put several apple slices on the plate. She set a glass of milk next to it.

"What about Callie, Mom?"

"Oh. You can share your sandwich with her."

"She needs her own; she's real hungry."

Pursing her lips, Meredith slapped another sandwich into the frying pan, thinking when lunch was over, she could always put it in a Ziploc bag and save it for tomorrow. She placed the plate in front of the empty chair next to Sawyer.

She sat down at the table and rolled her shoulders to relax her muscles. Questions about Sawyer ran through her head: *Is this a passing phase? Should I take him for counseling? Was it selfish of me to want to live outside of town?*

"We're done, Mom. We're going back outside."

The back door slammed. Through the window, Meredith saw him run to the tire swing and begin to push it, no doubt giving his new pal a ride. She turned to clear the table and noticed the extra sandwich was gone. *Wow, I guess Sawyer was super hungry today.*

* * * * *

Tilly dried her hands on the dishcloth after washing her dinner dishes. She moved into her cozy living room, where a trio of African masks hung on a wall. On a side table sat a collection of carved wooden giraffes, and in the corner was a hide-covered drum.

For the past several weeks, Tilly's favorite armchair sat askew, as she had moved it to face the ocean. She gave a little laugh; never before had a project required her to rearrange her furniture. As it was, she was condensing the motifs of ten quilts into one, but she wanted the process to be as traditional as possible.

She pulled the completed quilt squares from her tote bag and laid them across the couch. She then entered her dining room, where a table contained all manner of supplies needed for her craft: yards of ethnic kente fabric, batting, different colors of thread, and a rotary cutter. At her ironing board, she pressed the long sashing strips that would frame each square. The final step would be adding a wide border to the perimeter of the quilt.

Settling back into her chair, she began to piece the first square to a strip. Her skilled hands commanded the needle up, down, in, out, as she worked from right to left.

* * * * *

After brushing his teeth, Sawyer jumped into bed. Meredith smoothed his shaggy chestnut hair and tweaked his freckled nose as she sat down by his side.

"Tell me more about your new friend. Where did she come from?"

"She was in the ground, and her mother sent her brain a picture of boxes. That's when she looked for the monkey in the wagon with the big ducks."

"She told you this?"

"She puts words and pictures in my head."

"Where is her mother?"

"She's looking for her."

"I see." But Meredith didn't. She was confused and concerned. Caressing her son's cheek, she said, "It's not beach weather yet, but tomorrow we could go to Rehoboth and walk around town. We can stop in Browseabout Books, and I'll buy you a toy. On the way home, we'll check out the bake sale at St. George's Church."

"Can Callie come too?"

Meredith sighed. "Of course, sweetheart."

* * * * *

Sawyer ran ahead on the boardwalk, as the waves drummed their beat along the shore. Meredith noticed his left arm angled out from his body. *It's as if he is holding someone's hand.* He ran some more, stopping in front of the bandstand on the Avenue.

"Come on, Mom. Let's go to Browseabout!"

Sawyer took his time looking at all his options and eventually made his selection.

"Instead of a toy, can I get this book for Callie? She really likes the cover and has never seen a mermaid." He held up *The Mermaid in Rehoboth Bay.*

Hmm, this is getting out of hand. But Meredith also agreed the mermaid was darling, so she made the purchase and was now eager to hit the bake sale and get back to work on her vegetable garden.

Back in Lewes, they headed up Park Avenue. The crowd ahead

made the church easy to locate. Meredith approached a table laden with goodies, behind which sat a large woman.

"Welcome! Take your own sweet time; everything is delicious," Tilly said with a smile nearly as wide as her girth. She took a moment to appraise the trio. "May I give the children a treat?" She held out two *cinq centimes,* a popular African butter cookie.

It took Meredith a moment to respond as she stood, wide-eyed, gazing at Tilly.

"Can we, Mom?" pleaded Sawyer.

"Ah, sure, honey. Be sure to say thank you."

Sawyer grabbed the treats and ran to sit in the shade.

Meredith turned back to the woman and was drawn into vast dark eyes that seemed steeped in wisdom. Her words tumbled as she said, "This may sound like an odd question, but are you able to see my son's friend?"

"The little girl? I sure can and she's a long way from home. That child needs a heap of TLC."

Meredith was astonished. "She just appeared to my son yesterday and told him the strangest story about blocks and some kind of ducks in a wagon. I thought she was an imaginary friend but if you can see her why can't I? Don't tell me she's a ghost!"

Tilly rubbed her temples and looked over at the children. Her head began to throb as she considered all she had just heard. She said a quick prayer for guidance and then said, "If you've got the time, there's somethin' I want to show you. It might shed a light on what's goin' on." She turned to the woman behind the neighboring table of baked goods and said, "Nadine, can you handle my table as well? I need to leave and may not make it back."

* * * * *

Tilly opened the front door of her tidy Rehoboth home and moved aside to let her guests enter. They were greeted by the quilt squares laid out in a specific order done in a mix of vibrant kente fabrics of yellow, green, orange, and brown.

Tilly saw Callie's eyes grow wide and fill with tears. She pulled her close. "What's your name, child?" Tilly asked gently.

"Mkali Rebecca," she replied with quivering lips.

The quilter turned to Meredith and said, "Originally, each of these squares was its own entire quilt, that is, a quilt with blocks of just one pattern. They were displayed in a particular order and within a time frame as circumstances dictated."

Sawyer watched as Callie stepped forward and pointed to the first square. "Monkey," she said.

Tilly caressed the child's head. "That's right. Each quilt conveyed a secret message and was hung from a cabin window or perhaps over a fence. Put it all together and what you have is a travel guide for the Underground Railroad."

Meredith was stunned into silence. *What is this woman saying? Underground Railroad? That happened nearly two hundred years ago!*

Tilly squeezed the girl's shoulder as she said to the other two, "*Mkali* means 'bright' in Swahili. That's her birth name. 'Rebecca' was the slave name given to her by her owners."

"So Mkali is African-American? Sawyer didn't tell me that."

"Not surprisin'. Children are colorblind until they're taught different." Tilly picked up the first two squares, which had already been joined to the sashing strips. "Now, Mkali said she came here with a monkey in a wagon. This first square? It's called the 'Monkey Wrench.' It told the freedom seekers to start thinkin' about the tools they would need should they decide to escape. They would need somethin' to help build a shelter or use as a weapon to defend themselves."

"Monkey," Mkali said again and reached out to hold Tilly's hand.

"I see a wheel on the next square. Is that for the wagon?" asked

Meredith, still astonished by what she was hearing.

"Yes, the Wagon Wheel. Often times, a secret compartment was put under the bench seat where a runaway could hide. Or it could mean that a wagon was nearby, ready for someone to begin his or her escape. Every slave on the plantation was quietly educated on the meanin' of the symbols, even if they worked the fields and never laid eyes on a quilt."

Sawyer shifted his gaze from Mkali to Tilly, to his mom and back to the couch.

Without realizing it, Meredith reached out and caressed Mkali's head. Suddenly, the sensation of matted hair under her hand jolted Meredith. She gazed at Mkali, seeing for the first time the young child in a tattered blue dress with filthy bare feet and desperation emanating from her coffee-colored eyes. *What has this child been through?* Meredith shifted her gaze to Tilly, and again was swept up into the woman's face, etched by an intimacy with historic heartache and suffering.

Tilly returned Meredith's stare, her heart swelling with the significance of the moment. "Now you've got the eyes that can see."

"What about the ducks?" asked Sawyer.

"Ah," said Tilly. She picked up another square with a swirled *X* on it. "This is the Drunkard's Path. It was a warnin' to the passengers not to travel in a straight line but to weave here and there to lessen the possibility of bein' spotted and captured.

"As for ducks, I think Mkali was referrin' to the eighth square, Flyin' Geese. The triangles are in a formation. Its message was to watch the skies in the spring and follow the geese because they would be migratin' north, which was the destination of every passenger on the Railroad."

Meredith needed to sit down. She plopped into Tilly's armchair, still askew in the room.

"I want to say this is unbelievable, but now, seeing Mkali and hearing this fantastic history, I'm a believer."

"Well, this is oral history, so you won't find it in any traditional history book. Many folks disagree that there were ever any quilts at all because there is no documentation. But when you think about it, the slaves were not allowed to read or write, and the conductors who helped them along the route didn't want any evidence that could implicate them. When my quilt is finished, I'll donate it to my church to help keep the oral history alive."

Tilly paused for a moment. "You said Mkali showed up yesterday at lunchtime. That was just when I finished the last quilt square. So, here's what I'm thinkin.' Since there has been no more quilts hangin' over railings or out windows, Mkali was stuck where she was until my quilt had all the secret codes in one location. Her mother must have mentally sent her the picture of the box. Boxes meant it was time to pack up and leave."

Meredith's body was humming with the energy of the story: the tension of making the decision to flee, the physical toll of making the journey, the overwhelming fear throughout. "So, you're saying Mkali's mother told her to start her escape? Mkali probably learned the symbolism of the quilts by osmosis, hearing over and over the significance of the squares, even though she doesn't have the vocabulary to describe them. But why come to Lewes?"

"Why, indeed? Let's ask the child."

Meredith rose from the chair and kneeled in front of the little girl, taking her hands in her own. "Sweetheart, why did you come to our home?"

Mkali withdrew her hands and turned to the quilt, pointing to a log cabin with a small red square in the middle.

"As I thought," Tilly said. "That's the code for a safe house. If a house had a lantern shinin' in a second story window, the freedom seekers knew they could knock on the door and they would be taken in and given food and a place to sleep." She looked at Sawyer. "Your bedroom is upstairs, right?"

He nodded and asked Mkali, "Is that the light that you told me about?"

Mkali's eyes began to tear up again and she whispered, "Mama."

Now it was Tilly who needed to sit down and contemplate the big picture. She said to Mkali, "Don't you worry, child, we'll find her."

To Meredith she said, "I'm thinkin' Mkali's mom was dreamin' of runnin' away to freedom but could not leave her child behind; it was a dangerous proposition to take along a young'un who could cry out, not understandin' the gravity of the situation. At some point, Mkali must have taken sick and died on the plantation, so her mother then took the next opportunity to escape. You with me so far?"

"Are you saying that my house was a safe house on the Underground Railroad?"

"It's documented that Lewes was a stop on it."

"OK," Meredith said, taking a deep breath, "let's suppose Mkali's mom was taken in by the owners of my house; wouldn't she have kept moving on her journey?"

Tilly looked down and shook her head. "It was a courageous decision to become a passenger on the Railroad. Many slaves were caught and returned to their masters. Others died of exposure or became sick from hunger, infection, or disease. It's a wonder so many slaves made it to freedom."

"It boggles my mind." Meredith let out a long exhale. "So, what do we do now?"

"Why don't we go to your house? Perhaps we'll get some inspiration there."

* * * * *

Meredith and Tilly walked around the perimeter of the front yard. During the tour of the house, Tilly had to hold the handrail as she slowly mounted the stairs. She checked out the view from Sawyer's bedroom window and then both women proceeded to the backyard to walk its boundary as the children swayed on the tire swing.

"So now you've seen everything, Tilly."

"I had hoped somethin' might jump out at me, but no vibes are comin' my way." She tried to hide her disappointment. "I like your vegetable garden. You have a nice sunny spot for it."

"Yes, except I've been stymied by an obstinate rock that won't come out of the ground."

Tilly raised her eyebrows. "Really? Where?"

"Here! I remember now, Mkali appeared to Sawyer right after I struck the rock! I'll get a shovel."

"Wait," Tilly instructed. "Just clear off the surface so we know what we're dealin' with."

Meredith got to her knees, quickly brushing back the dirt to expose the entire stone. On it was a rough carving of a star.

A sudden gust blew through the backyard. The children stopped their swinging. A thin woman appeared beside the rock, standing tall, with a stately countenance. She was wrapped in white muslin.

"Mama!" Mkali ran to embrace the woman, smiling for the first time.

Meredith and Tilly gaped. Tilly stepped forward and took the hand of the woman. "Bless you, dear. What's your name?"

"Nyota," the woman proudly replied.

"Star," whispered Tilly.

"I will not speak my slave name."

"Of course not," Tilly replied.

Meredith stepped forward, placing her hands on top of the woman's, which still encircled the child.

"Can you tell us what happened?"

Nyota looked down at her daughter, pain flashing in her eyes. "I grew up on a plantation in the lower Carolina. Mkali took sick and I buried her in the little cemetery along the creek. The day before I escaped, I went to her grave and promised her that once I made it north I would tell her when to use the codes to come find me so we could be together again." Nyota gave Mkali a big squeeze. "I was already very sick from infection when I reached this house. The owners did their best to heal me, but I died a few days later. They kindly buried me."

The group was silent for several moments out of respect for the tragedy these two souls had endured as well as for countless others with similar stories.

"We must go," Nyota said.

Mkali hugged Tilly around her waist. Meredith bent down for a hug around the neck.

Mkali turned to Sawyer as he said, "Wait a minute!" He ran inside and came out with the mermaid book tucked under his arm. "Keep this. And come play with me any time you want. I'll miss you." They smiled at one another.

Mkali looked up at her mother and took her hand.

"Are you ready?" Nyota asked her daughter.

Mkali nodded her head.

They held hands as they stepped onto the carved stone and were gone.

* * * * *

Five hundred and thirteen miles to the south, in a little cemetery that bordered a creek, the groundskeeper was pulling weeds alongside a small headstone when a strong wind blew through the trees. He shielded his eyes, and when he opened them again, the little marker had disappeared.

* * * * *

One Month Later

Sawyer finished his lunch and told his mom he would be outside on his tire swing. When Meredith looked through the kitchen window, she smiled to see that Mkali had decided to come play with him that afternoon.

Tilly finished the border of her Underground Railroad quilt. She grunted as she shoved her armchair back into its regular spot. Proud to have carried on the tradition of her brave ancestors, she no longer needed to sit facing east so that her needle pointed north.

FIVE HUNDRED AND THIRTY-ONE MILES SOUTH OF LEWES, DELAWARE, IN MURRELLS INLET, SOUTH CAROLINA, THERE IS A DEVELOPMENT OF LUXURY HOMES. NESTLED WITHIN THAT DEVELOPMENT ARE TWO WOODED ADJACENT LOTS HARBORING A SMALL AFRICAN-AMERICAN CEMETERY WITH UNASSUMING GRAVE MARKERS. A HANDFUL OF YEARS AGO, WHILE WALKING THROUGH THE CEMETERY, CHRIS JACOBSEN CAME UPON THE GRAVE OF AN INFANT WHO SURVIVED A MERE TEN DAYS. WONDERING WHAT THE LITTLE GIRL'S BRIEF HISTORY WAS, CHRIS PROMISED THE CHILD SHE WOULD ONE DAY WRITE A STORY IN HER HONOR. "A STITCH IN TIME" IS THAT STORY.

THIS IS CHRIS'S FOURTH STORY TO BE ACCEPTED IN THE REHOBOTH BEACH READS CONTEST. THE OTHERS CAN BE FOUND IN *THE BOARDWALK*, *BEACH LIFE* AND *BEACH DREAMS*. A FEW OF HER OTHER STORIES ARE IN THE CAT & MOUSE PRESS SHORT STORY ANTHOLOGIES *BEACH LOVE*, *BEACH PULP*, AND *SANDY PAWS*. CHRIS FIRST BEGAN VISITING REHOBOTH BEACH WHEN HER BROTHER AND HIS FAMILY RELOCATED THERE ABOUT A DOZEN YEARS AGO. SHE LOVES THE FAMILY-FRIENDLY FEEL OF THE TOWN, THE PEACEFUL BEACH, AND THE BOARDWALK FOR MORNING STROLLS. CHRIS LIVES JUST OVER THE STATE LINE IN ROSE VALLEY, PA.

IF YOU HAVE NOT READ *THE MERMAID IN REHOBOTH BAY* BY NANCY SAKADUSKI, OWNER OF CAT & MOUSE PRESS, I HIGHLY RECOMMEND IT. IT IS ADORABLE.

This moving story draws from the Underground Railroad as Lewes history, in which enslaved African Americans were spirited to freedom by following coded images sewn into prominently displayed patchwork quilts. It's an incredibly thoughtful and well-researched story that dares to take the concept and typical setting of the beach read and morph it into something with great, literary substance. An essential story that takes the past and brings it poignantly into our present, providing food for thought and for the soul.

Tiny Solves the Case

By James Gallahan

The one-hundred-twenty-pound male Rottweiler growled and ran to the back door. He turned toward his human parent and barked.

Samantha Peterson pushed herself off the couch. "All right, I'm getting up." Then she froze in place. She held on to the sofa and stared wide-eyed at Tiny, as he barked at her. Sam looked at the urn in the curio cabinet and back at Tiny. *I'm losing it.*

Tiny barked again and vanished.

She glanced down at her ankle and sighed. The paw print tattoo was now fully healed, and Tiny's name, printed below it in a neat cursive, was perfect. *God, I miss you,* she thought as tears filled her eyes. *I can't believe it's been one week since I had to tell the vet to …*

Tiny reappeared, sitting at Sam's feet. She felt him lean against her leg. *I'm just imagining this. Think of something else.* She looked down. Tiny, her constant companion, the dog she'd had to put to sleep, was still there. *What's wrong with me?* She squeezed her head with both hands. "Snap out of it."

Tiny darted to the back door again, growling. He ran back to Sam and bumped her behind the knee. Her leg buckled. Tiny appeared at the door in the kitchen and snarled.

Sam made her way into the kitchen and saw two young men standing in her backyard peering in through the window.

Tiny bared his teeth as he stood between her and the door.

Sam's jaw tightened. "I've got a gun! I'm going to count to three. If you're not out of here by then …"

Before she could finish, she heard someone yell "run." Two teenaged boys stumbled and fell as they ran through the backyard. She glanced down at Tiny and smiled. "Thanks, big guy. Good thing they believed I had a gun. I don't know what I would have done if they had broken in."

Tiny licked Sam's hand and faded away.

* * * * *

The next morning, Sam unlocked the door to Petersons' Vintage Treasures and turned on the lights. She had inherited the jewelry and antiques store, and her parents' house, when they died two years ago. As she got things ready, she saw Laura Rhone come through the door.

"Hiya."

Laura scrunched her nose. "What's with the pink hair?"

"I'm trying out a new look." Sam glanced around. "So, why are you here today? You're not scheduled to work until tomorrow."

"I was worried about you. I overheard some of the customers talking about calling the police about a bunch of burglaries on and around Harbor Road. Don't you live in that neighborhood?"

"Yeah. I inherited my parents' house. No way I could have afforded it."

"Have you had anything taken?"

"No, but some kids were looking in the windows last night. I scared them away."

"I wonder if they're the ones who've been stealing from your neighbors. Apparently, someone is taking clothing from people's backyard decks—stuff like towels and shirts. I heard they even took a gardening glove that was left out to dry. They don't take all the items left outside, just some. Weird, huh?"

"Why would anyone report those things stolen?"

Laura shrugged. "I heard one of the ladies say that she was at a neighborhood party last weekend and they got to talking about their belongings missing and decided to call the police about it. Sorry, I guess you weren't invited."

"I had to work."

*****

Sam flopped on her couch later that night and thought about what Laura had told her. Sam loved solving mysteries and knew she wouldn't get a good night's sleep until she figured out who was stealing from her neighbors. *I'll talk to some of them tomorrow. I cracked the case of who was robbing jewelry stores in the area last summer. I can unravel this one too.* She closed her eyes and drifted off.

Sam awoke to a strange noise. She opened her eyes but didn't move. *Is someone in the kitchen?* She listened to what sounded like a person smacking their lips.

She crept to the wall, peeked around the corner, and dropped her head. Tiny was drinking from his water bowl. Sam hadn't been able to bring herself to put it away. It still had water in it from the last day he was with her.

"Hi, big guy," she said, crouching down and opening her arms. "Coming to visit your mama?"

Tiny walked over and put his head on her knee.

Sam smiled. "I'm glad you're still here. How'd you like to go with me tomorrow when I talk with a few of our neighbors? Some things were stolen and I'm gonna figure out who's doing it. You with me?"

Tiny licked her face and vanished.

*****

Sam knocked on the Milners' door the next morning. "Hi, Mrs. Milner. Got a few minutes?"

"Hello, Samantha. It's good to see you." Mrs. Milner adjusted the volume on her hearing aid before placing a hand on Sam's shoulder. "I'm so sorry about Tiny."

"Thank you."

"Come on in." Mrs. Milner held on to Sam's arm and led her inside the house. "How about a cup of coffee?"

"Sounds good. Hey, I heard some folks had things stolen recently. I wanted to make sure you were OK."

Mrs. Milner shook her head. "Thanks for checking on us. We're fine. I still can't believe it. I woke up early the other day and was sitting at the table here drinking my coffee before my granddaughter woke up. I glanced out back and noticed that the little shirt she wears to the beach wasn't there. I had left it out to dry overnight on the deck. Tom and I looked everywhere for it, but it was gone."

"What does it look like?" Sam flipped open a small notebook.

"You're just like a detective. I thought you owned an antiques and jewelry store."

"Sorry. Solving crimes is a hobby of mine. I thought I'd see if I could figure out who's stealing things in our neighborhood. I'm sure the police are on it, but it's fun."

"Well, be careful. Whoever's doing this could be dangerous."

"I will. So, what did the bad guys take?"

"The shirt is pink with a picture of a mermaid on it. Gabbi loves mermaids. She cried and cried when we couldn't find it. She's back home in Virginia with my son and daughter-in-law." Trudy held up a glove. "Oh, and I nearly forgot. One of my gardening gloves is also missing."

Sam nodded. "I see. Mind if I walk around your backyard?"

"No problem. I'll stay here and heat us up some scones."

"That sounds great, thanks!"

Sam roamed the backyard, whispering to Tiny as he walked by her side. He wagged his tail when he looked back toward the house. She turned around to see Mrs. Milner waving. Sam waved.

Tiny stopped and sniffed the air. He walked to the waist-high white picket fence along the side of the yard. Sam chuckled as she watched

Tiny walk through the fence into the neighbor's yard and disappear.

Mrs. Milner came out on the deck. "Scones are ready. Find anything?"

"No, but somebody probably hopped over your fence, snuck onto your deck, and took the shirt and glove."

"The world's gone crazy. Now people are stealing a little girl's shirt. Come on in, sweetie."

"Sorry, Mrs. Milner."

"Please, call me Trudy."

Sam nodded. "My friends call me Sam."

"Sam …" Trudy looked around as if someone might hear her. "You have to tell me about that tribal tattoo on your arm. I love it. I have a tattoo on my backside I got when I was a nurse in Samoa back in the sixties. Now don't tell anyone. I couldn't care less mind you, but Tom would die if anyone found out."

Sam laughed and jumped as her cell phone rang. She pulled it out of her pocket. "Sorry, Trudy," she said, looking at the phone. "I need to get this. It's Laura back at the store."

Sam listened while Laura stammered, "Um … Joel came in the store."

"So?"

"He was buying an item for his mom, and he told me someone had stolen a jacket from his back porch the other day. He asked about you and how you were doing … you know, since the breakup."

Sam rolled her eyes. "He's gotta move on. We just went out for a little while. It wasn't like we were engaged or anything."

"He asked if you would stop by and look around the house. He said he knew you were good at finding missing items."

"I don't know."

"Oh, come on. Help the guy out."

Sam frowned and sighed. "So, what kind of jacket was it?"

"Good. I knew you'd help him. It was a vintage World War II bomber jacket he bought as a gift for his father's birthday. He had it on his deck railing to get the mothball smell out of it. His dad was a pilot in the war and lost his coat years ago."

"So why doesn't Joel just buy another one?"

"He said the party for his father is in two days, and he can't get another authentic jacket that quickly. Go talk with him and see what you can find out. Maybe you two can get back together. He's rich!"

"Yeah, yeah." Sam hung up the phone and looked back at Trudy. "Sorry, I need to head out. Mind if I take your glove? It may help me find the other one."

* * * * *

It took Sam less than three minutes to arrive at Joel's house.

He opened the door as she was walking up the stoop. "Come in," he said with a smile. "Thanks for coming over. I know it's awkward, but it would help me out if you could find my dad's jacket."

She grinned. "OK, I'll try, but it doesn't mean things have changed between us."

"I understand."

"So, I hear it's a bomber jacket?"

"Yeah. It's got a hand-painted patch of a devil carrying a torpedo. I doubt there are too many of those out there."

"And your father's birthday party is in a couple of days?"

"Yes. I really appreciate you helping us out. The police are so busy. I heard the Hendersons got burglarized too."

Sam smiled and walked toward the door. "I'll do what I can. It was good seeing ya."

* * * * *

Later that afternoon, Sam rang the doorbell at the Hendersons' home. Sixteen-year-old Jennifer answered the door.

"Hiya, Jenny. Your folks home?"

"No, they're out grocery shopping."

"I understand you had some stuff stolen. A few other neighbors had things taken too."

Jenny waved Sam into the house. "Come on in. Whoever did it is probably some nut job. It's really not that big a deal. A pair of denim shorts I wear to the beach are missing. I put them out on the back deck to dry overnight. I hope whoever took my shorts has nice legs. They're pretty short."

Sam chuckled. "I'm trying to see if I can find out who did this and where everyone's stuff is."

Jenny shrugged. "Isn't that a job for the police?"

"Yeah, but I'd like to see if I can help out. Mind if I check around back?"

"No problem. It's that way. I'm in the middle of a *Game of Thrones* episode. Is it OK if I stay inside? My folks don't like me watching that show. I gotta binge-watch it while they're away. Don't tell 'em, OK?"

"Your secret's safe with me. I'll let you know when I'm done."

Sam walked out on the deck and Tiny immediately appeared and trailed her to the middle of the yard. She followed Tiny as he sniffed the ground and walked up to the wax myrtle hedge at the back of the yard. She smiled when he walked through the thick shrubs as if they weren't there.

Tiny returned a minute later, nudged Sam's hand, and barked.

"Find something? Good boy. Tiny ran through the hedge again and started to run down the street. "Stop, Tiny. I can't just go through people's backyards. I've got to say bye to Jenny first. Then I'll follow you in my car." Tiny sat in the street in front of the Henderson's house.

Sam walked into the family room. Jenny was sitting on the floor, eating popcorn, and looking wide-eyed at the TV. "I'm gonna head out, Jenny. I'll let you and your folks know if I find anything. Say hi to them for me."

"Thanks, will do." Jenny waved, her attention riveted to the screen.

Sam pulled up on the black replacement door handle of her rusty beige 2001 Camry. Tiny barked and ran down the road. Sam followed until Tiny stopped at a small wooded area.

She got out of the car and stood next to Tiny. "What's up, big guy? Did you find something?"

Tiny continued barking and tugging on Sam's sleeve.

"OK, OK."

Tiny ran to a nearby clump of trees, turned around, and bolted to an adjacent group of shrubs and stopped; his snout pressed to the ground.

Sam ran over and leaned against a tree, trying to catch her breath.

Tiny yapped and jumped back when a fox darted out from the bushes. He pushed his head into the bushes where the fox had been, pulled out a gardening glove, and dropped it at Sam's feet. She picked it up. It was an exact match to the one Trudy was missing.

Sam scratched Tiny's head. "Way to go, boy. Wonder what else is in these shrubs."

She pushed them apart and crawled to a small opening in the ground. "A fox den. I can't believe it."

She found a couple of towels near the den's opening. Farther in she saw a pair of denim shorts and what looked to be Trudy's granddaughter's shirt, but no bomber jacket. "A fox took all of these? That's a new one." She lay on the ground and stretched her arm deeper into the den. "Come on, jacket. Please be in here." Sam moved her arm left and right, then felt something furry. She screamed and jumped back. "Oh god, another fox!"

Tiny nudged Sam's arm and barked.

"I'm not putting my hand back in there."

Tiny pulled at Sam's sleeve.

Sam shook her head. "No way, big guy."

Tiny barked and crawled into the fox den.

"No, Tiny, no," Sam yelled. "It might bite you."

Tiny inched deep into the den until only his tail was showing. Then he crawled out backwards, dragging the bomber jacket with his teeth.

"You did it." Sam held up the coat, saw the fur collar, and laughed. "I'm such a baby. Wait a minute. How are you able to pick up stuff? Oh well. I'm glad you can. Thanks for being brave. Let's go return these."

* * * * *

Sam rang the doorbell at Trudy's house. When Trudy opened the door, Sam held up the shirt. "Look what I found."

Trudy hugged her. "How'd you find it?"

"You won't believe where it was. And, it wasn't stolen by a thief. Well, not a human one."

"What?"

"A fox took it and put it in its den. The shirt was there with a bunch of other things that had disappeared. I guess it wanted clothing to make its lair a little cozier."

"You're the best, Sam. Thanks, but how did you know where it was?"

Sam looked down. "Just lucky. I stumbled on it when I was walking near the park. I really should be going. I have other items to return to folks."

Sam got in her car and smiled as Tiny appeared in the passenger seat. "Hi there. I can't wait to see Joel's face when I give him the jacket. He really is a good guy."

* * * * *

Sam rang Joel's doorbell. He opened the door and hugged Sam when she held up the jacket.

"I knew you'd find it. You should be a detective. I don't know how you do it. You've gotta have a sixth sense or something."

Sam stepped back. "I'm just happy to have helped. Wish your dad a happy birthday for me."

"Wanna come to the party? He'd love to see you."

Sam shook her head. "I better not."

"Can I pay you for finding the jacket? How about dinner, just as friends?"

"I don't know, Joel."

"I promise I won't bug you about getting back together."

Sam looked at him and smiled. "Sure, why not."

"Great. How about dinner tonight at La Fable? I can pick you up at seven."

"Isn't that a little fancy for just friends going out?"

Joel touched her arm. "Please."

Sam nodded. "OK. It'll be fun. See you at seven."

Joel closed the door and yelled, "Woo-hoo!"

Sam shook her head and smiled.

* * * * *

One week later, Tiny sat on the floor next to Sam as she read a front-page article in the *Cape Gazette* with the headline, "Local Area Red Fox Behind Missing Items." The fox was now a celebrity. Apparently, people had started leaving clothing in their backyards for the fox to take back to its den.

She heard a knock on the front door and opened it to find Trudy holding a covered plate. "Hiya, Trudy. Come on in."

"I hope I'm not interrupting anything."

"No bother at all. It's good to see you."

"It's Saturday. Are you and Joel going out again tonight?" Trudy winked.

"How do you know Joel and I are seeing each other?"

"Oh, please. Everyone knows you two are dating again. Now that's one handsome man. And such a nice guy. You two make the perfect couple."

"We're giving it another try. We'll see how things go, but yeah, he's a great guy."

"I brought you some scones."

"Thanks. You really should sell them; they're that good."

"You're too kind," Trudy said, scrunching her nose and looking around.

"Is everything all right? You look like something's on your mind. Is Tom OK?"

"He's fine, but I want to talk with you about something. I'm just not sure how to begin."

"What is it?"

Trudy looked up at the ceiling. "Sam, I don't want you to close off your sensitive side."

"What do you mean?"

"I mean being sensitive to the spirits of those who have departed."

Sam furrowed her brow. "I still don't understand."

"I didn't want to tell you earlier because I was afraid you'd think I was foolish, but hear me out."

"OK."

"Here goes. I ... can see Tiny. He was walking around with you when you came over the other day."

"You saw Tiny?"

"Yes. I was waving to him when you were looking for clues in my yard. And I think you see him too."

Sam took a deep breath and looked away. "What makes you think that?"

"Either you talk to yourself or you were talking to Tiny when you were at my house."

"Oh, you saw that, huh?"

"Don't worry; I won't tell anyone."

"Can you see Tiny now?"

Trudy nodded toward the floor. "He's sitting to the left of you."

"You're right. I see him, too. All the time." Sam put her hand down and Tiny licked it. "So that's why his tail was wagging when he was looking back at your house. He saw you waving at him."

"Yep."

"Sorry I fibbed about how I found your granddaughter's shirt. Tiny's the one who really discovered it."

Trudy walked over to Tiny and scratched his head. "You're such a smart dog."

Sam's eyes widened. "Can you see dead people too? Sorry, that came out wrong."

Trudy chuckled. "Yes."

"I can only see Tiny."

"Just stay open to seeing others."

"I will. Hey, I've been thinking about something ever since Tiny found the missing items."

"What?"

"I was thinking maybe I'd get a private investigator's license and see about doing some real detective work on the side. Tiny could work the cases with me. Of course, I can't tell anyone he's helping me. What do ya think?"

"That sounds like a great idea."

"Would you be willing to help me by talking with people who haven't crossed over yet? It may help solve a crime."

"Absolutely. That would be neat. By the way, you remember when Sally Firmino died in a car crash and the newspapers said a deer must have darted out in front of her car?"

"Yeah, that was last year, right? She ran into a tree and died."

"Yes. I saw her near the crash site the other day. She told me it wasn't an accident."

Sam leaned in. "Can you take me to her?"

"I'm free now."

Tiny trotted over to Sam and Trudy, wagged his tail, and barked.

Sam laughed. "Looks like our crime-solving partnership just began."

JAMES GALLAHAN IS A MULTI-GENRE WRITER LIVING IN NORTHERN VIRGINIA WITH HIS WIFE. HE HAS HAD SHORT STORIES PUBLISHED IN THE CAT & MOUSE PRESS ANTHOLOGY, *BEACH PULP*; THE GREATER LEHIGH VALLEY WRITERS GROUP ANTHOLOGY, *REWRITING THE PAST*; AND THE *PILCROW AND DAGGER* LITERARY MAGAZINE, *THE SURVIVOR*. HIS SHORT STORY, "TINY SOLVES THE CASE," WAS CREATED IN MEMORY OF ONE OF HIS BELOVED DOGS. PLEASE CHECK OUT JAMES'S WEBSITE AT WWW.JAMESGALLAHAN.COM.

JUDGE'S COMMENT

This story would have been strong as a conventional whodunit: Samantha (Sam) Peterson is a charming everywoman who solves mysteries as a hobby, and her investigation of neighborhood thefts is fun to follow. But the addition of a supernatural sidekick in the form of Sam's recently passed dog's spirit gives the story a zippy flair that leaves me wanting more!

Incident at Canary Creek

By Justin Stoeckel

Dawn rises in a slow pull over the muddy green waters of the Lewes and Rehoboth Canal. Knee-high marsh grasses wave back and forth on a lullabied breeze that carries with it the bay's salty aroma.

Above, in a pink stretch of clouds, seagulls glide and circle and fuss, trading short squawks back and forth.

Down at the end, at the Lewes Public Boat Ramp, the fishermen are getting boats loaded, stacking braided, black crab pots one on top of the other on the stern, long looping lines of nylon connecting them together. Some of the fishermen trawl the waters already. The haggard and long-lived ones. Throwing out traps; pulling in lines from the Broadkill River.

A few of the seagulls are standing lookout on security lights. Tilting their heads, looking for forgotten bait. It's quiet except for the clang of the pots, the occasional grunted call of one fisherman to another, and the purr of outboard motors in their "slow, no wake" crawl.

A silver Chevy Tahoe, polished and marked with the Delaware Fish and Wildlife logo, cruises slowly over the drawbridge. Its tires hum against the grain of the bridge's steel grates. It pulls a gentle right at the stoplight and pushes lazily down Pilottown Road. The narrow street will be crawling with visitors and families in a few hours, but as the sun just starts to paint the canal orange, it's empty.

Up ahead, past the lightship *Overfalls* and Little League fields, and farther down past the boat slips running along the edge of the canal, the Broadkill River spills into the marsh reserve known as Canary Creek. The marsh snakes its way through to the Broadkill in a long, winding, unfolding ribbon of shallow water. There, at the end of the steel girder of the overpass, sits a black Silverado, parked on a turnoff at the end of the road.

It's dented at the fender well on the driver's side. Scrapes on the tailgate are gouged down to show shiny metal. Rust collects at the corners of the scrapes in raised, starfish clusters, already beginning the slow devouring of the metal it craves. The windows are cracked, and the stale stink of cigarettes floats out like a wave of bad breath.

Two men, Randy and Snoop, sit near the shallow black water, passively fishing. They are scruffy, in three-day-old beards and dirty jeans, looking as though that marshy scent never fully gets washed off them. A white Styrofoam cooler rests between them.

Snoop, gaunt and wiry, has his camo hat pushed up on his head, showing the line of pale, milky skin below his hairline. He looks around, uneasy and nervous. Twitchy, like the gulls on the light post across the road at the boat ramps.

Randy pushes a pinch of soggy tobacco down into his gums with his tongue, then spits into the water. As the little ripples run, a fish jumps. Randy plays with the line, gives the reel two slow turns. He's relaxed in a cool arrogant confidence.

Snoop dips his hand into his chest pocket, pulls a crushed soft pack of smokes, and brings it to his mouth, drawing a creased cigarette from it with his lips. He pinches the fishing rod to his side, finds the lighter, then tips the cigarette into the flame, cupping it from the wind, more out of habit than necessity. He closes the lighter with a snap and releases the smoke in a forced, impatient exhale. A blue-white vapor spreads out over the marsh. The quiet stillness of all it eats at him.

But then the Fish and Wildlife Tahoe crests the small hill and Snoop's heart pounds as if begging to get out of his chest as he sees the "Chief" logo on the front panel.

The Tahoe passes the two men at no faster than ten miles an hour, then loops around at the turnaround and parks behind the Silverado.

Snoop's leg starts going like his favorite bluegrass song just came to life in his head. He looks over his shoulder as the game warden's hand flashes up, putting the Tahoe in park. It's who they've been expecting, but Snoop wishes he hadn't shown.

Randy keeps his eyes on the water, with that cool and all-the-same arrogance jocks have at high school parties.

They hear the gear shift shoved up to park with an audible grind. The AC compressor on the Tahoe *whishes* on and runs with a steady, aggravated hum as the truck sits idle.

The door pushes open and DNREC Chief Fish and Wildlife Resources Officer Brett Stillwater steps out. At six two, 210 pounds, he is built for the uniform and his muscularity shows. He didn't let his early forties cut into his workouts. He pulls on his green cap and looks out over the string of narrow marsh and the two men fishing illegally within it. He slams the truck door, sending up a long-legged white crane. It flaps its wings in slow, loping strokes and lands back along the black muddy bank.

Brett steps off the road to the worn, sandy path cut through the marsh grass, his boots crunching over the spilled deposit of rocky sand at its edge. He walks easily toward the men. Randy launches another stringy tobacco spit and looks back at Brett with a sneering, cold grin.

Brett stops behind them, hands on his hips. "How's the fishing? Getting any bites?" His tone is even and relaxed.

Snoop flicks a look to Randy for an answer but gets nothing. He shifts from foot to foot. "Just a few nibbles. No takers." There's a tremble to his voice that he can't hide.

Brett eyes him. "Everything alright? Snoop, you seem jumpy."

"Sure," Randy hisses, cutting Snoop off before he can answer "All's good."

Brett studies Snoop. Sees him reach for the soft pack, then realize he has one going between his lips already. "That true, Snoop? All's good?" Brett asks.

Snoop jerkily reels his line, stops, wipes at his forehead with the back of his wrist. A dipping ash hangs from the end of the cigarette then dusts away as Snoop pulls it from his mouth. "Sure, sure. Yeah. Just a dumb idea coming out here, Brett. We know better."

Snoop starts packing up his lures and tackle in a frantic, busy way. It's all a bit overboard for just moving across the road.

"Just going to ask you to move it across the road. Take it to the river."

"Yeah, yeah. We're going to do that. Right, Randy?"

But Randy stays firm on the sandy creek edge. He spits again. "Just trying to earn a buck, Brett."

"I understand that. Times are harder this season with everything going on."

"Ain't all of us DNREC royalty like you."

Snoop stops mid bend. Looks at Randy. Then to Brett. The cigarette in his mouth short and close to the filter.

"Randy, no need for the hard role. Plenty of fish out on the river. Harold Gray swears they bite better over there."

"Don't have what we're after over there." *Spit.*

A hot surge runs through Brett. It wets his armpits and flushes his neck. It happens when he's frustrated and Randy's starting to push that button. He keeps an even tone as much as he can, but his words are sharp. "Nonetheless, you two gotta move out of here and over to the river."

When Randy casts a new line into the water, the surge comes again, and Brett moves closer. Snoop starts for the cooler, but freezes. Brett stops.

"Something got a hold of you, Snoop?"

"Nah, Brett."

Brett studies him, and Snoop, not able to bear the look, darts his eyes away.

"How about the cooler?"

"Ain't nothing in it but bunker cuts," Randy calls back, eyes shifting now from the road to the parking lot. A truck with a boat in tow comes toward them.

"Then open it."

"I told you. Nothing but a couple of bunker cuts," Randy barks.

"Still going from last night?" Brett asks. "Got a few more beers left to get into? Fine. Just don't get behind the wheel of that truck. Hell, I'll come back and give you a ride if you need one."

There's no response from either Randy or Snoop, just the flicking glare of Snoop to Randy and then to Brett and then down at the cooler again.

The truck with the boat bumps over the overpass and pulls past Brett's Tahoe. The driver looks on curiously and gives a small wave. Brett recognizes it's Harold Gray. He can tell by the long, stringy hair climbing down out of the meshed-back Vietnam veteran hat. He's going to have a talk with him, as he always does on this morning patrol. Ask Harold why he's on such a late start just as soon as he gets these two moved along.

Brett turns his attention back to Randy and Snoop and catches Snoop exchanging an uneasy glance, raised eyebrows, and pressed lips. He steps closer, thumbs the snap on his holster, feeling its leathery scratch over his skin. Brett holds his question, making sure he feels it. Not the leathery scratch over his thumb, but the tension on the creek's edge. It pulsates with an electric buzz.

"What's going here, boys?"

"Let's go, Randy. Come on." Snoop fumbles with the Styrofoam cooler.

"You can fish across the road at the river. Now pack your—"

The cooler suddenly dumps over, cutting the lid loose. A swarm of loose bills somersaults on the breeze, some catching in the marsh grass, a few twirling toward Brett Stillwater's boots.

"What the hell" are the last words Brett Stillwater says. The gunshot echoes across Canary Creek, reverberating off the maintenance shed across the road. Brett's right hand is torn apart by it. He grabs at the mangled, fleshy tendrilled skin and stumbles back, wondering still what exactly the hell is going on.

Snoop stands frozen, knowing, but not believing, what happened. The trailing line of cigarette smoke curls up and flattens out under the brim of his hat.

Harold Gray flinches as he unloads the jon boat, nearly spilling it onto himself. He looks to the maintenance building first, then back over his shoulder to the creek. What he sees when he does is Randy, stalking toward Brett with the Sig Sauer outstretched. That unwavering cool arrogance spilling off him. Brett extends his gnarled hand as a shield. Randy fires three quick shots. Brett is struck in the chest, side, and neck just below the jawline. The bullet catches the carotid, and blood fans the spindly marsh grass.

Harold stands stunned, his mouth open in a slung-jaw way. He doesn't hear the slow hiss leaking from Brett Stillwater's chest. He doesn't hear it spawn into a puddling, wet gurgle. He does see Randy swat the air toward Snoop and bark, "Get the damn money."

Randy squats and picks at the few random bills near Brett's boots. The ones that flittered past his head are spattered with assorted red dots. He shoves the money into his dirty jeans. Snoop has not moved, so Randy claps his hands and points. "I said, get the damn money. It was what we was paid to do."

Randy points the Sig at Snoop and this is when Harold Gray sinks behind the jon boat. Snoop frantically grabs at the bills. Randy tucks the cooler under his arm and marches toward the Silverado.

Harold's mind flashes back to the early morning. He had forgotten his bait. A consequence of six too many Budweisers the night before. He'd had to go back and get it. That's when he had seen the Fish and Wildlife Tahoe parked by the water. At first, he had thought it was Brett, but then saw it didn't say "Chief" along the front panel as Brett's did. One of Brett's wardens, then. He had gone back to rigging his boat and hadn't seen the driver pass off the Styrofoam cooler to Snoop. Nor did he see them exchange a few words. The Tahoe was gone by the time Harold pulled out. He would have to ask Brett about it when he saw him next.

Randy opens the door on the Silverado with a screech and slams it closed. Then the other door opens with its own metallic shrill and thuds closed. Randy twists the key, the engine whines, and then turns over, pushing a blast of power racing through the straight, glasspack exhaust pipes. The Delaware Fish and Wildlife Police Tahoe's low idle is lost to it. The Silverado tears off in a growling, relentless scream back up Pilottown Road and juts right, down Park Road in a screech, that monstrous scream of exhaust bouncing off the slate gray walls of the Virden Center.

Back at Canary Creek, the fishing poles lie like dropped toothpicks in the marsh grass, along with the leaking body of Chief Fish and Wildlife Resources Officer Brett Stillwater. The AC compressor of his Tahoe kicks over again with that aggravated *whish*. The sound sends the crane up. It circles over Canary Creek with its milky white wings.

Harold Gray tugs out his cell phone. He tries to put in his password. But it's difficult the way his hands are shaking.

Writing has always been a part of Justin Stoeckel's life in one form or another, but he turned a new corner on the Saturday morning in January 2019, when he stumbled into Rehoboth library for a Saturday morning Free Write with the Rehoboth Beach Writers' Guild. Since that January morning, he's completed two novels and is currently at work on his third. "Incident at Canary Creek" began as a writing prompt during a Saturday morning Free Write. Justin is an elementary school teacher and father of four children under the age of nine. Somewhere in the madness, he finds time to write at his home in Millsboro, Delaware.

What Lies Within Us

By Sarah Beth Harris

If you were reading a stranger's journal and realized it was the story of your life, would you read the whole thing? I was twenty-four when I had to make that decision, sitting stiffly in a large chair in my grandmother's old bungalow.

It all started a few months prior, with a phone call from a lawyer in Delaware.

"Is this Hannah Mae Lawrence? Born in Lewes, Delaware? My name is Kent Newcastle. I'm an attorney calling about your grandmother, a Mrs. Hannah Mae Bellmoor."

He said he'd been trying to find me for a couple of months.

"Oh well, that's my biological grandmother's name, but I never knew her," I said, confused.

In fact, I didn't know much of anything about my biological family, except that I had been named after my grandmother and then given up for adoption. My adoptive parents told me the day I turned fifteen, but I honestly had no interest in the people who decided *not* to keep me. Well, until now.

"Ms. Lawrence, I'm calling regarding your grandmother's will." He had an air of excitement in his voice.

I sat down, staring blankly at the wall of my New York City apartment, trying to digest what he was saying. My grandmother, with whom I shared a name, was dead. And apparently, I was in her will.

"I'm just not sure why she would have left me anything; I never even met her." My curiosity was growing.

"Ms. Lawrence, your grandmother passed away quite some time

ago, I'm sorry to say. However, her will stated her wish to leave you her home in Rehoboth Beach, Delaware, along with its rental profits, upon your twenty-fourth birthday."

Her *house?* In Rehoboth Beach? I'd lived in New York my whole life. I'd spent family vacations in Rehoboth Beach every summer when I was a kid, and I loved it, but I hadn't been back since I was about fourteen years old.

"What? OK, um … I'm sorry. I'm just a little shocked. This was supposed to be like … a birthday gift?"

"Yes. I understand. This is all sudden for you. We had a little difficulty finding you; it seems your grandmother did not know your adopted name. But as her will states: Ownership of the residence at Henlopen Avenue to transfer to my granddaughter, Hannah Mae Bellmoor (or adopted name), upon twenty-fourth birthday. It is my wish that Hannah does not know about the residence until her twenty-fourth birthday. The house is to be rented until then, with rental fees collected and profits passed on to Hannah at that time."

Mr. Newcastle told me he would be sending me some paperwork to sign and we said our goodbyes. A few days later, I received a packet in the mail, as promised. I snuck out of my office at *Harper's Bazaar* a little early that day to have it signed and notarized. I couldn't believe I was a homeowner—just like that! I spent the cab ride home conjuring memories of Rehoboth and flipping through my calendar to see when I'd have time to visit my grandmother's old house.

* * * * *

The following morning, I was late and distracted as I raced off the elevator, nearly colliding with James Norfolk, the senior copy editor from the sixth floor.

"Whoa, blondie, slow down," he chided, with an adorable grin on his face that made me turn into a blubbering idiot every time I saw it.

"And check your mailbox." He said something about lunch just before the elevator door closed.

Lunch with James today? Butterflies rose in my stomach as I floated to my desk, no longer concerned with my tardiness. We'd been having lunches together for well over a year now, and I was desperately in love with him. I snapped out of it when I heard my boss's prickly voice.

"You're late, Hannah." She was hovering near my cubicle, looking annoyed.

"I'm so sorry, Valerie, but actually, um, I really need to talk to you. Got a minute?"

Without saying a word, she spun abruptly on her pristine four-inch heels and trotted off toward her office, motioning for me to follow her. I explained what was going on and held my breath, hoping she'd grant the time off.

"Well, I suppose that would be OK," she said, adding, "I *did* just get engaged. You're lucky I'm in a good mood today."

"Oh, congratulations! And thank you so much." I made a beeline for the mailroom to find out what James was talking about.

My hope deflated when I discovered a memo about an office lunch today. *Maybe tomorrow,* I thought, assuming he and I had plenty of time for lunch dates. I was sorely mistaken. Valerie announced her engagement to James—*my* James—at lunch that day.

As I stepped into my apartment after work, disappointment and anger came pouring out. I'd spent hours with him the past few months—how on earth did I miss this? Eventually, my thoughts shifted to summers at the beach and my grandmother's house. Overwhelmed with nostalgia, I pushed James from my mind and began to pack for my trip. Maybe this was just what I needed.

Later, I burrowed into my favorite chair and picked up *Gone with the Wind,* which I was finally reading for the first time. I was successfully engrossed in a different world until Rhett told Scarlett he was divorcing her and going back to Charleston: "No, I'm through with everything here. I want peace. I want to see if somewhere there isn't something left in life of charm and grace. Do you know what I'm talking about?"

I knew. I wanted it too. *Surely this is all happening for a reason. What if I belong somewhere else?*

The next morning, I made the drive to Rehoboth. When I pulled up to my grandmother's house on Henlopen Avenue, I was smitten. It was completely charming—a little white house that had a bright-red, arched door with a tiny window in it—like a fairy-tale cottage.

Almost right away, I knew I was going to stay. Perhaps it was a bit rash; I can't really defend what I did except to say it just felt right. I got a job at the *Cape Gazette*, threw myself into my work (an excellent distraction from the devastation of James) and settled into a new rhythm.

Thankfully, my new home had been kept up impeccably for years by a man named Munson Stockley. He's the one who showed me the little closet hidden behind a panel under the stairs. That's where I found the journal. Well, it didn't look like a journal. It was big and thick as a dictionary, leather bound with yellowing pages and a worn cover with a single, faded rose etched into it. When I opened it, the name was written in neat, beautiful script: Hannah Mae Hickman. *Maybe Hickman was my grandmother's maiden name.*

Intrigued, I hugged the book to my chest, left the cramped space, and sat down in the living room to investigate further. I'd never cared about my biological family—or wanted to leave New York, for that matter—but things were different now. I opened it to the first page.

June 28, 1936

Henry David Thoreau said, "What lies before us and what lies behind us are all small matters compared to what lies within us. And when you bring what is within out into the world, miracles happen."

I have always been a writer, but never kept a journal. I suppose that ought to change today! I am twenty-four years old and unmarried. But I have decided if I have a family of my own, I want them to be able to read about my life, in my own words. Mostly because I did not have that. You see, I never really knew my family. Family by blood, that is. I was adopted as a baby. My parents were lovely people. I always felt cherished, taken care of and safe with them, so I never wanted to know about my biological family. Until recently.

As a child, I did not know I would someday long to hear about the lives of my family. I will get to that, all in good time. But for now, to my unborn children, grandchildren, great-grandchildren, and beyond, this is for you. I am "bringing what is within out into the world." Within these pages, you will find my stories and my thoughts, and hopefully, learn a little something about who you came from.   With love, H

Goosebumps rose on my arms as I put the journal down. *I'm twenty-four and single. I was adopted. I never used to be curious about my biological family.* At first, the coincidences felt strange, but serendipitous, just like being back in Rehoboth after all this time. I turned the page.

July 8, 1936

Well, hello again. Now then, where shall we begin? I was born in Lewes, Delaware, on May 18, 1912, but my adoptive parents lived in New York, so off I went. I lived there my whole life, though we always spent summers in Rehoboth. Oh, how I loved those summer days—quite a departure from loud life in the city. Now I have always adored the city, but I suppose the change of pace was kind of magic to me when I was little. I loved to play in the sand and wander the boardwalk. It was a happy childhood, bouncing between the bustling city and serenity of the beach.

When I was fifteen, my parents explained my adoption. I am not sure how they expected me to react. I certainly was not expecting it, but I felt no anger—more of a blank indifference toward the family that left me behind and a large swelling of love and affection for the family I knew loved me so well.

The day I turned twenty-one, my father told me a friend of his at Harper's Bazaar was willing to interview me for an administrative position. (Remember how I told you I have always been a writer? I thought this would be my big break.) I was hired! That is where I met James. Oh, James—the man I hoped to someday have a family of my own with. We spent hours together, between long lunches and the occasional chat on the telephone. But he failed to mention his engagement to another woman. I found out with the rest of our office over lunch one day. I was devastated. He must have known I was in love with him—he must have.

I wonder sometimes if I will ever truly get over him. But ah, what was the line from that new book I just read, Gone with the Wind? Yes, it said, "I'll go home. And I'll think of some way to get him back. After all, tomorrow is another day." Indeed, it is. Perhaps it is not too late?

Well, I suppose that is enough for now. But fear not, I have much more to share. With love, H

I slammed the book shut, jumped up, and stuffed it in a cabinet across the room. This journal was describing *my* life. She had the same birthday as me. She worked at *Harper's Bazaar*. James. This was all just a *really* crazy coincidence, right?

In the weeks and months that followed, I kept shutting the journal away in that cabinet, only to have my curiosity get the better of me. Each time, without fail, it described yet another event that had happened to me too. Not all of it was identical, of course, but most of it was. Even my grandmother's thoughts echoed my own.

She wrote about James—how much she missed him, but also how it was easier to be away from him. She wrote about how her biological mother bought this house and left it to her on her twenty-fourth birthday, and about searching for her only to learn she'd passed away. She wrote about discovering she had space in her heart, both for the parents who raised her and the family she'd never gotten to meet.

She wrote about the Great Atlantic Hurricane of 1944, when a ship called the *Thomas Tracy* ran aground atop the remains of the *Merrimac*, a ship that wrecked in 1918. Another massive coincidence. She wrote about coincidence, too.

September 15, 1944

Albert Einstein once said, "Coincidence is God's way of staying anonymous." I rather like the thought of that. It makes me think deeply about this journey of my life. It is not mere coincidence that I ended up back in this place. I like to believe there is something bigger at work here. And today, despite the devastation to our beloved boardwalk and town, I feel hopeful. Where there is destruction, there is also rebuilding. And I think that is what I am doing. Rebuilding me.

I could almost picture her on the beach, staring in awe at that huge ship, split right down the middle.

Sometimes, I would put the journal away for weeks or even months at a time, not sure if I should continue reading. It was a heart-pounding, sweat-inducing experience each time I picked it up; I never knew if it would be the day I peeked into my own future.

Then, one day, it happened.

August 12, 1946

This afternoon, I was strolling along the boardwalk, relishing the sound of the ocean and pigeons chattering away, when I was suddenly gripped with a need for sweets. Of course, I made my way to Dolle's for some taffy. After carefully selecting my candies, clumsy as I am, I tripped over a bin and landed in the arms of a man with the kindest eyes I have ever seen. Truly, it was like a scene from the movies. He said his name was Ray Bellmoor, and before we went our separate ways, he invited me to dinner, and I have accepted. Oh, how I love surprises! I am hopeful I will have another story to tell after our evening together. (James who? Ha ha ha.) With love, H

This must be how my grandmother met my grandfather. I stuffed the book away for the millionth time and wondered if our parallel lives would continue.

Sure enough, eleven days later and despite my best efforts, I tripped (over nothing, I might add) at Dolle's and was helped up by a man named Ray Scarborough, who, before we went our separate ways, asked me to dinner the following night.

I raced home, desperate to read the next journal entry. My grandmother described Ray as a perfect gentleman—respectful, kind, and full of insightful questions. She was clearly enamored with him. For a moment, I was relieved. But I soon realized the gravity of the choice I needed to make. Was I going to read the rest of this thing?

I didn't make the decision lightly, but I did make it definitively. I was going to read this story of my grandmother's life, this story of *my* life. But I was going to read it slowly. And that's exactly what I did.

Some things were still a surprise, like the night Ray proposed to me under the stars on his boat at the West Bay Park Marina. Others, I was expecting, like the news we were pregnant with our first and only child, a girl I named Laurel, the same name my grandmother chose for my mother.

Ray knew about the journal, of course, and as the years went on, having him with me made it easier to handle whatever I read about my own life or our lives together. I'll never forget the night we read my grandmother's words about Ray's death. We cried together, grateful for the time to prepare, but fully aware it wouldn't make the loss any less devastating. Ray was the love of my life, and he passed away from cancer when he was just fifty-nine.

When we learned what would happen to him, we threw away the rules about reading the journal. If we would be learning about my fate in these pages, too, we wanted to do it together. So, before he died, the two of us sat down and finished it, side by side. That's how I learned cancer would take me from this world too.

But perhaps most heartbreaking of all was the day I realized my grandmother had likely died the day I was born. Which meant I would probably die the day *my* granddaughter was born. The last thing my grandmother ever wrote was on the day before my birth.

May 17, 1975

I feel so weak, I can barely write. I know my time is coming soon, so forgive me for how short this will be.

My Laurel is due any day now, but she has decided not to keep the baby, since the father is out of the picture. I know she believes it will have a better life with two parents. It grieves me that I will not be here to help her deal with all of this, but I have made peace with my fate. I have also set in motion a plan to make sure my granddaughter is well taken care of.

In the words of Seneca, "The day which we fear as our last is but the birthday of eternity."

When Laurel gets here today, I am going to tell her why I wrote this journal to begin with. I hope whenever she or my granddaughter read it, they will feel like I am still part of them, even after I am gone. Because I will be. Forever. With Love, H

And then, just last week, I was shuffling around in the kitchen, trying to find my muffin pans, when the phone rang. It was my own Laurel. She wanted to meet for dinner later; she sounded insistent and a little strange.

"OK, I'll see you at Salt Air at six," Laurel said after I agreed, and quickly hung up.

We had barely settled in at the table when Laurel blurted out the two words I was hoping she wouldn't say, at least not yet.

"I'm pregnant."

For a moment, I couldn't breathe. I wasn't ready. I knew my diagnosis, and the end, were near. I'd have to find a way to tell Laurel.

"Who's the father?" I asked, already knowing he wouldn't be around.

Laurel's eyes filled with tears.

"Just this guy … Mom, I only dated him for a couple of weeks, and now he's gone, and I didn't think … I mean, I never meant to …"

In an instant, I was next to Laurel, putting my arm around her.

"Shh, shh now, it's OK, sweetheart. You don't have to have it all figured out right away," I cooed, not wanting to believe the moment I'd dreaded had arrived.

"I'm two months already, but I've been so busy I didn't even realize I was late."

"Oh, honey. I know it's scary, but you're going to be just fine, OK?"

Laurel slumped back in her chair, unconvinced. And then, she brightened the tiniest bit. "Well, there *is* one thing that's kind of cool. My due date is actually your birthday, May eighteenth."

I squeezed my eyes shut, as fresh tears began rolling down my cheeks. I pulled my only daughter in close. Everything in the journal was true. I'd never get to meet my grandchild, and Laurel would be grappling with new life, death, and adoption all at the same time. I felt like the *Thomas Tracy*, split down the middle and irreparable.

Suddenly, it hit me that perhaps Laurel could choose a different path. In that moment, I knew I'd leave the special house on Henlopen Avenue to her *and* my grandchild. Maybe Laurel's fate wasn't written in my grandmother's journal. Right now, I needed to be strong for her. I wiped my own tears away, held my beloved girl's face in my hands, and said the first thing that popped into my mind, the very first thing written in my grandmother's journal.

"Henry David Thoreau said, 'What lies before us and what lies behind us are all small matters compared to what lies within us. And when you bring what is within out into the world, miracles happen.' You have a miracle inside of you, sweet girl. And you are so much stronger than you know."

SARAH BETH HARRIS HAS LIVED IN THE ATLANTA AREA SINCE 1996 but used to visit her maternal grandparents at REHOBOTH BEACH every summer as a kid. SHE OWNS A SMALL FREELANCE marketing, writing, and web design business, has published articles on the minimalist website *NO SIDEBAR,* AND IS CURRENTLY working on her first novel. HER STORY "WHAT LIES WITHIN US" was inspired by the magical feeling of childhood memories in and around REHOBOTH. IN HER SPARE TIME, SARAH WORKS ON HER fiction writing and creates acrylic paintings. YOU CAN VIEW her artistic works and read her personal blog on her website, WWW.SARAHBETHHARRIS.COM.

The Sound of Lightning

By Kim Biasotto

Luca Angelo De Rossi was born March 21, 1995 at 4:59 a.m. He weighed six pounds even and had a head of dark-brown hair. His eyes, which were hazel, were wide open when he entered the world, as if trying to take everything in. Once he had scanned the entire area, however, he shut them tightly and began to wail.

When Luca turned two, his brother Mario, who was four and a half, gave him a large red fire truck with seven small black buttons on it. It required two C batteries. Luca was thrilled to discover that each of the buttons made a different sound when pressed. Luca wore out the buttons before he did the wheels, as his favorite way to play with the toy was to sit in the corner, shut his eyes, and listen to sirens blare.

When Luca turned four, his mother arranged for him to see an ophthalmologist. She was convinced the child had something wrong with his eyes. He kept them closed much of the day and was constantly tripping over things directly in his path. When she asked Luca why he walked into a wall, he answered, "I didn't hear it." The doctor assured her that his eyes were perfectly fine.

When Luca started kindergarten, his teacher appeared nervous at the fall parent-teacher conference. She began by telling his parents what a delight Luca was to have in class. They smiled in response. She then went on to ask them if they noticed anything peculiar about him at home. As no parents want to hear the word *peculiar* used when discussing their child, they bristled.

"What do you mean?" asked his mother in a clipped tone.

"It just seems like sometimes Luca sort of drifts off?"

No one responded.

"He is smart," she quickly added. "And doing well. He just seems to be very in tune with the sounds around him and less so with what is actually going on. He will notice the noise a pencil makes when it hits the floor, but totally miss the fact that someone is trying to hand him a crayon."

"So, what's your point?" asked Luca's father. "I thought you said he was doing well."

"He is … it's just that there is something different about him. He's unique," she added, hoping that sounded more positive.

"Well, I would hope you find all your students unique," said Luca's father, as he stood to leave, motioning to his wife that the meeting was over.

The summer after Luca finished kindergarten, his parents began to see what the teacher had been trying to convey. One rainy day, his mom decided to let the boys watch a movie. This was a rare treat, but she was busy and the idea of ninety uninterrupted minutes appealed to her. Disney's *The Emperor's New Groove* had been released on VHS a few months before and she had purchased it and tucked it away.

The boys were thrilled and quickly sat down next to each other on the sofa. Unfortunately, about twenty minutes into the movie the bickering began. Their mother could not hear what was being said and chose to ignore it until Mario burst into her bedroom, interrupting her laundry folding.

"Mom, make him stop!"

"What's wrong?" his mom asked.

"Luca is ruining the movie."

"How is Luca ruining the movie?"

"He keeps telling me that the sounds are wrong."

Their mom stopped sorting socks and followed Mario down the hall.

"What's going on, buddy?" she asked Luca. "Is something wrong with the TV?"

"Not the TV," he said. "The movie. They have the sounds wrong."

Confused, she asked him to explain.

"They were out in a storm and there was lots of lightning."

"OK, so what is the problem?"

"That's not at all what lightning sounds like!"

Mario lifted his arms in the air and gave his mom a see-he's-being-crazy look.

"What do you mean?" she asked, ignoring her eldest son. "What was wrong with the way it sounded?"

"It was all weird sounding. Lightning is different. This was not right!" He slammed his small fist on the sofa.

"OK. I guess that could be frustrating. But look, the storm scene is over. Just enjoy the movie."

Mario jumped in. "Oh, it's not just the storm. It's everything." He imitated Lucas: "A llama wouldn't sound like that when it runs. A vine would never make that sound if it wrapped around a tree. Scorpions don't click when they walk."

"OK," said their mom, resting a hand on Mario's shoulder. "I think I understand what you're saying." Turning to Luca, she smiled. "Buddy, this is just pretend. It's a cartoon. They add funny sounds to make it, well, funny." She added a small laugh for effect.

Luca started to tear up. "But it's not funny," he said quietly. "It's just wrong."

When the Fourth of July rolled around, Mario ate his dinner in record time. He was eager to walk the two blocks to the beach to watch the fireworks. The De Rossi family lived in Rehoboth Beach, Delaware, and always celebrated Independence Day the same way.

First, they went to Candy Kitchen and purchased large amounts of red shoestring licorice. Next, they visited the kite shop to buy glow sticks. Finally, they set up chairs on the beach and waited for what seemed like hours for the sky to explode with light.

This year, their mom was running late and told her husband and the boys to go on ahead; she would meet them on the beach. As she walked out onto the screened-in porch, she was surprised to find Luca reclining on one of the cushioned chairs.

"Whatcha doing, buddy?"

"Well," said Luca. "This year, I have decided to watch the fireworks from here. Dad said it was OK if you stay with me."

"But we can't really see them from the porch, bud. We need to get closer to the beach."

"No, we don't. I can totally see them from here."

"Really?"

"I just shut my eyes and watch them with my ears." And with that, he stretched out and closed his eyes.

As the years went by, Luca became more and more fascinated by sounds. He could tell when the UPS truck was a block away. He learned to identify neighbors by the sound of their gait and knew the local dogs by the noises they made. Snickers, the fat corgi, had a collar with tags that jingled when he walked. Bagel the beagle always needed a nail trim, thus causing a tapping sound as he approached. But his favorite was Sasha the German shepherd.

Sasha was three years old and lived around the corner. She had not made the cut at police dog training school and now resided with a nice family of five who, much to Sasha's delight, often forgot to close the gate. Sasha would patrol the neighborhood until one of her family members noticed she was missing and tracked her down. She walked so stealthily that even Luca often didn't hear her approach. If it were not for her new dog tags that occasionally clinked as she walked, he would never hear her. He respected her greatly because of this.

One warm August evening when Luca was fourteen, he went to the Lake Gerar park to listen to the cicadas. He would spend hours there on warm summer nights and then meet Mario when he got off work so they could walk home together. While sitting in the grass, Luca heard the wind shift in the trees and noticed a change in the cadence of the bugs. He knew this meant there was a good chance for a storm and smiled, as lightning was still one of his favorite sounds.

He decided to head to Nicola's early and wait for Mario. Thick clouds were rolling in quickly, turning the sky dark. As he prepared to cross the small bridge on First Street, he heard a funny, buzzing sound. Looking for the source, he discovered one of the bridge lights was out. He stood quietly, trying to determine why a streetlight would make so much noise if it was not producing light. He wasn't sure how long he stood there, but his concentration was soon interrupted by another sound.

The gunshot broke his train of thought. He wasn't sure what direction it had come from, so he closed his eyes, replaying all the sounds that had occurred in the past minute or two. He recalled a soft cry, a gunshot, a thud, and a shuffling sound coming from somewhere near the other end of the bridge. He opened his eyes and moved forward slowly.

When he had crossed the bridge, he looked down the path to his left and saw a figure lying on the ground. He walked over and stopped about two feet away. Blood pooled around the young woman's head. Her eyes and mouth were open. Luca shut his eyes and listened. He could not hear her breathing. He did not move until he heard the patter of rain and the rumbling of thunder.

When the police arrived, Luca was overwhelmed by the number of sounds that accompanied them. The equipment they wore rattled as they walked. Their shoes squeaked on the wet pavement. The lights on their cars clicked as they blinked on and off: red, blue, red, blue. One of the officers ushered him away from the woman's body and had him sit in the back of a squad car out of the rain.

When Luca did not appear at Nicola Pizza, Mario figured he had gotten distracted at the park and headed that way. The rain was becoming heavy and Mario laughed to himself. *Luca is probably comparing the sound of rain on water versus grass.* It was typically a ten-minute walk, but when Mario saw the cop cars he broke into a run. He found Luca sitting in the back of one of the cars, eyes closed, not saying a word.

"You know this guy?" one of the officers asked him.

"He's my brother," Marcus replied.

"Something wrong with him?"

"No, not really. He's just really sensitive to sounds. What happened?"

"A woman got shot. We think your brother might have seen something. Would you mind talking to him? He hasn't said anything to any of us yet."

"Sure. Do you mind if I get in the car with him? It's kinda wet out here."

The officer went around and opened the back door on the other side. Mario slid in next to his brother.

"Hey Luca, it's me."

"I know, I heard you walking up."

Mario found that hard to believe, between all the rain and other sounds, but then remembered who he was talking to and smiled.

"So, what happened?"

"A woman died."

"Did you see it?"

Luca didn't answer.

"Did you hear it?"

Luca nodded.

"Want to tell me about it?"

Luca shook his head. "I am still trying to separate all the noises, but I need to be someplace quieter to do that."

"Let me go talk to the officer and see if we can get you away from here." Mario knocked on the window and the officer opened the door.

"So, did he tell you anything?" asked the officer.

"No, not yet. But I am pretty sure he has information that can help you. He just needs to get away from all of this."

"Let me see what I can do." The officer walked away and came back a few minutes later. "Why don't you guys head home, get dry, and then have one of your folks bring him down to the station. Will that work?"

Mario said it would.

"You guys need a ride home?"

"No, it's not too far. Plus, he loves the sound of lightning," Mario added with a slight grin.

When they arrived home about twenty minutes later, their mom was beside herself with worry. Mario explained as much as he knew. Luca had already gone to take a shower and put on dry clothes.

Luca and his dad went back to the station, but not until Luca had eaten a large plate of lasagna and three slices of garlic bread. The officer who had been at the scene was waiting for them. He introduced himself as Sergeant Ghent and led Luca and his dad down a narrow cinderblock hallway to a room in the rear of the building. They sat around a wooden table and the officer asked if he could record the conversation. Luca and his father agreed.

"Tell me about tonight," said the sergeant.

"The light was out on the bridge," said Luca.

"Go on."

"It was still making noise even though it was out."

"OK, but what about the woman who was shot—did you see her?"

"Not exactly."

"I don't understand."

Luca looked frustrated. His dad jumped in.

"You need to understand," he said. "Luca doesn't process things the way the rest of us do. He has an acute sense of hearing. He can pick up the slightest sound and often perceives more than someone who was looking at the same thing."

The officer looked doubtful. "So, what did you hear?"

Luca closed his eyes. He went back to the park in his mind. The cicadas singing, the wind shifting, the broken bulb on the bridge humming. He tried to focus. "There was a man," he began. "He said something like 'give it to me.' Then there was the sound of a zipper that wouldn't open. The man said, 'Hurry up.' The woman started to cry. Then the gun made a loud noise, someone fell to the ground, and then someone limped off."

"What do you mean *someone limped off*?"

Luca opened his eyes and looked at the officer. "Do you not know what *limp* means?"

"I know what it means," said the sergeant. "I want to know how you know someone was limping."

"I heard it."

"You could hear a limp?"

"Yes," said Luca. "It was clear that someone was putting more weight on their right foot and sort of dragging their left one. Limping," he added.

"How can you know it was their left foot that was dragging?"

"OK, so I can't be one hundred percent sure, but most people lead with their right foot and this person's second step was the one dragging, so I am theorizing that it was the left one that was hurt."

"Amazing," mumbled the officer.

Luca's dad smiled and gave him a pat on the shoulder. "You're doing good," he said.

"Anything else you remember?" asked Sergeant Ghent.

Luca closed his eyes and thought back.

"Gum," he said. "The person with the limp was chewing gum."

"You could hear him chew?" asked the Sergeant in a skeptical tone.

"No," said Luca. "I heard him popping his gum. You know, blowing a bubble then popping it."

"So, we are looking for a gum-popping man with a limp. "Well, I've started with less." He laughed.

When Luca got home that night, he was tired, but restless. He kept his bedroom window open, hoping the sound of the rain would calm him and help him fall asleep. It took some time, but eventually the sound of the rain, wind, and swaying of the leaves helped him drift off.

There was a break in the storm, but the breeze was causing drops to fall from the drenched leaves onto the walkway outside Luca's window. This was the first sound he noticed when he woke, but it was not the sound that actually woke him. Closing his eyes, he listened closely.

A twig snapped. Luca sat up. There was a shuffling sound. Luca moved toward the open window, with his eyes still closed. The clouds had momentarily parted and as the moon was nearly full, it provided a fair amount of light should he decide to look around. He strained his ears, looking for other noises.

When he heard a gum-popping sound, he froze. When the man spoke, Luca opened his eyes and peered through the screen.

"You the kid that was on the bridge tonight?"

Luca said nothing. Too afraid to move or call out, he closed his eyes as the man continued to talk in a quiet but gruff voice.

"You don't have to answer. I know it was you."

Luca heard the man cock a revolver. The gum popped again, along with a small sound of metal on metal. Luca smiled.

"What are you smiling about?" asked the man, his gun pointed at the screen Luca was standing behind.

Still smiling, Luca answered, "You don't see what I hear."

When the police arrived, they found Sasha the German shepherd sitting on top of a screaming man in the yard. Her long white teeth were clutching the man's right wrist, and his gun was in the grass a few feet away. Luca's mom and dad were on the front porch along with some curious neighbors. Mario was in the kitchen eating leftover lasagna, and Luca was on the sofa, his head resting on the floral cushion. His eyes were closed, and he was smiling, listening to sounds of the distant lightning.

KIM BIASOTTO IS A WIFE, MOM, AND *MORAI* (IRISH FOR "GRANDMOTHER") LIVING IN WILMINGTON, DELAWARE. SHE HAS SPENT HER SUMMERS AT THE BEACH FOR AS LONG AS SHE CAN REMEMBER. HER FAVORITE PASTIMES, WHEN NOT WRITING, INCLUDE SPENDING TIME WITH HER HUB, PLAYING WITH HER GRANDDAUGHTER, CO-LEADING A TENTH-GRADE GIRLS GROUP, AND HELPING HER YOUNGEST GET READY TO LEAVE THE NEST. KIM'S PASSION IN WRITING AND SPEAKING IS TO INSPIRE OTHERS TO NOT JUST "HANG IN THERE" OR "MAKE IT THROUGH" BUT TO THRIVE. "THE GREATER DANGER FOR MOST OF US LIES NOT IN SETTING OUR AIM TOO HIGH AND FALLING SHORT; BUT IN SETTING OUR AIM TOO LOW, AND ACHIEVING OUR MARK." — MICHELANGELO

JUDGE'S COMMENT

Tight beginning, an interesting setting, and a strong narrative arc. Dialogue moved both plot and characters forward. Overall a well-constructed and executed short story, enjoyable as a mystery beach read!

Treasured Time

By Michele Connelly

Despite the relaxation podcast and the scent of lavender essential oil wafting through the Honda Pilot, Caroline Brooks was finding the five-hour drive from Connecticut exasperating. She breathed in, held it for five seconds, and exhaled for seven. Glancing over to the passenger seat, she spied her camera bag and laptop case. Work had become monotonous and Caroline needed a break; however, never knowing when inspiration would occur, the photojournalist was compelled to take both tools of her trade.

Once she arrived, she knew her anxiety and stress would melt away. Caroline had visited Rehoboth most of her forty-nine summers. Her favorite aunt lived in nearby Lewes, and every summer included at least one trip to Rehoboth for sun, sand, and Thrasher's fries. This time, however, there would be no visiting family or eating french fries on the boardwalk. Instead, this was a much-needed girls' getaway weekend. At the realization that she and her four lifelong friends would reunite in less than an hour, Caroline smiled and continued driving south.

They used to see each other all the time for spring breaks, vacations, and clubbing. Then it became bridal showers, weddings, and babies. Now that they were turning fifty, their reunions revolved around funerals for parents and even siblings and classmates. She still felt as if she were twenty, OK, maybe thirty. They were still too young for this, thought Caroline as she shook her head in denial.

Making a left turn into the condo community where they were renting, Caroline spotted two closed iron gates and a sign warning that a code was needed for entry. Meg was the one who made the reservations, but she wouldn't be arriving until later. Caroline navigated onto the shoulder and called Julianne, who, according to the extensive group texting that had been happening all day, would be first to arrive.

"Julianne, are you in? How do I get in?"

"Oh, I can get you in, but good luck finding the place. I've been circling for like an hour." Julianne sighed in frustration. "Enter 1-7-9-8 on the keypad, and the gates will open. I'm circling somewhere to the right."

"OK. I'll see you soon … hopefully." Caroline tried the code.

The gate opened, and immediately Caroline understood what Julianne was referring to. The development was still under construction. Roads were barely marked, and when they were, they often led to a dead end. Her GPS kept saying it couldn't find Starfish Circle.

A gray minivan with a bumper sticker that read "Superheroes Wear Scrubs" was making a five-point turn.

Must be Julianne. Caroline smiled. Julianne Taylor was a nurse as well as a nerd. There were no other cars around, and none in the parking areas of the few completed buildings, which she supposed wasn't too odd, considering it was off-season.

Lowering their windows and giving the universal signal of confusion with upturned palms, the two exchanged hellos.

"These roads are the craziest I've ever seen," Julianne said. "It's like they all radiate from the center, but then dead end."

Just then, a group text alerted them that Margo was in the house. Caroline and Julianne looked at each other, puzzled.

Texting back, Julianne asked how she got there. Margo instructed them to go to the center of the development, and their GPS should work. Once at the hub, looking at the map on the screen, Caroline saw that they were in the middle of a circle with five prongs.

Ohhh, I get it now. Caroline opened her car window. "It's like a starfish," she called to Julianne.

"So which leg of the starfish is our condo building?" Julianne called back. "I'm running low on both patience and bladder strength."

"Top right one. I've got it," Caroline said as she located it on the map. "Want to follow me?"

Looking relieved at the idea of arriving at the destination versus circling through the deserted development again, Julianne nodded.

Margo Martinez and Dessa Simmons had driven together. They would say it was because they both still lived in Pennsylvania where they had all grown up, so carpooling made sense, but the real reason, as they all knew, was that Margo was the only one who could tolerate Dessa's nonstop talking. It was the same reason the two of them would be sharing a room, while the others all had singles.

After shrieks, hugs, and hellos, the four started gathering bags from their cars.

"I need wine," Margo said.

Looking at Dessa, Caroline joked, "I'm sure you do!"

"Hey! I made the three-hour trip fun," said Dessa.

"Where's that wine?" asked Margo, raising her eyebrows.

Laughter ensued. They had known each other for decades, graduated together, and were still friends after college and work and kids and moving.

By the time the fifth member of the group, Meg Ward, arrived, they had decimated two bottles of wine, all of the chips and salsa, and made a considerable dent in a Costco-sized bag of Reese's peanut butter cups.

"This place is super cute, Meg," said Dessa.

"Yeah, once we finally found it," chimed in Julianne.

"I was a little worried about the development still being under construction, but this place—it's called "Daulton's Place"—looked fantastic online," Meg said, smiling. "And Daulton seemed nice over the phone."

Margo held up her wine glass, "To Daulton, cheers!"

After a few hours of catching up, the group ventured out for dinner.

Meg was the designated driver. Before leaving, she grabbed a key fob that resembled a flash drive from a porcelain bowl near the door. "Daulton said that sometimes the keypad doesn't work, so we should keep this with us at all times. He said if we didn't, we could have a *situation*.

"Well, nobody wants a *situation*," Julianne said mockingly.

Being off-season, they figured restaurants wouldn't be as busy; therefore, they had not made reservations. As Meg drove, the other four had phones in hand, utilizing Google and GPS while looking out the windows to get their bearings as they headed down Coastal Highway.

Margo suggested Blue Coast. Dessa squinted and looked at her map. "Blue Fin?"

"Blue Coast," Margo repeated.

"I don't see Blue Fin," Dessa replied.

"Coast. Coast!" screamed Margo.

"Big Fish is coming up," Caroline said.

"Blue Fish?" asked Dessa.

"Remind me again why I get stuck with her," implored Margo as she elbowed Dessa.

Deciding for the group, Meg pulled into the restaurant parking lot.

Big Fish Grill had trendy, fresh food but with a relaxed atmosphere. The wait for an open table was less than five minutes. Chad, a waiter who looked like a surfer, introduced himself by writing his name on the paper tablecloth. Next to his name, he drew a starfish. From the starfish to the opposite end of the table, he drew dashed lines without missing a beat, as he told them about the drink specials.

Everyone ordered drinks and appetizers. When it was Caroline's turn, she said, "I'll have a pot of the Spicy Diablo Mussels."

Margo and Dessa looked horrified.

"*Spicy diablo?*" Margo asked. "Do you not get heartburn?"

"No," Caroline said. "Do you?"

"We're almost fifty. All fifty-year-olds get heartburn. Don't they?" Margo looked at the rest of the group for validation.

Opening her purse, Meg pulled out a village-sized bottle of antacids. "I never leave home without them."

Everyone sitting near them in the restaurant turned and stared at the outburst of laughter that followed.

"What the hell did Chad draw?" Julianne asked, looking back at the starfish and dashes.

"Maybe the starfish is dancing?" Dessa guessed, doing a little seated dance.

"Maybe the starfish was drunk," Julianne said, as she drank her Dogfish Head India Pale Ale.

Conversation flowed over the delicious dinner. No one would have guessed it had been years since they'd all been together. They shared memories, told stories, and laughed so hard they cried.

Chad returned to the table, cleared plates, and asked if anyone wanted more drinks or dessert. Yes, to both. Whipping out his crayon again, he added some embellishments to his masterpiece. Opposite the starfish, he drew some sort of box with a round top. Next to it were the words, "Read between the lines."

The blond college student turned to leave the table, but not before Julianne whispered, "What has Chad been smoking?"

"Looks like a treasure chest," said Margo.

"Oh, I love a good mystery!" exclaimed Caroline, as she took a photo of the wacky tablecloth art.

The laughter continued as they left the restaurant and piled into Meg's brand new, white Mercedes SUV. *Meg's tech company must be doing well*, thought Caroline.

Julianne, Margo, and Dessa were all talking at the same time in the backseat. From the front passenger seat, Caroline smiled at the sight of the empty highway. She completely understood why the masses were drawn to Rehoboth in the summer. After all, what's not to love about sun, sand, and surf? But she loved the off-season with the emptier beaches and quieter town.

Two of the three backseat drivers were begging to go thrift shopping the next morning. Everyone knew this was coming. Dessa owned an antique store and was known to spend hours upon hours looking for the next treasure she could resell for a mint. Meg, Caroline, and Margo were less excited.

"Is there something else we could do while Julianne and Dessa search for treasures?" asked Caroline.

"I saw in the brochures at Daulton's Place that there's an antique store right across from the outlets," Meg said, "We could drop them off, and the rest of us could go outlet shopping."

"Tax-free shopping? I'm in!" said Margo.

Arriving back at the condo community, Meg pulled up to the keypad and entered 1-7-9-8. The gates opened, and Meg headed right. Moments later, they were circling, lost again.

"Why is this so challenging?" Julianne asked. "It's a development with cul-de-sacs for crying out loud."

After three U-turns, they were finally back at Daulton's Place.

After a late night of additional talking and more wine, the friends woke early and spent Saturday morning lounging on the deck drinking coffee and tea in the cool, crisp early autumn air. They soaked in the smell of the nearby saltwater.

Even with the lazy start to the day, by ten o'clock they were all showered, dressed, and ready to continue their weekend celebration.

Before checking out the beach and then outlet and antique shopping, caffeine was required. Caroline recommended The Coffee Mill. It was an unpresumptuous little shop with a million varieties of coffee. But what Caroline liked most was the display of local vintage photographs that covered the walls.

"You weren't kidding, Caroline. It'll take me an hour to figure out what I want," said Margo, looking at the extensive chalkboard menu before finally deciding on the Copper Canyon blend.

"Is the Peruvian organic?" Dessa asked the owner. Margo rolled her eyes.

Julianne and Meg each ordered the decaf almond amaretto coffee and avocado toast.

"What are we, latte-drinking, coastal-elite millennials?" asked Caroline, smirking at her two friends as she squinted at a photo on the wall.

"I wish. I'd rather be turning thirty than fifty," said Julianne.

"Hey, look at this," Caroline said, pointing to the picture she had been inspecting. Embedded in the image of an old sailboat with puffy white sails was a clipart starfish with a raised, bent right hand.

"OK, this is freaky. Chad? Chad, where are you?" asked Dessa.

Before they left, Caroline snapped a photograph of the image. Something about the boat seemed familiar.

After dropping Dessa and Julianne at a strip mall with three thrift stores, Meg, Caroline, and Margo headed to the nearby Tanger Outlets. They had been to Ann Taylor, Francesca's, and Talbots when Meg's phone rang.

"I can't find Dessa," said Julianne.

"What do you mean you can't find her?" asked Meg.

"I mean she was shopping in the store with me and then she was gone. I've been texting and calling, but there's no answer."

"OK, we're on our way back."

When they arrived at the thrift store, they found a distraught Julianne. They tried to calm her and then searched for signs of Dessa but found nothing.

"Hey, guys," squealed a chipper Dessa, emerging from the back room of the shop.

"I've been searching all over for you!" Julianne shouted.

"Oh, sorry. I found this cute starfish coin," Dessa said, holding up the small gold coin with a raised image of a starfish, which of course, had a waving right hand.

"Not the freaking starfish again," Margo said with a sigh.

"And Susie," Dessa said, pointing and waving to the woman at the front desk, "Susie and I were looking in the back room to see if there were any more like this."

"Can I see that?" asked Meg.

Meg turned the doubloon over, and on the back, they saw a large boat.

"That's the same boat from the coffee shop, isn't it?" asked Margo.

"And, it's the same as the boat in the painting at Daulton's Place," replied Caroline, suddenly remembering where she had seen it before. "I think it had the name *De Braak* written below it."

"*De Braak?*" Susie asked.

"Yes, I think so," Caroline said.

"The HMS *De Braak* is legendary. It's a ship that sank off the coast in the 1700s. There were rumors of treasure on board," Susie said with a mischievous glint in her eye.

"Treasure!" exclaimed Dessa, imagining all the antiques.

"They raised the ship in 1986 or 1987, but they didn't find much of value," Susie said.

After Dessa paid for the starfish sailboat coin, the group returned to the outlets for more shopping. Several stores and a Starbucks pit stop later, the friends were exhausted.

"I'd be fine just getting pizza and hanging out on the deck or by the fireplace for the night," said Margo.

Caroline suggested Grotto's. After much deliberation, they decided on one Mama's Pizza and a Bianco White Pizza. Sitting at the table on the deck and watching the sun go down was the relaxation they all needed.

"So, Meg, how's single life?" asked Julianne, flinging her long legs onto a nearby chair.

"It's rough out there. I'm just looking for a fifty-year-old Ed Sheeran. How difficult is that to find?"

As they laughed, devoured their pizza, and drank their wine, Meg regaled them with stories of her recent dating fails.

"I'm glad I don't ever have to date again," said Margo. "I think I'll just keep what I've got."

"It is nice being here without the husbands and kids, isn't it?" asked Caroline.

"You don't have a husband or kids," Julianne said.

"I know. I meant it's nice being here without all of *your* husbands and kids." Caroline, still smirking, picked up her phone to check her texts. After she did, she searched for *De Braak*.

"Guys, listen to this," she said, waving her hand at her friends to get their attention.

"The *De Braak* sank in 1798."

Her excitement was met with blank stares.

"What numbers have we been entering into that keypad? One-seven-nine-eight!"

"OK, that's a little weird," admitted Dessa.

"So, we have a stoned waiter, waving starfish, sunken ship, and hidden treasures," Margo said, trying to tie it all together.

"And don't forget, we're staying in a starfish-shaped development," Julianne added.

Retrieving her camera, Caroline flashed back to the photographs of the starfish at the restaurant and the one in the coffee shop. "Look, it's always the starfish's right hand waving. If you were looking at this development from above, where we're staying would be the right arm of the starfish."

"This is where the treasure is!" screamed Dessa.

"*Read between the lines,*" Margo said.

At the same time, they all yelled, "The library!" They ran from the deck to the library, looked around the room, and began reading the book titles.

"What are we looking for?" Julianne asked.

"Something to do with a ship, *De Braak*, the year 1798, a treasure," suggested Margo.

"Hamilton!" shrieked Caroline, pointing to a book.

"The play?" asked Dessa.

"No, the man. He would have been around then," Caroline said. "And yes, I only know that thanks to the play."

"In the late 1700s, he was secretary of the Treasury. Treasury! Money!" said Margo.

"You saw *Hamilton* too?" asked Julianne, getting sidetracked.

"No, I'm a teacher," Margo said, grabbing the book about Alexander Hamilton.

As Julianne, Margo, and Dessa gathered around the book, Caroline noticed photographs on the bookshelf and walked toward them. They were of a nerdy but cute man with shaggy red hair and thick glasses. In the most recent picture, he looked to be around their age—a fifty-year-old Ed Sheeran.

Caroline turned and looked at Meg, who was watching her intently. A knowing smile crept across Caroline's face.

"Oh my god, there's money in here!" Margo shrieked, as she leafed through the book.

On the last page of the book was a note: "Congratulations! You solved the mystery and are a true-life super sleuth. Your reward? This hidden treasure."

"This is so cool," said Dessa, fanning herself with one-hundred-dollar bills.

"What's going on, Meg?" asked Caroline.

The others looked confused. Before she could deny it, Caroline picked up the photo, turned it toward the group, and said, "A fifty-year-old Ed Sheeran. Daulton, I presume?"

Meg paused, started to protest, then smiled. Just then, the man in the photograph walked through the library door.

"Meet Daulton, my boyfriend," Meg said, smiling as the two hugged and Daulton greeted the group.

"We had an idea to offer real-life escape room mysteries—a destination vacation with a twist, using local stories and legends to make it educational and interesting. This whole development will be part of the escape," Meg explained. "And that is your reward is for being our beta testers."

"The fob tracks where the participants go," explained Daulton. "Everyone wants more off-season tourism, so several businesses signed on. The fob technology notifies them when a treasure hunter is in their restaurant or store, and they're given clues to drop."

"Chad and Susie were in on it?" asked Julianne.

Daulton nodded.

"I thought it would be a fun way to remember turning fifty," said Meg.

On Sunday morning, Caroline pulled onto the highway. She had a one-hundred-dollar bill in her wallet, her share of the treasure. She smiled, feeling inspired, as she reflected on the time with her lifelong friends. Her mind raced, pondering the story she could write about their treasured weekend. Maybe turning fifty wasn't so bad after all.

For Michele Connelly, who currently lives in Pennsylvania, every summer since childhood has included at least one visit to Delaware and Maryland's Eastern Shore. Her first published short story, "Treasured Time," was inspired by a recent vacation to Rehoboth Beach with a group of lifelong friends to celebrate their fiftieth birthdays. A nonprofit administrator by day, Michele has found writing to be her passion. In her spare time, she enjoys photography, reading mysteries, spoiling her niece, and rescuing old dogs. She can be found on Instagram @ MICHELECONNELLYWRITES.

A Whole New World

By Jennifer Walker

I was there the day the mermaid washed up on Rehoboth Beach. It was a Saturday in the middle of July, and like everyone else I was sprawled under an umbrella listening to the surf crash down on screaming children and laughing adults. I had a weekend off from my horseshoe crab research at the University of Delaware and was spending it entrenched in the sand, eating Grotto's pizza and Fisher's caramel popcorn like a real tourist.

It was a luxury to relax and watch the ocean instead of breathing through a snorkel in it. Above me, a squadron of pelicans plunged through the air again and again with the brutal gracelessness of warplanes shot from the sky. Sunlight dazzled the humps of unbroken waves, and the horizon shimmered as if it were desert instead of sea that met the sky. The smell of hot boardwalk, like the inside of an ice cream sandwich wrapper baked in the dunes, was just strong enough to edge out the tropical scents of a dozen sunscreens. The cloudless sky was that ridiculously bright periwinkle even sunglasses can't dim.

And then the whistles started. At first, they sounded like something to ignore if you aren't in the water or watching someone who is. But then they got so urgent, so fast, I sat up to see what the lifeguards were so excited about. They were pointing to something the shape of a small log, rolling in and out of the water some distance from shore. As it came closer, its iridescent sheen was unmistakable. It had to be some kind of fish but was shaped more like a seal. As the lifeguards frantically tried to get everyone out of the water, people up and down the beach shouted out guesses: "It's a marlin!" "Some kind of shark!"

"No, it's a manatee!"

No one was right. I knew that from all the years studying marine biology, but that didn't mean I knew what it was. I joined the growing crowd near the water's edge and was just as dumbfounded as everyone else when a mermaid washed up and landed on the beach with a foam-framed flop.

The lifeguards moved the crowd back, but I shouldered my way to the front. That gave me a clear view of the little girl on the boogie board still in the water, and I saw her ride the wave in that dropped her almost on top of the creature.

Her name, I later learned, was Stephanie Miller. According to subsequent news reports, she was a soon-to-be fifth grader from Buck's County, Pennsylvania, at the beach with her family for the week. Her parents had left her in the care of an older brother who, the employees of Funland confirmed, had spent the afternoon trying to get the attention of the girl running the bumper cars. The family declined to be interviewed, but there were lots of other interviews about Stephanie. Teachers described her as a dreamer, a student who got easily distracted by a squirrel or a bird outside the classroom window. Her classmates said she was nice but quiet, and I got the impression she was the kind of kid who sat alone at lunch reading a book. She wasn't particularly good at sports, she didn't seem to have any hobbies outside of reading, and in every picture, she had that sort of wistful, far-off look that made me think her imagination was stronger than her reality. She reminded me a lot of myself at that age. I could see how a girl like that might not have heard the lifeguards or noticed the mass exodus around her. She was probably too busy watching the kamikaze crashes of pelicans or the whirling dervishes of light on the water. I think she caught that wave purely by chance.

If Stephanie looked surprised to find a mass of people screaming in front of her when she rubbed the saltwater out of her eyes, she

Rehoboth Beach Reads

was even more shocked by the grotesque creature next to her. For the mermaid was nothing like the nubile creatures of lore. Her tail resembled the short, clumsy back end of a grouper instead of a dolphin's sleek posterior. Her upper body ballooned out from her tail with no discernible waist and ended in a neckless head positioned in front of two small arm-like appendages. Her face was flat like a flounder's, somewhat triangular, and both her eyes bulged from one side like a cubist nightmare. Her stringy hair was made of fine writhing tentacles. Her entire body was covered in slimy gray-green scales. She was about five and a half feet long—although later reports exaggerated her length up to ten feet—and despite her hideousness, there was no mistaking her humanlike qualities, even as she lay there, eyes-side up, her mouth opening and closing like a fish.

The crowd shouted hysterical warnings at Stephanie, as if the chubby nine-year-old was the abomination and not the horrendous beast next to her. The fearful girl shrank back and moved closer to the mermaid. This caused even more rabid shrieking and arm waving, especially from the lifeguards whose piercing whistles intensified the din. But the girl just stared at the gasping mermaid, who was clearly dying.

There was some debate later that the earplugs the child was wearing might have prevented her from hearing properly, but I doubt it. Looking back on it, the way we were all raving, it's not surprising she wanted to get as far away from us as possible.

With a good deal of awkwardness that is a specialty of little girls who prefer to sit, read, and dream instead of run, climb, and jump, Stephanie lifted the scaly monster onto her boogie board and started to push her back into the sea. A lot of folks later asked why, with all those people standing around, someone didn't do something. But that thing was so horrific, and the sight of it slung over a bright-pink boogie board decorated with unicorns and rainbows—a boogie board that had only a week before been prominently displayed in a surf shop just two blocks away—was so ghastly it stifled the bravest impulse. I didn't even have the wherewithal to record what was happening on my phone; my shock and terror erased every scientific instinct. I watched the whole thing, rooted in place, unable to distinguish the sound coming out of my throat from the helpless wails around me. People ran to their cars, ran down the beach, ran into the shade so they could see their phone screens to call 911, but nobody ran to Stephanie.

That's why she was able to get so far out before anyone came after her. That, and the fact that there was a strong northerly current just beyond the breakers that had been building all day. The last I saw the girl, she was propped on her forearms at the front of the boogie board, kicking like mad, while the mermaid lay over the back with her head and tail in the water. Every now and then that unglamorous tail slapped the water with surprising power.

The Rehoboth police and the Coast Guard eventually sent boats to look for the pair, but they never managed a sighting. A couple of bird-watchers at Gordon's Pond did report seeing a pod of dolphins leaping like silver acrobats around a tiny fuchsia dot, and a family surf fishing saw a group of pelicans dive-bombing near some hot-pink debris.

The final time the duo was spotted was just beyond Cape Henlopen. About a dozen passengers standing on the starboard side of the Cape May-Lewes ferry on its way to New Jersey swore they saw a blur of pink rising in and out of the Atlantic swell, headed north. It really could have been anything, except for how every few seconds, until it was out of sight, a tiny gray tail fin crashed into the ocean and sent up a spray that made rainbows in the air.

Stephanie and the mermaid were never found. The boogie board might have broken up on some rocks along the coast in Maine later that month, but there were a lot of those boogie boards sold that year. It was never verified. The story stayed in the news cycle for most of the summer and blurry pictures of the creature made waves throughout the marine biology world. Every expert had a theory and the federal government even gave our University of Delaware marine biology department a million-dollar grant to do more research. We never turned up anything on mermaids, but the extra money did allow me to explore previously unrecorded sections of the Delaware Bay and I discovered a new species of horseshoe crab. I named it *Limulus stephanieus* and got to personally present to the little girl's family a taxidermic specimen, which they keep on their mantle to this day.

Most people think the girl is dead. When they're optimistic, they think she drowned, but they can easily imagine her viciously devoured by the repulsive aberration she tried to save.

At first, nobody in Rehoboth dressed up as a mermaid, even for the yearly Sea Witch Festival around Halloween. But slowly, over time, in that defiant way memory rewrites the horrors of history, sinuous sequined tails, shell bikini tops, and impossibly flowing hair began to resurface. There are still some people who refuse to swim in that section of Rehoboth Beach, but every summer it stays packed with bright umbrellas, lolling bodies, and families sharing greasy bags of Thrasher's fries.

I never stopped swimming there. Even now, I rent a house every July just down the street, no matter where I might be teaching. I love that ocean. It's the kind of ocean that can beat you down until your chest hurts to breathe, or it can lull you to sleep as you float under a cloudless sky. It invigorates and calms. Frightens and soothes. It's the kind of place where a little girl who loves to look around and imagine the beauty and mystery in everything could one day find a whole new world, open only to those, like her, who can see it. If you ask me, that's exactly where Stephanie is.

Even though she now lives on a small rock in the Virgin Islands called St. John, Jennifer Walker still thinks of Lewes, Delaware, as home. She wishes the smell of the marsh came as a room fragrance diffuser. She spent a long time staring at the sea but never saw a mermaid, so she had to make one up. This is her first published story, but she's in serious discussions with her imagination about upping production. Stay tuned for more weirdness to come.

The Dripping Man

By Will Eichler

The alarm wakes me at four thirty in the morning. I slam my hand down on top of my phone, doing my best to remember what could have compelled me to get up at an hour when I wasn't even sure God was paying attention.

With a good amount of groaning and cursing, I push myself up and walk to the bathroom, careful to avoid kicking the dresser and tripping over the dog's bowl as I pass. I start the shower, stepping in before it even has a chance to warm. The cold water shocks me into complete consciousness, and I release a long shiver that frees up what little energy I have.

After standing in the torrent for long enough that my skin begins to feel as if it might just peel off my body, I step out of the shower and grab a towel. Burying my face in it, I feel the fibers rub against the coarse hairs of my beard and scratch against my eyelids. I dry my body robotically before tossing the towel into the bin next to the sink. I see that the fog on the mirror has begun to dissipate, but before it is completely gone, I doodle a small smiley face as a smile appears on my face as well, and I think about why I have dragged myself out of bed this early.

In an hour, I will be watching the sun come up over the ocean in Rehoboth. I had done this a handful of times before, each time with a small collective of friends to share the journey. But the friends have scattered to the winds, pursuing lives that still included me, just in a smaller capacity. So now, I'm going to do it alone. I'm not sure what compelled me to do it again, but I suppose there are worse ways to start the day; besides, the school year would be starting soon, and seeing a beautiful sunrise and buying an egg sandwich at Kaisy's is as good a way as any to say goodbye to summer vacation and hello to my next classroom of students.

The small house my aunt owned was situated just a few blocks from the beach, and I leave it while the moon is still over the horizon. The walk is short, and as I step onto the boardwalk, I grab my blanket and a book from my backpack, and head toward the beach. It's surprisingly chilly for an August morning, and I'm grateful for the happy coincidence that my jeans were the only clean pair of pants I had ready for today.

I kick off my sandals as I approach the sand and place them in my bag. I refuse to set foot on the beach with shoes on my feet. I step onto the pathway and feel each grain between my toes. It shifts and parts as I walk, and my soles quickly become covered in the granules that were being squished beneath them. I scan the shoreline for the perfect spot to watch the dawn, and eventually I place my blanket on a little stretch where the sand is flat. I sit down with my legs crossed, listen to the crashing of waves, and wait for the sun to greet me.

But the sun is not the first thing to greet me this morning. I see a wave break on the beach, carrying something that's disturbingly person shaped. I get up and run to where the tide is coming in, and find a man lying face down, gripping a large piece of driftwood. I turn him over and see he's middle-aged, his silver-streaked hair sticking to his face in long thick locks, his clothes completely soaked through and falling apart. He's wearing a dark-blue, collared shirt that's riddled with holes over a white T-shirt, and a pair of cargo shorts, which hang loose on his hips. His skin is red and raw, covered in blisters that ooze and cracks that bleed. He's disturbingly thin, his ribs visible through his soaked shirt, and his face almost skeletal. His chest rises slowly, and he releases a tough, wheezing breath, which is followed by a harsh cough that wakes the man from unconsciousness. The man's coughing continues, and he rolls over and pushes himself up to his feet. Once he is standing, he begins walking in circles, mumbling under his breath, and releasing loud retching coughs. As he trips over the sand and himself, I pull my phone from my pocket and punch in 9-1-1.

"What's your emergency?" the dispatcher asks.

"Hi," I say, my own heart threatening to beat out of my chest as I watch the man stumble around on the beach. "I'm at Re … Rehoboth Beach, in front of the main shopping strip, and a man just washed up on shore. I think he needs an ambulance."

"OK, is the man conscious?"

"Y … yes, he's walking around the beach right now, but he's stumbling." I begin to move toward the man, and the dispatcher's voice barely registers in my ear. As I try to approach him, he seems to sense me and turns to meet my gaze. He falls forward and I drop my phone to catch him. I can hear the dispatcher saying paramedics are on their way, but it is drowned out as the dripping man's deep, gruff voice enters my ears and I am finally able to make out what he is saying.

"Silently, he approaches." The man pulls back and looks at me with eyes that have sunk deep into his skull. By the light of the moon, I can see that the man's pupils have expanded into deep black pools, while the rest of his eyes are a bloodshot red. "Silently, he gazes upon us," he continues, and despite his frailty he is able to push me back toward the water. He keeps repeating the same phrase and pushing me, and I keep giving him ground, afraid of what he may do if I try to stop him.

As we get closer and closer to the shoreline, the sound of crashing waves becomes louder and louder, and my heart begins to pound harder against my ribs until it drowns out the ocean itself. Finally, I feel the surf flow beneath my feet, and the ocean threatens to take us both, me for the first time and the dripping man for the second. As I sink into the soaked sand, I grab hold of the man's wrists and toss him to the side of me. He stumbles and falls to his hands and knees, the water crashing around him. He wrenches himself upward and turns back toward me, still saying the same thing,

"Silently, he approaches. Silently, he gazes upon us."

I move backward, but I trip, landing hard on my back on the same piece of driftwood the dripping man had washed up on. He walks toward me, and I crawl farther and farther away. My chest becomes tighter as my lungs gasp for increasingly shallow breaths. I kick into the sand to push myself away from the dripping man, and I reach backward, grabbing for whatever purchase the beach can give me. I grab at the edge of the driftwood, but as I try to pull myself away, the wood's jagged edge slices open my palm. The dripping man is now right in front of me, his eyes bearing down on me and his voice cramming itself into my ears.

"Silently, he approaches. Silently, he gazes upon us."

He drops to his knees in front of me, and his pupils distort, no longer disks, but writhing forms, pushing past his irises and encroaching into his bloodshot sclera. He continues to approach me, crawling forward as I try and fail to move backward. I reach back again but grab nothing but sand, and I can feel the grains force themselves into the gash on my hand. I grab a handful of sand, throw it in the dripping man's face, and with a slick *thud* it connects. But the man just claws the grime away, his nails ripping open some of the blisters on his face so trails of red mix with the dark brown of the sand. He keeps saying, "Silently, he approaches. Silently, he gazes upon us."

He reaches me, reaches the driftwood that he had floated to shore on, and says one more time, "Silently, he approaches. Silently, he gazes upon us." Then he grabs the edge of the wood and pulls, and pulls, and pulls, until finally, with a splitting *crack*, a wicked piece of wood wrenches free from the man's makeshift vessel.

He stands and looks down at me, the sun finally rising as he does so. He walks toward the surf as if to greet the approaching dawn, and now I can see only his back and the shadow that stretches far behind him. I watch the man's motions reflected in it. His arm rises, his hand clutching the wood so tightly that it cuts into his fingers, and he turns his face upward toward the sun.

I run and grab my phone; I can hear the dispatcher still calling out to me, but I don't answer. Instead, I stand captivated by the dripping man.

"We have not the words to welcome him," he says, his voice dropping to just above a whisper. "We must gain new ways to speak, we must open new mouths to greet him." And he jams the wood into his throat, dragging the wood across his neck and opening a huge gash that disappears behind a waterfall of reddish black. He collapses onto the sand, gargling on the blood that flows from the wound. I get to my feet and run to his side, trying to put pressure on the massive hole he has opened in his neck.

As the sun continues to float upward into the sky, the paramedics rush in and push me aside, doing their best to keep the man alive, but it takes only a few moments for them to see that there is no saving him. Soon, he takes in one final, rasping breath that escapes through the opening in his neck before it ever reaches his lungs.

* * * * *

I have been waiting at the police station for two hours, the powerful fluorescents showcasing every flaw in the face of every officer and every supposed wrongdoer. I've been passing the time by counting as many things in the office as I can. There are forty-eight ceiling tiles, six lights, and twenty officers with twenty desks with two chairs each, one fitted under the desk and one off to the side for the various people that are brought in. I'm sitting in one of those cheap rolling chairs, struggling to resist pulling at the stitches one of the paramedics was kind enough to weave into the gash the driftwood had opened on my hand.

The officers had taken my statement not long after I arrived, but the rest of the time has been taken up by them commenting on the strangeness of the incident. Apparently, the man had been lost at sea off the coast of Maine weeks ago and presumed dead. They didn't know how he managed to survive for as long as he did, nor could they figure out how he managed to end up as far south as Delaware, but there he had been, riding a massive piece of driftwood and preparing for the death he inflicted upon himself when he arrived.

Finally, an officer tells me I am free to leave, saying they will call me if they need me to return, but he mentions that one of the paramedics saw the man inflict the wound himself, so they know I wasn't involved.

The sun is now sitting comfortably in the sky, bearing down on the beach town and reminding me that I had not been allowed to enjoy my revived tradition. I'm not sure if I will ever be able to again.

I move in the direction of my aunt's home, not bothering to turn on music or do anything at all to break the silence or cover the sound of my feet slapping against the sidewalk. Instead, I just absentmindedly walk and dwell on the sight of the dripping man carving open his throat, calling out to whatever strange being he claimed was "approaching and gazing upon us."

Eventually, I get to the door, and I think of all the ways I can force down the memories of the dripping man's death and keep my mind blank. When I walk into the house, I do the first thing that comes to mind—I turn on the TV to find the most mindless show I can stream and turn up the volume as loud as I can.

The day passes quickly, the sun casting shadows across the living room that move and shift in a pattern all too similar to the shadow of the dripping man when he brought the wooden shard up to his neck. I stare at the television until my eyes force out tears, and when that happens, I put on music so cheery and sweet that it could rot my teeth. The bright guitars and chipper vocals pound my ears and the bass reverberates in my chest. I pay painstaking attention to the lyrics so my mind cannot wander to the events of the day's dawn.

When the sun does set, I do not bother to try to stay awake. I walk to the bedroom and collapse, falling asleep above the covers in the clothes I have been wearing all day. I leave the light on.

* * * * *

When I awake, the light around me is different. It is not all-encompassing; instead, it is just a small circle surrounding me. I look around and see that I'm standing under a streetlamp, the boardwalk just ahead of me. I feel the rough concrete beneath my bare feet and hear the crashing of the tide on the beach. I know where I am. Just behind me is Penny Lane, and directly ahead of me is the spot on the beach where the dripping man washed ashore that morning. There are no cars on the strip, and aside from the light of the streetlamps, it is pitch dark, without so much as a star in the sky.

It would only take me a few minutes to walk back to my aunt's house, but instead I find myself moving toward the beach, the tide entering my ears like a siren's song. The water has overtaken the sand, and when I step forward, I am soaked up to my ankles. I have never seen the beach like this before. The water pulls the sand away from my feet and I feel myself sink down, little by little.

It is silent except for the breaking of waves, and as I stand alone, I scan the beach for any sign of the events of the morning. Sticking up out of the water is the piece of driftwood that had brought the dripping man into my world. I move toward it, the water racing past my legs as I walk, the cold dampness of it crawling up the legs of my pants.

As I draw closer to the massive piece of wood, the cut in my palm begins to radiate pain up my arm. I lift my hand to my face and see that the stitches that had been holding the gash closed have all broken. Blood seeps from the opening, but what is flowing forth is not its normal crimson, but instead a dark, inky black. The blood flows out and down my arm, rivulets of it turning my arm into a piece of nightmarish calligraphy.

I bring my hand closer to my face, as if that might cause what I'm seeing to make sense. When my hand is directly in front of my eyes, I see that the cut is moving, opening and closing, over and over, and the blood keeps flowing. I can make out small, white objects within it, and at first I think I am seeing the bones of my hand, but then the cut opens once again, wider than before, and I hear a quick sucking sound from within it, as if it were taking a breath. I realize I am staring at a mouth. Teeth have grown into my hand, and while the newly opened maw on my palm continues drooling its black blood, it moves one more time and begins to speak.

"Silently, he approaches. Silently, he gazes upon us," it says, in a voice I do not know. Deep and sonorous, it repeats, "Silently, he approaches. Silently, he gazes upon us."

* * * * *

I wake up for a second time. I am lying on the bed in my aunt's home, the light is still on, and my stitches are intact. I let out a quiet sigh and begin to wipe away the cold sweat that had drenched my body while I was dreaming. For a moment, I revel in the safety of the bedroom. I let the light shine onto my skin, close my eyes, and take a deep breath. But this respite lasts only a moment. When I open my eyes, I see that while I slept, a black, jagged scrawl has appeared on the wall opposite me. It reads "He approaches."

I drag myself backward on the bed until I am over the pillows and pressed against the wall. The cut on my hand throbs and burns, the kind of low, relentless pain that pushes into the back of your mind until it devours all your remaining thoughts and you can think only of that feeling. I force myself to look at my palm, and see the cut pulling against the stitches. There is a muffled voice coming from within it, and while I cannot make out its message, I know what it wants to say. As the wound continues to pull against its restraints, the same black blood from my dream begins to drip through the opening in my skin.

"STOP IT!" I scream into my palm, "SHUT UP!" I climb out of the bed, screaming the same message at my disobedient hand over and over again until I reach the kitchen.

"FUCK YOU! SHUT THE FUCK UP!" and I stumble over to the knife rack. I grab the largest one I see, place my left arm on the counter, and swing.

The pain nearly causes me to black out, but the rage and fear I feel at my own body push me onward, and I swing again. Blood now spills from my wrist in such volume that it drips onto the floor, but I keep swinging. I can see the muscles and sinew that I am trying to chop through as I bring the blade down again and again. The blood flows beneath my feet and I slip. I fall to my knees, and my next swing misses my wrist as I do. The knife goes directly into my palm. The stitches tear as I pull the knife free, and my hand strikes up its maddening chorus once again.

The sound of the dark voice causes my rage to burn even brighter, and I make one final chop, and my hand falls to the floor with a quiet *thud*. The room finally goes silent, and I lie down on the kitchen floor in a pool of my once-again-red blood. My vision begins to fade, and the rush of the tide fills my ears.

William Eichler has lived in Delaware all his life. He was born in Dover in 1996, graduated from Dover High School in 2015, and received a bachelor of arts degree in English from the University of Delaware in 2019. Since then, he has begun working as a freelance copywriter and as the editor of the newly created literature and arts website, *Next Page Ink*. His work has been featured on *Next Page Ink*, but this will be his first piece to be published elsewhere. His story "The Dripping Man" was partially inspired by trips to watch the sunrise at Rehoboth Beach that he took with his best friends, although those trips involved notably fewer encounters with the horrifying and unknown. He is incredibly honored to have been selected for this year's anthology.

Judge's Comment

A lot of words could be used to describe this story. Grotesque. Repugnant. Unrelenting. Nightmarish. And I absolutely loved it. The dread that builds in this story is exquisite. Starting innocuously enough with the main character's morning routine, it's hard to see this story coming until it's too late. The story's quiet murmur of discontent becomes a howling scream of violence and rage, one that's hard not to hear echoing in your ears as you read. I like to imagine this sinister story rolling in with the tide like a piece of alien driftwood. It's unforgettable, and I'm tickled to be able to share it with you as my judge's pick.

Teething Toddlers Tell No Tales

By Rachael Tipperman

It began, as many bad decisions do, with alcohol.

Amelia Carpenter, six days into a two-week family vacation and needing a respite from both the heat and her older sister's screaming toddler, had fled to one of the dozens of beach bars dotting downtown Rehoboth Beach.

"Another glass of rosé?"

Amelia held out her glass with a sheepish grin. "Pour up, Nick." The bartender laughed, making a show of looking around before he ever so slightly over-filled her glass. She glanced down. "Your generosity knows no bounds."

"You know what they say about big hearts."

Amelia waved her hand. "Goodbye. Try using that line on actual customers and see where it gets you."

Nick laughed again, shaking his head as he made his way down the bar. "You're going to miss me when Eddie gives you a regulation pour."

Amelia rolled her eyes. Her family had been coming to Rehoboth each summer for as long as she could remember, and Nick had been a constant in her life just as long. Their parents were close friends— Amelia's mother had set up their beach chairs and umbrella next to a family on the beach over two decades ago and walked away with a lifelong friendship. The relationship, quite literally, served Amelia well when she visited Nick at his bartending gig. He had a habit of over-serving and under-charging his friends. It would have made him unpopular with his boss if it hadn't ensured a steady stream of repeat customers.

"Don't listen to him," a bartender Amelia didn't recognize called to her. "Any friend of Nick's is a friend of mine." He held out his hand for Amelia to shake. "I'm Eddie. I'm new around town. Are you a local?"

"Amelia," she replied. "Not a local, just a very persistent tourist."

"Ah, so part of the summer set."

"Guilty as charged." Amelia took a sip of her wine. "So, what brought you to Rehoboth?"

Eddie shrugged. "Oh, you know. Nice people. Nice weather. Buried treasure. The usual."

Amelia raised an eyebrow. "Buried treasure?"

"Eddie's really into the pirate lore in the area," Nick explained. "You've heard the stories about Blackbeard, right?"

"I mean, I know he used to hang out somewhere along the Delaware coast, but didn't he die in South Carolina? I sort of thought all his treasure was down there."

"Maybe," Eddie said, "but maybe not."

"Definitely not," said Nick. "Next you'll tell us that you think the Sea Witch from the festival is real."

That made Eddie laugh, a loud harsh sound that rang through the nearly empty bar. "We'll see," he murmured. "We'll see."

* * * * *

The storm that hit that night seemed to appear out of thin air. Amelia was half-asleep when the first bolt of lightning tore across the sky, followed by thunder so loud it seemed to shake the house. Her older sister, Natalie, appeared in the doorway to her room.

"This isn't a hurricane, is it?" Natalie asked, as her son Max began wailing in his room. Another thunderclap made both sisters jump.

Rain battered the window.

"No. We would have heard if a hurricane were coming. This is just a really bad storm."

Natalie grimaced. "I'm going to check on Max."

"Girls!" their mother called from the master bedroom. "Come here!"

"Go get Max," Amelia offered. "I'll go check on Mom and Dad." She walked down the hall to her parents' bedroom and called out "Is everything OK?" as she opened the door. They were huddled against the large picture windows.

"Look at the ocean," her father said, awestruck. "This is one big storm."

Amelia came up behind them, peering over their shoulders. White-capped waves hit the sand with enough force that she could faintly hear the crashes over the sounds of the storm. Roiling black water seemed to blend into the horizon.

"Wow," Amelia exclaimed.

"Wow is right." Her mother sighed. "Last time it stormed this badly, it seemed like the beach was scattered with half the shells in the Atlantic Ocean. Who knows what this will wash up tomorrow? Hopefully not horseshoe crabs." In the darkness of the storm, with the ocean heaving violently outside of their window, Amelia couldn't help but wonder if Eddie was right. Maybe there was something out there, far below the surface, just waiting to be dredged up.

* * * * *

By the time Amelia woke the next morning, the sun was already high in the sky and the thought of pirate treasure washing up on shore was as distant as a dream. She found a note from her family at the top of the stairs:

> *Sea (haha) you later! We got Green Man for breakfast. Your sandwich is in the fridge. We didn't want to wake you.   - XoXo*

Amelia sighed. She couldn't blame them for going without her. The storm had kept her up most of the night, and she knew that her parents liked to be among the first on the beach in the morning. She would get coffee and catch up with them later, she decided. She headed down the stairs and into the living room, which offered the quickest route to the breakfast nook. Her brow furrowed at the sight of Natalie fussing over a blanket on the couch.

"Back early from the beach?"

Natalie startled, turning around and revealing that the blanket was, in fact, her toddler. "Max started throwing a fit because we took away something he picked up and started teething on. If I have to deal with a feral three-year-old, I'm at least doing it in air conditioning."

"Fair enough." Amelia laughed. Max was sleeping on the couch now, his curly blond hair splayed against the cushion like a halo, but she knew as well as Natalie that peace with him was always tentative and hard fought.

"I put it in my tote because he kept grabbing at it." Natalie dug through her beach bag and pulled out an irregularly shaped gold medallion or coin, slightly larger than a silver dollar. "Wow. Take a look. I've never seen anything like it. I'm guessing it washed up with the storm."

Amelia wrinkled her nose. "He had that thing in his mouth? It looks ancient!"

"It's filthy, but probably not going to make him sick. It kind of looks like real gold, but it's probably just an arcade token someone dropped in the water."

Amelia held out her hand and Natalie deposited it willingly. "Now if you'll excuse me, I'm going to go make a screwdriver and force Jack to be the parent-on-duty today."

"A screwdriver," Amelia repeated with a laugh. "Glad to see you're taking the threat of scurvy seriously."

Natalie raised her hand in mock salute before disappearing into the kitchen, leaving Amelia alone with a sleeping toddler and a strange bit of gold from the depths of the Atlantic.

Amelia turned the relic over in her hands, admiring its weight and the way it caught the light from the window and sparkled faintly as she spun it. Things washed up from the ocean all the time. It was what kept the metal-detecting crowd showing up to the beach at the crack of dawn. Blackbeard had been in the Delaware Bay. Ships had vanished somewhere beneath Rehoboth Beach's glittering seascape. The gold object was just one more piece of flotsam and jetsam that had reappeared on the sand, and one of the hundreds of thousands of curios resting on the muddy sea floor. It wasn't special.

And yet.

Amelia slipped the gold piece into her pocket and double-checked that Max was still sleeping before she made her way to the kitchen. "Can you let Mom and Dad know that I'll be back for dinner?" she asked Natalie. "I have some things to take care of today."

"We're going to Henlopen City Oyster House for happy hour, so either meet us there or I'll text you when we're home and Dad starts on the crabs."

Amelia nodded, then looked at her sister's half-empty glass. "If you don't make it to happy hour, can you tell Jack to pass the message along?" That earned a laugh from Natalie, who waved her off.

"Parent rule," she called as Amelia turned toward the door. "It's five o'clock whenever you need it."

* * * * *

While Amelia appreciated her sister's enthusiasm for an afternoon cocktail, it had barely cracked noon by the time she got to Nick and Eddie's bar. Eddie grinned when he saw her, his teeth stark white against the dark black of his beard.

"Found something?"

Amelia slid onto a stool, pulling the piece of metal from her pocket and placing it on the bar. "It's probably nothing, but I thought you might find this interesting given how old it looks. My nephew found it on the beach. Apparently, he was using it as a chew toy."

Eddie barked out a laugh. "That's disgusting."

"It is."

He held the object up to the light, squinting at it. Despite the harsh sun outside, the inside of the bar was dark and lit with neon. Still, the gold seemed to glow in the dim room. Amelia couldn't blame treasure hunters for growing obsessed. There was something eerily beautiful about holding something so old and so foreign.

Eddie let out a low whistle. "This is the real deal. A gold doubloon. I'd stake my life on it." He handed it back to Amelia, who tucked it away in her pocket.

"A doubloon? Really?" Amelia shook her head in disbelief. "Well, you must be happy to see that your treasure theory was correct."

Eddie raised his eyebrows. "Theory? It was never a theory. Your coin right there?" He tapped the bar with his index finger for emphasis. "That's proof."

Farther down the bar, Nick groaned, setting down the wine glass he was cleaning. "Eddie, no one is going out into the bay with you."

Eddie threw his hands up. "Why not? We could look for more pirate booty. Who knows what else the storm dredged up?" Eddie looked at Amelia. Amelia looked at Nick.

Nick sighed and put his face in his hands. "What time?"

* * * * *

Amelia never made it to happy hour at Henlopen City Oyster House. She never made it to dinner either. Instead, she and Nick found themselves on a boat with Eddie, somewhere in the Delaware Bay in the middle of the night, after a long day spent poring over maps of the bay (of which Eddie seemed to have an unlimited supply) and eating nothing but leftover crab cakes (of which Eddie seemed to have a mercifully limited number). The fog was thick, and the boat's lights seemed to bounce off the cloudy gray mist, illuminating only a few feet of pitch-black water.

Amelia shifted nervously as Nick tugged up his makeshift salvaging device. They had been scooping sand and debris out of the water for hours, painstakingly sifting through each haul by hand once it made it to the deck. So far, their search had turned up nothing but trash. The doubloon felt like it was burning a hole in her pocket. "Find anything?"

Nick sighed and shook his head, tossing the salvage gear back into the water. "Empty. This has been a fun little excursion, but Eddie's delusional if he thinks we're finding anything." The man in question was sitting on the bow of the boat, eyes closed and humming quietly under his breath.

"I feel like we're in a bad horror movie," Amelia said.

Nick let out a low laugh. "You and me both." He tugged the hood of his sweatshirt down and cupped his hands around his mouth. "Ed! Let's call this, huh?"

"A few more minutes," he murmured.

In the absence of his humming, Amelia realized that the night was strangely silent. Save for the occasional sound of the water lapping against the side of the boat, Amelia heard nothing. No birds. No breeze. No signs of life. She caught Nick's glance. He had noticed it too.

"Eddie," Amelia began, "I really think …"

The words died in her throat. A dark shadow was growing against the mist, at first so faint she thought it was her mind playing tricks on her. Eddie picked up a large flashlight. Its beam caught dark wood, a porthole, and a glittering black cannon. Amelia's mouth fell open.

There was a pirate ship in the Delaware Bay.

"There she is!" Eddie hollered. His victorious whoop echoed, sounding as though it had come from the throats of a thousand men.

Amelia stumbled back into Nick, who caught her with trembling hands. This was no hallucination, she realized. The hammering of Nick's heartbeat against her back emphasized that, no matter how impossible it seemed, he saw the ghost ship too.

Eddie turned to them suddenly and Amelia froze. Nick's grip on her upper arms turned painful, but Amelia was too terrified to make a sound.

"Friends!" Eddie's cheeks were bright red, and his black eyes seemed to glow in the dark. "Friends, I cannot thank you enough. You betray a sea witch and she traps part of your soul underwater for three hundred years. A bit unfair if you ask me."

"What—" Nick tried.

"A curse!" Eddie crowed. "A curse that I could never set out on the water without a piece of the treasure I stole from her and trusting men to steer a ship in my name. The men, that was easy. But the treasure …" Eddie broke off on a laugh. "I have you and your teething nephew to thank, dear Amelia."

A ship. The treasure. The wheels in Amelia's head began to turn, before coming to a grinding halt. "Oh my god." The words tumbled out of her mouth. "Blackbeard. You're Blackbeard."

"Edward Teach at your service." Eddie bowed.

A glowing rope fell from the side of the ship. It was too difficult to see the top deck through the thick mist, but Amelia could hear the faint noises of men at work, talking and singing far above them.

"And now, friends, I bid you farewell. You have done me a great service." He tugged once on the rope.

Edward Teach and the *Queen Anne's Revenge* vanished in a blink.

Amelia all but collapsed back into Nick, whose own knees gave out and they both dropped to the deck.

"Nick," Amelia said, "tell me you put something in those crab cakes."

Nick shook his head. "I wish I could."

They drove the boat back to the marina in stunned silence. Neither of them had much interest in staying out on the water, which had grown silent and placid once more. "Well," said Amelia as they arrived at the dock, "let's never speak of that again."

Nick nodded. "Fine by me."

"I lied. I need to talk about it," Amelia blurted. "So how are you going to explain to your boss that Eddie can't clock in tomorrow? I don't think he'll buy the 'Eddie was actually the trapped spirit of an eighteenth-century pirate that Amelia and I inadvertently laid to rest' excuse."

"Stop," Nick muttered. "You just said we'd never have to talk about it again."

"I can't believe Eddie was a spirit." She paused, suddenly horror-struck. "Oh my god. He mentioned a sea witch. Do you think he meant *the* Sea Witch? The Sea Witch Festival legend might actually be based in reality?"

Nick blanched. "Shut up. Stop talking."

"Do you think she looks like the parade float? Do you think she knows about the parade? Maybe in October we'll have to free one of the balloons to set her soul free and—"

"Amelia." Nick grabbed her hand. "Please, for the sake of my sanity, no more talking. No more mysteries. I am going to go to bed and wake up in the morning and pretend that none of this ever happened."

Amelia tugged her hand away. "That's fair." She paused as they reached Nick's car, turning around to take one last look at the bay. The mist had cleared. Now the moonlight cut through the clouds and made the dark water glisten.

Nick unlocked the car and pulled the door open, before going completely still. "Amelia." The panic in his voice snapped her attention back to him. "I take it back. This definitely, definitely happened."

Amelia followed his gaze to the backseat and her jaw dropped. Gold doubloons spilled out of the seams between the seats. Rubies covered the floor. Necklaces looped around the headrests. But it was the word *Thanks* spelled out in strands of pearls arrayed on the cushions that told Amelia that, while Nick's car might have looked as if he had raided a pirate movie set, what they were looking at was the real deal.

She let out a disbelieving laugh. "Forget having to tell your boss that Eddie can't clock in." The smile on her face was so wide it hurt her cheeks. "Looks like you'll never have to clock in again either." Amelia let out a shout of joy. Somewhere, far out in the bay, the ghost of Edward Teach whooped back.

RACHAEL TIPPERMAN HAS BEEN VISITING REHOBOTH BEACH WITH HER FAMILY FOR AS LONG AS SHE CAN REMEMBER, THOUGH SHE HAS YET TO ENCOUNTER ANY PIRATES OUTSIDE OF THE ANNUAL SEA WITCH FESTIVAL. WHEN SHE'S NOT WRITING CODE AT HER DAY JOB AS A SOFTWARE ENGINEER, SHE LOVES TO WRITE STORIES. "TEETHING TODDLERS TELL NO TALES" IS HER FIRST PUBLISHED WORK, BUT RACHAEL HOPES TO TELL MANY MORE STORIES.

Hiawatha's Smile

By Doug Harrell

September 2019

"I never thought I'd feel sad pulling up to Lucky 13," said Amanda.

Zoë agreed. "Yeah, it's so different without Grandmom Rae standing at the door waiting for us."

Amanda drove up the narrow driveway at 13 Brooklyn Avenue, Rehoboth Beach, Delaware, and stopped just short of a large blue dumpster. The house, a side-by-side white-shingled duplex, was set well back from the street and shaded by several large pines. As much as the sisters wanted to keep it, they simply couldn't afford it.

As Amanda was unlocking the door, Zoë reached over and stroked the house number. "Amanda, don't forget to rub it for luck."

Amanda lovingly ran her fingers over the numbers. "And Grandmom would never forgive us if we didn't go straight up and thank Hiawatha." Giggling, the two women ran up the stairs into a small back bedroom. On the wall was a painting of a proud Native American chief pointing toward a woman nursing an infant. "Thank you, Hiawatha."

"Yes, thank you, Hiawatha," Zoë echoed. Then, turning to her sister, "Amanda, do you know why we thank Hiawatha?"

Amanda shook her head. "Because he's a great chief? I don't know. I asked Grandmom once, but she said she didn't know either. Great-grandmother Alice taught her to thank Hiawatha when she was a girl, and she taught mom and then us."

Zoë reached out and touched the young mother in the painting. "That'll be you soon."

Hiawatha's Smile

"Not for six more months. It's so sad to think of never being able to come here again. I always dreamed we'd spend summers here with our own children, you and me, next door to each other. They'd be thick as thieves, building sandcastles on the beach and going on rides at Funland. Any luck convincing Jack to give my baby a cousin to play with?"

"Not yet. Jack says he needs a promotion first—either that, or we need to hit the lottery."

After a quick lunch, Amanda and Zoë began the sad task of going through their late grandmother's apartment and the guest apartment next door. They labeled some items "keep" or "donate," and everything else went into the dumpster.

Amanda was tackling the kitchen when Zoë hurried down from the attic, carrying a red leather book with a gold "1931" embossed on the cover.

"Amanda, I found great-grandmother Alice's diary. I know why we thank Hiawatha!"

May 1931

Memorial Day was approaching, but the weather seemed not to care. The curtain of clouds overhead looked like the underside of a bulky quilt, and a chilly breeze was blowing off the Atlantic. A hand-painted sign, "Furnished house for rent—inquire next door," stood crookedly in front of the right half of 13 Brooklyn Avenue. In the backyard, Alice Gaines leaned over her basket and picked up one of Rae's sopping-wet rompers. She threaded it into the wringer and cranked the handle with vigor, squeezing out all the water but none of her worry.

The Joneses hadn't paid the rent since March, and Alice had finally put them out. Since Charlie died, that money was Alice's only source of income, and with a new baby and no husband, Alice was falling behind on the mortgage. Summer would bring renters, but after the summer was over, how long before she and little Rae were out on the street? Alice was hanging the romper on the clothesline when a loud voice called out from behind her.

"Hey, lady …"

Startled, Alice turned to see a well-dressed man coming around the house. He was wearing a gray pinstripe suit and a gray fedora, but what really caught her eye was the flash of white from his two-toned oxfords every time he put a foot forward. He advanced within a few feet of her.

"Hey, lady. I saw your sign out front."

Alice wiped her hands on her apron. "Yes, are you interested?"

"Could be. Your husband around? Maybe I oughta talk to him."

Alice's throat clenched. "My husband died in March."

"Oh, ain't that a shame. I'm sorry." The man touched his hand to the crown of his hat and waited for a respectful moment before continuing. "So, yeah, I'm interested, but I gotta have it right away, and I need it for the whole summer, maybe longer. Can you do that?"

Alice almost choked. "Yes. Give me a few hours and I'll get it nice and clean for you."

"Whaddaya want for it?"

Alice steeled herself. "I'm asking fifteen dollars a week." Then, unsure of herself, she stammered, "But, you'll want to see it first."

He replied without flinching, "Naw, I'm sure it'll be fine." Then he raised his arm, pointing to the back of the yard. "That garage empty?"

"No, our car's in there."

The man shook his head. "I gotta have the garage too. Twenty bucks."

"I'm sorry, what?"

"Twenty bucks a week for the house and the garage." The man extracted a tight roll from his pants pocket, and peeled off four twenty-dollar bills, extending them toward Alice. "Here's for the first month."

Pocketing the money, Alice replied, "Yes, that will be quite satisfactory, Mr. ...?"

"Feldman. Benjamin Feldman."

"Alice Gaines."

"I'm gonna need to do some work in the garage. A little noise won't bother ya, will it?"

"I shouldn't think so. What kind of noise?"

"Just some hammering and sawing. I'm an art dealer down here to buy pictures. I hafta crate 'em up before I ship 'em back to Brooklyn. That's part of what I like about your place—Brooklyn Avenue. That and the street number—thirteen. Most folks don't like it, but thirteen's my lucky number."

Alice was beginning to feel lucky herself. She handed him the key.

"I'll be back later. Just take your car out and leave the garage open for me, will ya?" With that, Mr. Feldman touched the brim of his hat, turned, and walked out of sight. A moment later she heard a car start up and drive away.

Back inside the house, Alice collapsed onto the sofa, sobbing. She and Rae would be OK—at least for now.

* * * * *

Alice marshalled her mop, bucket, and brushes, and attacked the long-neglected grime in 13-B like a woman possessed. The cleaning done, she opened the padlock on the garage leaving the key in it, and swung the doors wide open. With a lump in her throat, she backed out the car and parked it on the street in front of the house. Charlie had been so proud of that car, one of the new Chrysler coupes. She knew she was going to have to sell it eventually, but she couldn't bring herself do it. Not yet.

Hours later, as Alice was undressing for bed, she heard a car. Looking out, she saw a black sedan backing rapidly up the driveway and straight into the garage, facing out. Given his style of dress, Alice had expected

Mr. Feldman's car to be fancier. After a moment, he emerged and swung the doors closed. He removed her padlock and tossed it into the garage before snapping on a new one and walking up to the house.

In bed, Alice lay awake pondering Mr. Feldman. She'd seen plenty of New Yorkers when she and Charlie used to play the ponies at the track in Havre de Grace. Still, it seemed strange that, as an art dealer, Mr. Feldman was so *exactly* like the kind of person you'd meet at a racetrack. Finally, exhausted, she fell into a deep and well-deserved sleep.

* * * * *

The next morning, Alice was weeding the front garden when Mr. Feldman returned with a large framed picture across his back, holding it by the wire.

"Good afternoon, Mr. Feldman. I hope everything is to your liking."

"Everything's swell. Thanks."

"I see you've bought your first picture. Can I look?"

"Sure thing." Rather than take the picture off his shoulder and hold it out, Mr. Feldman turned his back so Alice could see the painting. It was a colorful scene of a small harbor with houses and boats and a flock of seagulls hovering overhead.

"Oh, how pretty. What's it called?"

"*Herring Guts*. Makes sense, I guess, all them seagulls."

Suppressing the urge to laugh, Alice gently corrected him. "You know what? I bet it's a painting of Herring Gut. That's a creek about an hour south of here."

Mr. Feldman shrugged and turned back to face her. "Whatever."

"Do New Yorkers enjoy country scenes like that?"

"Oh yeah … sure. They can't wait to get their hands on 'em." With a grin, he added, "Especially when they're big. The folks in Brooklyn like big paintings."

To her surprise, Mr. Feldman locked the painting in the garage.

Over the next few hours, Alice noticed Mr. Feldman come and go repeatedly, bringing back paintings, all large.

Alice was up nursing Rae just after midnight when she heard Mr. Feldman take his car out. At that time of night, he could only be on his way to a speakeasy.

Four hours later, Alice was awakened by the sound of tires on the gravel driveway. Looking out, she saw Mr. Feldman walking toward the house as purposefully as always, so either he hadn't drunk too much or he could hold his liquor.

Early the next morning, Alice heard voices. She peeked through the curtains as Mr. Feldman pulled his car out and led two men carrying boards into the garage, closing the doors behind them. Soon, she heard sawing and hammering. Alice wondered why they had closed the doors. Surely, it would be more pleasant with them open.

Curious, Alice snuck over to the garage window, but she couldn't see anything because the shade was down. As her shadow fell across the window, the sawing stopped. Alice was wondering whether she could make it back inside when she heard the garage door creaking open.

Embarrassed, she only had two alternatives: let Mr. Feldman catch her snooping or disappear. Quick as a cat, she climbed the nearest tree and froze. Below her, Mr. Feldman crept forward, arm extended, sunlight glinting off a chrome-plated revolver. After looking around, he returned to the garage. Alice gingerly climbed down and tiptoed back into the house.

Oh my god. What have I gotten myself into? Alice considered calling the police. Then she thought about Rae. Even if Mr. Feldman's money was dirty, it was all she had. Alice decided to mind her own business.

Later that day, Alice saw a white delivery truck backing up the driveway. Two men loaded it with thin rectangular boxes as Mr. Feldman looked on. The boxes were only slightly larger than Mr. Feldman's paintings. Alice felt silly. Apparently, the art world was more dangerous than she knew. After loading the last painting, the men shook Mr. Feldman's hand, climbed into the truck, and drove away.

All summer, this was Mr. Feldman's routine. He would bring paintings back to the garage, and every five or ten days he would take his car out at night and spend the following day supervising the crating for pick up by the same white van.

September 1931

Alice worried that Mr. Feldman had decided to return to New York. September first had come and gone, and while he had not left, he had not paid either. Later that week, Alice decided to lie in wait for him by weeding the front yard. After a while, he came bounding up the walk with an enormous canvas slung across his back.

Leaping to her feet, Alice blurted out, "Oh, Mr. Feldman. I hope you'll be staying with us a bit longer."

"Yeah. Don't worry," he replied before adding, "I landed a big one today—take a look." The painting was beautifully rendered and quite different in style and subject from anything she had seen Mr. Feldman bring back before. In it, a Native American chief stood proudly, chest out, a defiant look on his face. His left arm was outstretched in the direction of a squaw seated in front of a bark-and-timber longhouse, discreetly nursing the baby she held in her arms.

"Oh, what a dear picture."

"Dear's the right word. Cost me sixty bucks, but it was worth it. Look how big it is."

Alice was amused at Mr. Feldman's obsession with the size of his paintings and the way he never seemed to know or care about the titles. "What's it called?"

"Some Indian name. It don't matter." Then he smiled. "Wait, he's Hiawatha!" At that, Mr. Feldman laughed so hard that Alice rushed forward to steady the painting lest he scrape the frame on the sidewalk.

Composing himself, Mr. Feldman straightened up, and still laughing, he carried the picture to the garage.

Around midnight, Alice heard Mr. Feldman take out his car, and the next morning she heard the familiar sounds of his men sawing and hammering. They hadn't been at it long when a black sedan screeched to a halt in the driveway, and the driver ran to the garage, banging heavily until Mr. Feldman opened the door. Immediately, all four men began carrying paintings out of the garage and tossing them haphazardly into the back seats of both cars. Then they jumped into their cars and drove away, leaving behind a crate too large to fit. Alice began to cry. Not only hadn't she gotten the rent for September, but the frantic nature of Mr. Feldman's departure left no doubt he was gone for good.

Alice closed the garage and put the sign back out front. The next day at the market she nearly fainted when she saw a picture of Mr. Feldman on the front page of *The Sunday Morning Star* next to the banner headline: "Prohibition Agents Bust Alcohol Smuggling Ring: High-Speed Motor Launch *Hiawatha* Seized Near Taylors Island, Maryland." With quivering hands, Alice paid for the paper before clutching Rae and dashing out of the store, leaving her shopping and a confused grocer in her wake.

The article was about a New York outfit that had been evading the Coast Guard vessels patrolling the mouth of the Chesapeake Bay and landing illegal booze by night along the Eastern Shore. Leading the operation was the boat's owner, Benjamin "Little Bennie" Feldman. No wonder Mr. Feldman had laughed so hard when he called the chief in the painting "Hiawatha." Even with them all safely in jail, it took three days for Alice to work up the courage to put her car back in the garage. It was a week before she decided the day had come to deal with the crate "Little Bennie" had left behind. If it held liquor she could just dump it—no one need know.

As she pried off the boards, she was delighted to find not hooch, but Hiawatha. Afraid of what people might think if they saw a poor widow with such an expensive-looking painting, she waited until after dark to sneak it upstairs. Alice hung it in the nursery, where Hiawatha could keep her company, at least until she had to sell him.

Alice was ashamed her rent money had come from crime. Hiawatha always seemed to be looking at her with a conspiratorially cocked head, as though he and Alice were "in on it" together. No matter how often she straightened Hiawatha, the next time Alice came into the room he was crooked again. Alice had begun talking to Hiawatha like a friend, and one day she asked him, "Why are you so crooked? Are you a crook?" Then, it hit her.

Initially, Alice hadn't found it odd there was a thin wooden board fastened across the back of the frame. Now, she wondered if something was hidden behind it making the picture off balance. With trembling fingers she removed the screws and lifted the panel to reveal bundles of cash aligned in neat rows—five thousand dollars in all.

Alice now understood that while the gang had been smuggling and selling liquor, Mr. Feldman had overseen the shipments of cash disguised as art. She felt guilty keeping the money, but who was she going to give it to, gangsters? And if she turned it over to the police, maybe they would make her give back the rent money too. If that happened, she would lose the house.

Alice decided the best thing to do was to say nothing. With no need to sell him, Alice kept Hiawatha hanging in the nursery where together they shared their guilty secret.

September 2019

Amanda walked over to the painting. "Imagine that, five thousand dollars."

"According to this app, that's eighty-five thousand in today's money," replied Zoë. "Say … you don't suppose there's still any money back there, do you?"

"No, but we ought to take a look just to be sure."

Zoë carefully lifted Hiawatha off the wall. After removing the screws, eyes squinting with hope, they leaned in and gingerly lifted the panel. All they found was a cavity. They had not really expected to find any money, but it was still a letdown.

"Well, that would've been fun, but even the whole five thousand wouldn't have been enough for us to keep the house," said Amanda.

Zoë nodded. Still hovering over the back of the painting, she ran her finger along the bottom corner. "Look, there's something written here in pencil. 'Magua said her bosom cannot nurse the children of a Huron.' What do you suppose that refers to?"

"One way to find out." Amanda did a quick search on her cell phone. "According to Project Gutenberg, it's from *The Last of the Mohicans*."

"Maybe this was an illustration. That would explain why it's not signed."

"It looks similar to the ones shown here." Amanda swiped upwards several times, then began hyperventilating. "Oh my god … Oh my god … Oh my god …"

September 2020

With both their babies asleep, Amanda and Zoë paid their nightly visit to thank Hiawatha in what was now Amanda's apartment.

The new painting of Hiawatha was a faithful copy of the original. The artist had succeeded in matching the style and getting all the colors exactly right. The only flaw was with the mouth of the imperious chief the sisters would forever refer to as Hiawatha. He now appeared to be smiling.

Their great-grandmother Alice's painting had turned out to be the lost N. C. Wyeth illustration Scribner's had found too risqué to include in their 1919 deluxe edition of *The Last of the Mohicans*. All those years,

"Hiawatha" had hung there, appreciating in value to well over half a million dollars. The proceeds from the sale of the original had been enough for the sisters to keep 13 Brooklyn Avenue. The money had also helped Zoë convince Jack it was time to have their own child, born a few months after Amanda's.

No wonder Hiawatha was smiling.

DURING THE FREEWHEELING DAYS OF PROHIBITION, A VERITABLE NAVY OF SMALL CRAFT PLIED THE WATERS BETWEEN "RUM ROW" AND THE MYRIAD INLETS AND COVES OF THE DELMARVA PENINSULA. THE MOTOR LAUNCH *HIAWATHA* WAS ONE SUCH CRAFT UNTIL SHE WAS CAPTURED BY FEDERAL AGENTS IN 1931 IN THE CHESAPEAKE BAY NEAR TAYLORS ISLAND.

WORLD RENOWNED ARTIST AND ILLUSTRATOR N. C. WYETH STUDIED UNDER HOWARD PYLE AT PYLE'S WILMINGTON AND REHOBOTH STUDIOS, AND MANY OF THEIR FABULOUS ILLUSTRATIONS CAN BE SEEN AT THE DELAWARE ART MUSEUM. WYETH'S *THE HARBOR AT HERRING GUT* NOW HANGS IN THE BRANDYWINE RIVER MUSEUM. WYETH'S ILLUSTRATION OF MAGUA AND THE SQUAW HAS NEVER BEEN FOUND.

DOUG HARRELL IS A RECOVERING ENGINEER WHO HAS TAKEN UP MYSTERY WRITING AS A SECOND CAREER. DIVIDING HIS TIME BETWEEN PIKE CREEK AND LEWES, HE LOVES WEAVING HISTORY AND LOCAL LORE INTO HIS STORIES. "HIAWATHA'S SMILE" IS HIS FOURTH STORY PUBLISHED BY CAT & MOUSE PRESS. VISIT HIM AT WWW.DOUGLASHARRELL.COM.

JUDGE'S COMMENT

An engaging mystery, this story captures several elements of the 1930s in Rehoboth and telescopes them into the present, where they happily resolve—by weaving together the legacy of a famous illustrator and equally famous writer, both of whom remain icons of American culture.

Baba's Flying

By Paul Geiger

Sixteen umbrellas are crammed in a circle on the same pristine beach our forefathers originally set foot on in 1952. Or was it '51? It really doesn't matter … unless you're Grandpa or one of his brothers, sisters, or cousins. Like the swallows of Capistrano, or more aptly the wildebeest of Karoo in search of the lush savannah, here we are. The Callahan Clan yearly migration has ended at the water's edge in Rehoboth Beach.

To the average beachgoer or even day-tripper, we are sometimes viewed as a strange lot. Maybe it's our size. It can't be the array of multicolored umbrellas, can it? Did someone say Ringling Brothers are in town?

As of ten thirty this morning we were seventy-one strong. I counted fifteen oldies, that is, folks fifty-four to eighty-six years old. Seventeen out of twenty-three children, ages nineteen to forty-eight, were present, plus fourteen mates. Twenty-five grandchildren, ages newborn to twenty-three, scrambled from beneath bumbershoots to bright sand to wet surf and back to base umbrella for food and drink. The actual constituency of our tent city may change over the three-week encampment, so a plus or minus ten percent is quite normal.

If one were to observe our bedouin settlement from Ryan's mini-golf or the Greene Turtle, I'm sure one wouldn't comprehend how we're all related. Just like at the animal shelter, we may all be dogs, but we certainly look and act different.

The oldies group, of which I would consider myself a member, spend most of the day trying to see which of us can most closely mimic a sloth. Once the main job of setting the umbrellas and directing the placement of coolers is accomplished, we park ourselves for the duration. Of course, our daily respite gives way around noon to gathering provisions. A run for twenty pizzas and twelve boxes of fried chicken will usually suffice.

Any medical professional would give the advice that while on the beach you need to drink, drink, and drink. Dehydration can have devastating effects on the young as well as old. Today we have seven coolers for the children and nineteen for the adults. I don't count the two just holding ice and whipped cream. The way Cathy and Karen drink those orange crushes we need to buy Lewes Dairy.

Each day at the beach seems to have one common theme. The parents, grandparents, aunts, uncles, and older cousins tell the younger kinfolk what constitutes acceptable behavior. Explaining to the kiddies what worked the day before and what didn't usually takes about two minutes. I wonder why we bother to do this when by two o'clock the grown-ups either aren't paying attention or have completely forgotten their children are with them. I call this the Cooler Effect. This debilitating disease seems to hit some families harder than others. Must be a genetic thing. We are somewhere in the middle of the scale.

It's nearly 4:20 and Uncle Dennis is roaming around aimlessly, looking as if he'd lost his best friend. I had to ask, "Hey Unc, what are you searching for?"

He didn't answer, but as he got nearer I heard, "Where are you? Where the hell are you? Don't you hide from me."

The guy might be in his seventies, but he's not usually like this. Finally, he yells, nearly knocking my niece and cousin off their chairs. "There you are! There's my damn gin!"

Don't need an ancestry kit for him; he's surely one of us.

Scanning our crowd, I noticed Mason was seated on the sand next to his dad. Must have been some trouble between him and his older sister, Emily. Their dad was always ahead of the game with the father-son time-out. He'd distract the boy until his urge for annoying his sister subsided.

Emily is seven and Mason is five. The annoying behavior of a five-year-old is always repaid with a smack by an older sister, so why does he ride her all the time?

The older cousins and their friends were joined by a few onlookers as they assembled a huge shark kite. Last night, before they hit the boardwalk, they decided the family needed this monster. It was close to five o'clock when the seven-footer made its maiden voyage. Resembling the Hindenburg, it drew the attention of all nearby.

Once the kite was aloft, Mike pulled two rolls of kite twine out of his pocket. Alex had two more and this gave them five rolls. Ethan, paying close attention as one roll expired, tied on another … and another and another until the shark had three thousand feet of line attached.

With almost a half mile of line stretching eastward over the Atlantic, the shark was still visible. While the airborne division worked their kite, the rest seemed preoccupied with making the coolers lighter to carry back home.

Some of the younger members were in a nap-time mood, aka cranky. Mason sat next to me and asked for a sip of my Guinness. One small taste and his face showed the telltale sign he'd rather stick to his water or two percent milk.

His expression was as if a bulb had gone off in his head. Up and gone he was, only to be back in a flash. "Uncle Brett, can you fix Baba?"

Looking down, I saw the most disheveled, sand-covered, worn-out, stuffed sheep on the planet. Besides its years-of-usage body, it only had three legs. Well, maybe an inch of the fourth. I had to inquire: "Where did this sheep come from?"

Mason replied, "Its a lamb, not a sheep. It's for Emi. Can you fix that leg? She'll be nice to me if you fix it."

I was thinking, why not help the kid? Maybe his sister and the others will be more understanding. Maybe even let him play with them. So, I reached into the cooler for another hydration device and scanned the surroundings for useful tools to aid the job at hand.

One long swig. "Ah. Here we go, lad. Grab that string over there and we'll make a knot on this stub." Holding the lamb on my knee, I pushed the protruding stuffing back inside and tied the string around the tiny appendage.

Good as new. Well, as good as its gonna be today." I threw the lamb underhand toward the boy's outstretched hands. As if by magic, the sheep abruptly disappeared. Gone. Vanished.

I choked out, "What the?"

Mason yelled, "Baba's flying!"

Yeah, truer words were never spoken. Baba was flying.

The crew working the kite wanted to see just how high over the ocean their shark would go. Ethan had let go of the string at the exact time I let go of Baba. While still holding my beer, I nearly fell over backward.

The guys in charge of the kite wondered what was following their shark upward. Was it a snag? Could it be a potato chip bag? Had the string wrapped around a piece of garbage? No, quite the contrary. That wasn't debris pulling a Mary Poppins—it was Baba.

Rearranging my backside in my chair, I pulled two cans out of the cooler. Pulling both tabs, I called Stevie over. "Here, have a Coke. Don't tell your Mom or Dad what just happened. And especially don't tell your sister."

While we enjoyed our calm comradery after the debacle, the rest of the clan started packing up. Each family had its coolers and umbrellas neatly arranged and ready to go. The speed and organization resembled troops departing Camp Lejeune ... except for one family. Emily, along with her mom and dad, were walking a thirty-yard circumference from where they had sat.

I finished my beer, took Mason's empty can, and headed toward the trashcan. "Hey, guys. What are you looking for? Can Mason and I help?"

Emily's Mom turned. "Sure. Seems Emi's misplaced her Baba."

Paul Geiger lives in, and enjoys the world of, Ocean City, Maryland. He and his wife spend the majority of their time at the water's edge, either in Ocean City or Key West. Paul's writings are mostly mysteries from familiar places: Ocean City, Maryland; Baltimore, Maryland; and Key West, Florida. "Baba's Flying" could be a typical observation of why everyone loves to visit our Delaware and Maryland beaches.

Catching Up

By Susan Towers

Gladys Evans and Florence Wingate meandered along the Rehoboth Beach boardwalk, arm in arm, just as they had done on August mornings for the last ten years. They arrived early for the sunrise and relished watching the vibrant orange hues stretch across the sky and reflect upon the wet sand.

"I feel so spiritual. It's as if we are being reborn." Gladys stopped and watched the sun peek over the horizon before it disappeared behind wafer-like clouds low in the sky.

Florence dropped her arm and held her hands closely to her chest. "Magnificent." She closed her eyes and took a slow deep breath. She had felt a twinge in her knee after walking so long from where they parked the car.

"Aren't we lucky to experience such an inspiring sunrise? I have to get a photograph." Gladys pulled her cell phone out of her Baggallini shoulder bag and focused on the horizon.

"Don't forget to send it to me. Are you going to post it on Facebook?" Florence couldn't help herself. She was hooked on Facebook. Who would have thought she had a doctorate in nineteenth-century British literature? She enjoyed seeing herself as someone different than what one would expect of a retired professor.

"I'm not completely sure how to do that. You do it." Gladys handed her cell to Florence. Technology stumped her. She had only agreed to take the phone because her son bought it for her and said she needed it "in case something happened." She didn't want to think about what that "something" might be.

Florence quickly tapped the phone several times with her index finger. "There," she said, handing it back. "Gladys, you have to learn how to use it."

"I know. Michael says I need it for emergencies. He says he worries about me."

"It's a far cry from the old black rotary, isn't it?" Florence, steering the conversation away from possible medical emergencies, smiled at her friend, whom she had known since the sixties when she was at Brown and involved in the feminist movement. They had met at a protest and spent many a night drinking cheap red wine and discussing Virginia Woolf and Gertrude Stein.

How remarkable that after losing contact for more than thirty years, they had ended up living around the corner from each other in Old Town Alexandria. Both were retired and widowed, and they had run into each other at Sacred Circle book store on King Street.

"I wish I had kept that old phone. It would go in my living room." Gladys had decorated her townhouse with an eclectic mix of Persian rugs, rosewood furniture from China, and framed posters of works by Klimt and Dali. She had taught twentieth-century history and had written several books on artists of World War II Europe. "Besides, that phone was so easy to use."

"It didn't have Siri, though." Florence chuckled.

"Siri? What's that?" Gladys scrunched her nose as she tried to figure out what Florence was talking about.

"You can ask questions of your cell phone. Just push the button at the bottom."

The two women, who some might refer to as "elderly," stood in the middle of the Rehoboth boardwalk as Florence tried to explain how Siri worked.

"Watch out!" Florence yelled, as she pulled her friend out of the way of a group of speeding cyclists.

"Can you imagine coming all the way to Rehoboth, only to get run over by a bicycle?" Gladys couldn't stop laughing. Anxiety-prone, she had managed the DC beltway, maneuvered the Bay Bridge (barely breathing), avoided a truck while turning left too quickly off Route 50, and now faced potential injury from a bicycle.

"That would have been something. I'm starved. Breakfast at Robin Hood?" Florence knew Robin Hood would be open and guided Gladys forward, even before she had time to answer.

The aroma of fried bacon and fresh coffee met them as they walked into the small diner. The place was bustling with waitresses pouring coffee and taking orders as dishes clattered in the background.

Gladys and Florence ate at least one breakfast at Robin Hood every summer. The family-owned diner served the kind of breakfast they had enjoyed as kids: real scrambled eggs, thick and meaty bacon, home fries, and toast slathered in butter.

"When I was a child, my mother used to let me sip her coffee when we sat at a restaurant counter." Gladys smiled and shook her head as she thought of the creamy flavor of her mother's coffee, which was mostly half-and-half.

"I wasn't allowed to drink coffee." Florence, who had ordered two eggs sunny side up, broke the yolk with her fork so it could run onto the home fries. Something else she figured a professor wasn't expected to do.

"So, what's on the agenda today?" Gladys poured strawberry syrup on her French toast. *Pure decadence.*

Their annual August week together at the beach was like a college girls' vacation. It was a time to catch up with each other and have fun at the same time. They'd visit their favorite stores on the Avenue and walk the path near Gordon's Pond, binoculars hanging from their necks, in hopes of seeing an egret, heron, or any other waterfowl. They'd write poetry on the beach and read it back to each other. They'd argue about who had the best sushi. They'd drink loads of wine and more than a few cosmos, which had been recently added to their list of favorite beverages.

"It's going to be hot today. Maybe we should hang out at the pool and take in a movie later." Florence finished the last bit of home fries. *Better not have those every day.*

Gladys noticed Florence was reaching under the table and rubbing her leg. It was something she hadn't seen her do before. "Are you OK?"

"It's nothing. My right knee hurts now and again. It happened to have picked this morning."

"Why don't you sit on the bench outside and I'll go get the car." Gladys was surprised to see Florence admitting to any kind of pain. She was the athlete of the two of them. Gladys had not liked sports much and had avoided exercise. Her doctor had lectured her about living a healthier lifestyle while prescribing her cholesterol medication. She was heavier than she wanted to be and had made herself walk a mile every morning.

"That might not be a bad idea. I'll sit over there." Florence pointed to a nearby bench as they walked out of the restaurant. The parking spaces were filling up. Two small children with buckets in hand ran alongside a woman pushing a stroller.

"I'm sure I remember where we left the car. It's not far." Gladys headed toward First Street. Since they had decided to stay in a hotel on the highway this trip, they had driven to the boardwalk for sunrise. No problem getting a parking place that time of the morning.

She walked to Baltimore Avenue as fast as she could and to Café Azafran, where she was sure she had parked the car. It was one of her favorite spots, right around the corner from the Avenue, down from the boardwalk and under some shade trees. It wasn't there. "Oh no."

She walked to the middle of the street and looked up and down in search of the tan Prius. She closed her eyes to try to picture where it might be. She could see herself parking it, right in front of Café Azafran. But it wasn't there. *Impossible*. She and Florence could not have walked any farther with Florence's knee acting up. *Well, maybe*. She walked back onto the boardwalk and went another block to Maryland Avenue. It wasn't there either. *We couldn't have walked this far*. She began to panic. She pulled out her cell phone and called the police.

"I think my car has been stolen." She felt tears forming in her eyes and a pain in her chest. Panic made her dizzy and nauseated.

"Let's hope it wasn't stolen. It would be unlikely, especially in the daytime. Quite often, our visitors forget where they park."

Gladys felt herself getting angry. The dispatcher sounded like he was patronizing her, patting her on the head like a good little grandmother. Her heart was racing. Had she left anything of value in her car?

"I'll send an officer over. What is your location? And what's your license number? I'll check to see if it was towed."

Gladys told him where she was on Maryland Avenue, noting the number on the adjacent, newly renovated house, and stood looking around. Her trousers and zippered sweatshirt were making her warm. She unzipped the jacket and pulled it off, feeling cooler in her light sleeveless cotton shirt. She stared down the street, willing the Prius to appear. *What must Florence be thinking?* She saw the police car driving slowly toward her. Stepping into the street, she waved at the officer.

"Thank you for coming." He looked so young and had a broad smile on this face.

Leaving the motor running, the lanky young man walked over to her and asked her to describe what had happened. Gladys recalled every detail and emphasized that her favorite place to park was in front of Café Azafran, where she and Florence had paella with Spanish wine at least once every summer. You had to make reservations.

"Ma'am, we checked, and it wasn't towed. People forget where they park all the time. Why don't you get in my car and let's see if we can find it."

Gladys reluctantly got into the cruiser. He was so young that he could have been a grandchild if she had one. Her son and daughter-in-law, both professionals in New York City, had decided on having dogs instead. She had two doodle grand dogs.

The policeman drove to First Street and then back to Baltimore. "Do you see it?" He drove slowly past each car.

"I already looked on Baltimore. It's not here." She was growing impatient with the young policeman, wondering if he had graduated the academy or if he was just a summer intern dressed in a uniform.

He then drove over to Olive Street and slowly headed toward the boardwalk, inching past each car. "See it yet?"

The rear of her car, with its "Read History" bumper sticker, emerged from behind a red pickup truck. It was nowhere near where she remembered parking it, positioned in front of a large white house she swore she had never seen. She suddenly felt embarrassed. Was that young man thinking she was an old lady who was getting forgetful? Suffering dementia? Oh god, he must. He was smiling at her as if she were his grandmother.

"I bet you didn't think you could walk so far, did you?"

The smile broadened across his baby face. He was probably too young to shave. He seemed genuinely empathetic, but Gladys was even more furious now. He was insufferable. What could she say? She took a deep breath and forced a smile. "Thank you for helping me."

"Glad we could help, ma'am. No bother. It happens all the time. You be safe, now."

Gladys got out of his car and into hers. She felt the tears again. *I wish the damn car had been stolen. At least I wouldn't look so silly.* She grabbed the hot steering wheel, started the ignition, and turned on the air conditioning. She backed up slowly so as not to run into anyone. How embarrassing to have lost her car. How stupid of her. She felt so old. Almost frightened. Was she getting senile? How could she have forgotten where she left the car? Had she and Florence been so distracted that they hadn't noticed they had turned onto Olive instead of Baltimore? She recalled they were talking about all the new houses, marveling at how big they were getting. They had talked about the flowers, and Florence had said she liked the baskets of geraniums someone had put on their front porch.

Florence. Florence was sitting on a bench near Robin Hood waiting for her. How long had she been gone? What must Florence think? Gladys had no idea. Should she stop the car and call Florence or keep going? She was driving slowly down Rehoboth Avenue, being careful of jaywalkers and cars backing out of their spaces. No. She couldn't stop. Not now. She inched through the turnaround to head back to Robin Hood. The First Street light turned red in front of her, giving her a chance to fish her phone out of her purse. Looking down at it, she realized Florence had called, and more than once. The phone had been on silent ever since she had been in the restaurant. *Oh god.* She hit "call back" and suddenly Florence's voice blared through the car's speakers.

"Where are you? I've been trying to call you." Florence's voice was agitated.

"I'm at the corner and coming your way. Look for me. I see you." Gladys could see Florence standing on the sidewalk and stopped in the middle of the right lane. It would only be for a moment. Honking began from behind.

"I thought something happened to you. Where did you go?" Florence settled into the passenger seat and slammed her door. Her face softened when she saw how distraught Gladys had become. There must be a joke in the situation somewhere. Isn't that what they promised each other years ago? To find ways of laughing in difficult situations.

"The only mystery here is why you didn't ask Siri. I told you she knows everything."

Susan L. Towers is a native Californian and a freelance writer who made Lewes, Delaware, her home in 2003. She's been a journalist for daily newspapers, and a public relations representative for Beebe Healthcare. In 2010, She earned the Lewes Public Library Florence Coltman Award for Creative Writing for an essay on the secrets of her birth. Susan, who was adopted, learned of her birth family in 2019 through DNA testing and has turned to fiction as a way to examine relationships in an anonymous way. "Catching Up" reveals a friendship between two women. Visit her website HTTPS://SUSANTOWERS.COM.

Judge's Comment

In this slice-of-life story, a small event serves as a window into decades of companionship between two lifelong friends. The seemingly low-stakes mystery is transformed into a universal commentary on aging and the anxieties of everyday life. The author captures genuine human emotion and conjures a real depth of feeling that is both specific to the characters and relatable to any reader.

Thalassotherapy

By Carolyn Eichhorn

Maeve paused at the bottom of the weather-worn ramp to slide her sandals off. The wood was rough against the soles of her feet and her left palm, which gripped the handrail as she leaned over to scoop the flip-flops with a finger. She gently shook the sand away before dropping them into her cheap plastic beach tote. The sand was soft and deep this far away from the water, and Maeve made her way slowly. It wouldn't do to lose her balance and maybe twist an ankle. No, that wouldn't do at all.

A mild breeze smelling of salty sea flapped the loose sleeves of Maeve's worn hoodie and tugged at the tote. The sun was just creeping up, and the air was pink and blue and unexpectedly warm for October. Maeve absorbed the scene, mentally cherishing the moment. When the sand became firmer, she took a towel from the tote and spread it on the sand, still folded, so her toes were free to wiggle through the dry top layers to the cool packed grains below.

She settled herself and breathed the morning in, closing her eyes to the sun, losing herself to the sounds of the waves meeting shore and the wind in her fading red hair. Unconsciously, her palms opened skyward at her sides, the backs of her fingers grazing the powdery surface. This is what she'd come for, this rejuvenating, solitary immersion in the elements. *Thalassotherapy.* The healing effects of the sea. Of course, she had no intention of going in it, but she already felt better. Not cured, but better. All in all, this was pretty good. Then she realized that both hands were empty and that wasn't right.

"God damn it!"

Maeve opened her eyes. She'd left her thermal mug of coffee on the kitchen counter. She hadn't realized that she'd cursed out loud until she noticed a man with a metal detector avert his eyes and shuffle away without even looking back. What did he think she was going to do? Chase him down the beach? Not likely. She looked up the beach in the other direction.

A surf fisherman cast his line out before placing the rod into a section of white PVC pipe. He was about fifty yards away, too far away to have heard her, she supposed, though she wasn't sure why she cared. Wearily, Maeve stood and shook the sand from her towel. She'd settle for her coffee on the narrow porch this morning.

*****

Charlotte, or Charlie as she preferred to be called now that she was back in Delaware, stared at the nearly empty fridge as if groceries might magically appear if she were hungry enough. This was no magic refrigerator though. Even the light bulb flickered a little, demonstrating a general lack of enthusiasm shared by nearly everything in the slightly shabby condo. Her uncle rented it out during the summer, saving his visits for the unprofitable off-season. He made enough to cover the mortgage but not much else.

Charlie doubted that the place had been renovated since the eighties, but it was free, at least for a while, so she tried to think of this as a phase she would overcome. She had her job at the outlets, selling work blouses and cardigans to female business professionals—the women who matched earrings to their uncomfortable shoes.

That kind of life wasn't for Charlie. Neither was college. College meant getting a real job. That's what her dad called it—a real job. Her writing was a hobby, not something to be taken seriously. Certainly not something that would pay the bills. He had no idea that Charlie hadn't been at school since April.

It wasn't that hard to stay with friends here and there. Lots of people had a couch free for a few days. Charlie always left before wearing out her welcome, cheerfully tidying up, or buying a pizza, or baking a pie, leaving her friends happy before moving on to the next basement or guest room until the summer ended. With her friends back in school, Charlie was left with little choice but to return to the Delmarva region and get a job, but she caught a break with Uncle Harry's condo being unrented.

Charlie was Harry's favorite, partly because she was the first niece and partly because they'd both felt the loss of her mother more than the rest of the family. Charlie's dad had retreated into his work, avoiding home. Avoiding Charlie. Harry had been there for her from that terrible day when she was thirteen, through high school and her attempt at college, never chiding her for drifting, never criticizing her dreams of writing. Uncle Harry was her safe space.

"Charlie girl," he'd said when handing her the condo keys, "you have to find your place in the world. Find where you fit and what you want to do. Do it soon though. Otherwise, Christmas is going to be super-awkward."

That was his way of telling her that her secret was safe for a short while longer, but not to piss this chance away. Charlie filled her water bottle from the tap and added a few ice cubes before tucking it into her roomy shoulder bag. After a glance back to the stack of filled composition books on the coffee table, she threw in a few protein bars, vowing to stop for real groceries after her shift. Then she pulled the battered metal door closed behind her.

* * * * *

Sweat prickled Jeff's back and he shrugged, instantly annoyed. *Breathe.* He stopped, tugging the bulky headphones off before carefully placing his metal detector on the packed sand, out of reach of the morning tide. He tugged the University of Maryland sweatshirt over his head with only minor difficulty and then stood there wondering what to do with it. The morning was not as cool as it should have been, as cool as he had wanted it. Irritation welled again. Jeff was annoyed far too much lately. These were supposed to be his halcyon days of retirement. At fifty-eight, he was still young enough to get out and about, to enjoy his life, but so far it had kinda sucked. He tossed the sweatshirt onto the metal detector, a gift from his sons when he announced the relocation to the beach. They'd called it *El Jeffe*, pronounced "Jeff-eh," a long-standing family joke about his love for gadgets.

You're at the beach, asshole. Jeff breathed the sea air in and out until he felt his tension subside. The water was pretty calm, just shy of glassy. *Figures.* Not likely much would have washed up overnight. He heard his wife's voice in his head: *You could find the splinter in any situation. I swear you want to be disappointed.*

Was it true? His sister always told him that he had complete control over how he reacted to the world and that it was up to him to be happy or … well, whatever he was. He wasn't sure what he had expected his retirement years to be like after shedding his career, his too-empty house, and his proximity to the boys, but it wouldn't have been this quiet, he was sure of that. Even with the wind in his ears, the near solitude felt empty.

Jeff glanced up the beach and saw a woman on her towel regarding him without expression. How long had he been standing there like an idiot? He reached for El Jeffe and his discarded shirt and headed away in the direction he'd come without a look back.

* * * * *

Charlie skirted around the cluster of middle-aged women clogging the sidewalk and ducked into the alley between Rehoboth and Baltimore Avenue to get to the Coffee Mill. She splurged on a large iced coffee instead of her usual small and continued through the alley, leaving the crowded sidewalks for the quieter neighborhood beyond. Charlie had gotten pretty good at slipping through almost any neighborhood without much notice. Even Baltimore City had been manageable if she put a fuck-you attitude on like a cloak and kept her head down. Earbuds and a deliberate avoidance of eye contact kept her safe in most situations. For the other times, she had pepper spray and a speed run earned from track team and occasional jogs.

She hadn't needed either since she'd been at the condo, having had only one close call, and that was some drunk college boys in the elevator. Egged on by his snickering douchebag friends, one guy had cornered her, leaning in until she felt his beer breath on her cheek, a shock of blue-black hair tousled over his eyes as he asked her name.

He didn't touch her, but he braced his weight on ringed fingers on either side of her head, looming over her petite frame, his pendant swinging toward her chin. She focused on it, some sort of coin with a star shape on a heavy chain. She refused to look up. Fear coursed through Charlie, but she kept her eyes on the lighted numbers, willing the old elevator to move faster. The boy stank of sweat and smoke and it filled Charlie's nose. He moved his lips close to her face, his repulsive breath sliding across her cheek to her earlobe, infecting her skin. When he spoke, Charlie tried not to flinch.

"Come on baby, wanna go to a party?"

She didn't. She scooted out at the next floor on shaky legs, face aflame while the laughter echoed out of the elevator, and hid in the cinder-block stairwell until she felt safe enough to climb the four flights to get back to her temporary home. After a few minutes safely inside, Charlie's adrenaline turned to focused rage. Keeping the lights out, she slipped onto the narrow balcony and listened in the dark. Many of the balconies were shuttered for the season with aluminum accordion doors, most of the rest were dark. But two floors down and a few balconies over, she heard them. They talked too loudly, occasionally yelling toward the sea, until quieting down to murmurs and the glow of a cigarette or joint. When Charlie crept back inside, it was a little after 1:00 a.m.

For three days, Charlie had been careful in the afternoons and evenings, choosing the stairs on her way to and from work. There had been no sign of them aside from their nightly balcony parties. It had stormed last night, so Charlie had not kept vigil on the balcony, and she assumed they had moved the inane banter indoors. The rain had lulled her to sleep early and Charlie had slept hard, waking early to bright sunshine for her day off.

Fortified with her cold caffeine, Charlie walked to Cranberry Park, scoring a bench under a tree. She balanced her coffee on the bench beside her and pulled a blank composition book from her bag. After tucking her dark hair behind an ear and taking a healthy draw on the coffee straw, Charlie clicked her pen open and wrote.

Death comes for all of us. For Johnny, it arrived instead of the normal morning hangover, though in much the same way. He was high, he had no idea where he was, and his dumbass friends had laughed and left him behind after he'd thrown up the fireball shots in the alley beside the bar. He'd just gotten turned around in the dark, pausing to rest on the beach. All the condo buildings looked alike from here, vague, white concrete buildings, mostly dark. His arms and legs were heavy, so Johnny lay back and looked up at the stars until he could no longer keep his eyes open. Then he was choking, struggling to breathe, taking salty water in his nose and mouth, unable to rise, to get away, until the pain in his chest finally subsided and there was nothing.

Rehoboth Beach Reads

*****

Jeff swung El Jeffe back and forth over the wet sand in the early morning light. The storm had meant a pretty intense high tide overnight, so he was more optimistic or at least less pessimistic about what he might find, as long as he got out there first. Over the last few days, Jeff had noticed three other dudes with detectors, all older than him he noted, wandering up and down the beach. They looked like lifers, browned as acorns from the constant sun, hunched and gnarled, perhaps a glimpse of his future self.

But today would be his day, he felt certain. He started on the north end of the beach, carefully covering all the wet packed sand washed in overnight. In several places, the water had rushed in and then out again in a narrow river, carving a ditch into the beach sand that might run all the way up to the dunes. Jeff was especially excited about the dunes, carefully sweeping El Jeffe and scratching at the sand. A few wrecks were noted in the literature of the area, lost near the Indian River Inlet. It would not be impossible to find an old coin or remnants from wreckage washed up after a storm.

After an hour, Jeff had collected six bottle shards and a couple of flattened beer cans but not much else. He was working his way up another washed-out area when he started to pick up something. El Jeffe was practically screaming. Jeff set the detector down and combed through the wet sand with a small hand rake. It caught on something. Jeff still had his headphones on, so all he heard was the sound of his own rapid breath as he scraped at the sand with his hands until a glint of silver winked from the wet grains.

He could hardly believe it. This was it; he'd found a once-in-a-lifetime discovery like a coin from a pirate galleon or something. Pieces of eight? Wasn't that a pirate treasure coin? He carefully dug around the object. It was round and shiny and had something stamped on it he couldn't quite make out. Then his fingers caught. The object was attached to a chain. With a whoosh of disappointment, Jeff realized he'd found a necklace. Not a pirate treasure necklace, no jewels or gold, but a modern heavy medallion on a chain.

He sat back on his heels in the wet sand, looking down at the necklace in his hand. Only then did he tug the headphones off and realize that a woman stood at the top of the sandy ditch. She was sturdily built, wearing clam diggers and a flowy blouse. She was turned away from him slightly, bare feet splayed as if she needed to brace for balance. One hand clutched at a lime-green plastic tote and the other was pressed across her mouth.

"Just an old necklace," Jeff said. "I mean not *old*, but, well … It's nothing …"

"I wouldn't say that," the woman said, her voice sounding raspy in the sea breeze.

* * * * *

Maeve had not forgotten her coffee a second time. The Yeti tumbler had been worth every penny. Even after she walked the five blocks from her tiny but adorable rental house to the beach, her coffee burned a little going down. Maeve decided to walk a little, her bare feet giving her tingles from scraping against the wet grainy sand. It was a pleasant sensation, like having one's soles salt-scrubbed at a spa. Maybe she should forgo chemo for spa treatments. Spend however much time she had left getting pampered instead of poked and prodded.

Even as she thought it, Maeve knew she wouldn't do that. This week was supposed to clear her head, give her time to think about her options, allow her to formulate a plan for her care needs. Part of her screamed *run away, see the world*, but Maeve had already named her tumor "Andy" after an old boss she'd hated. She would take a few days to enjoy the quiet of the shore and then every fiber of her being

Rehoboth Beach Reads

would be dedicated to eradicating that sonofabitch. She was picturing flamethrowers as she picked her way across the beach, which was somewhat in disarray from the deluge the night before. The metal detector guy was back, and just as she recognized him, he dropped to his knees behind a ridge of sand. Slowly, she drifted that way, curious. It appeared that the incoming storm surge had brought trash to the beach or uncovered trash or ... wait.

"It's nothing," she heard the man say.

"I wouldn't say that," she replied, before pulling out her cell phone and dialing 9-1-1. At her feet, a tangled mass of blue-back hair peeked from the wet sand, which almost covered unseeing eyes. "Hi, yes, I need to report a body."

* * * * *

Charlie filled fourteen pages before her coffee and attention span ran out. She felt lighter and inspired, though it might have just been the caffeine. Still, she smiled a little as she headed back to the cluster of shops and restaurants to find some lunch, without making eye contact of course. She settled on a sandwich shop with outdoor tables and ordered an iced tea and a turkey club.

* * * * *

Maeve pushed her cobb salad around until it was adequately mixed and coated in dressing. Might as well cram in whatever antioxidants and vitamins she could. She looked at the man across the table. He wasn't eating the sandwich he'd ordered.

"Jeff? You should eat something. This has been a terrible morning and your body needs to recover." She gestured with her fork at his untouched Reuben. "Is there someone I can call for you?" She chewed, feeling weirdly alive, as if all her senses were tuned to the right frequency. She practically hummed. Not a normal reaction to finding a dead guy, if there were such a thing as a normal reaction. Perhaps seeing the end of a life made her more intent on feeling and defending the one she still had.

Jeff looked up and sighed. "No, thank you. I … lost my wife last year."

"Oh my goodness. I'm so sorry to hear that." *Don't say cancer. Don't you fucking dare.*

Jeff nodded his thanks and continued. "And my sons, well, they already worry too much about me. You know the phrase 'helicopter parents'? Well I have helicopter sons. I'll talk to them in a few days." He picked up his sandwich and took a bite. "They got me the metal detector. This isn't really what any of us expected though." He managed a smile.

"No, I suppose not. So terrible. I bet that young man couldn't have been more than twenty-two or twenty-three. Such a shame. Way too young to die like that."

"What did the police tell you?"

"Well, nothing really. I don't even know his name. Maybe he just had too much to drink and passed out on the beach."

"That was a pretty intense storm."

Maeve nodded and the two ate in silence for a few minutes.

"What was it, by the way?" she asked.

"What was what?"

"The thing you found. Obviously, not the dead guy, the other thing. What was it?"

"Oh, a necklace, I guess. A man's, I'd say. A silver medallion with a compass rose on a rope chain."

"A what now?" Maeve's brows furrowed.

"A compass rose, like an eight-pointed star in a circle."

* * * * *

Charlie felt a funny compression in her chest, as if she were falling, but here she was, still in the metal chair under the umbrella. Her fingers gripped the table's edge. She thought she might be sick. Quickly, she scrambled for some bills from her wallet, leaving them on the table, though her check had not come, and stumbled toward the street, passing the man with metal detector and the woman with him. She avoided eye contact and once clear of the tables and chairs, dug through her bag for her phone.

"Millsboro Police Department, Detective Simmons."

"Daddy? It's Charlotte. I want to come home. Please, Daddy, I just want to come home."

CAROLYN EICHHORN HAS LOVED MYSTERY AND THRILLER FICTION SINCE SHE DISCOVERED NANCY DREW AS A CHILD. NOW SHE WRITES HER OWN TWISTY FICTION. HER STORIES BEEN PUBLISHED BY OSCILLATE WILDLY PRESS AND GIMMICK PRESS, AND SHE WON THE PLANT HALL SPOOKY STORY CONTEST AND PLACED IN THE TALES OF THE DEAD EVENT. HER COLLECTION OF SHORT STORIES, TEN DYSFUNCTIONS OF MY TEAMS: DISTRESSING TALES OF THE CUBICLE BOUND IS AVAILABLE THROUGH AMAZON. YOU CAN FOLLOW HER ON TWITTER AT @BMORECAROLYN AND FIND HER BLOG AT GROUNDSFORSUSPICION.BLOGSPOT.COM AND HER WEBSITE AT WWW.CAROLYNEICHHORN.COM.

JUDGES' COMMENTS

A tossing sea has the power to destroy, and the ability to calm. Some of its therapeutic powers depend on inward transformations, and some on external events. The distinction is not always a neat one when refracted through a troubled soul. And it's not always sunshine and rainbows at the beach. "Thalassotherapy" weaves a brooding, mysterious narrative from characters that seem disparate when we first meet them, only to all come together right as everything falls apart. The composition and structure of this story is especially impressive.

Murder at
The Sea Wall

By Pat Valdata

Most locals prefer Rehoboth Beach during the off-season, but I like it better in the summer, when it's alive with teenage girls in skimpy bathing suits, who are trying to impress teenage boys, who are playing volleyball trying to impress teenage girls. There is something fresh and vital about all those hormones sunning themselves on a hot beach that smells more of coconut oil and french fries than salt air.

Not too many years ago, I had been one of those teenage girls. Now, I was twenty-five, not exactly an old lady, but as a single mom I was further from the teenage crowd than the age difference alone.

I was on my way to my full-time job, waitressing at The Sea Wall. I made good money there in the summertime, enough to feed my daughter, Julie, and me and pay the rent on a one-bedroom apartment on First Street, far from the million-dollar beachfront homes. Most of the year, though, I supplemented my off-season tips by selling cosmetics. Julie stayed with her grandparents all weekend, as she did on summer weekdays until I got off the dinner shift.

It was the first warm day we'd had in a while, so I decided to walk to The Sea Wall on the beach instead of on the street. The wet snow that had fallen days ago was melting and shimmered with little rainbows up and down the empty beach. The ocean had lost the dull gray patina it gets any time the temperature dips below freezing. Even the gulls looked a little cleaner than usual, so when I came to the bloodstains, they really stood out.

It took me a minute to realize what I was looking at—a line of rusty-colored footprints, as though someone had stepped in a puddle of … I swallowed hard and followed the line to the water's edge.

Something shiny was being tossed by the incoming tide, something rectangular with a dark handle. A biggish wave sent it sliding on the wet sand, landing nearly at my feet. It was a cleaver. I could see the little brand—an *L* in a circle. It was the symbol Chef Louis had stamped on all his kitchen tools. I picked up the cleaver and turned around, looking up the beach. The line of bloodstains led straight back to The Sea Wall.

When I walked around to the front of the building, I saw the police cars and the flashing lights and a lot of blue uniforms. One of the uniforms was blocking the door with that crime scene tape you see on the TV news. Another uniform saw me coming, noticed what I was holding, and got a funny look on his face.

"Hey, Lieutenant," he called.

Lieutenant Bill Armstrong came out from one of the police cars. He was a nice enough guy, late thirties, came into The Sea Wall once or twice a year, usually on his anniversary and his wife's birthday. Ordered scotch, straight up, prime rib, cheesecake. Pretty good tipper.

"Where'd you get that?" he asked, without even saying hello. That wasn't like him.

"I found it on the beach," I said.

"You shouldn't have picked it up." He reached into his pocket and pulled out a white handkerchief. He shook the handkerchief out and reached for the cleaver with it.

"Haslett," he called. "Evidence bag."

The uniform who'd given me the funny look came over with a plastic bag. Armstrong dropped the cleaver into the bag, then turned back to me.

"Show me where you found it," he said.

I led him to the line of footprints and pointed at the surf. "Right there."

The tide was coming in, but the clear line of prints stood out in the wet sand. An incoming wave washed over one of them.

Armstrong looked down at the bloody footprints and put his own right foot next to one. The print was smaller than his shoe.

"Not a size twelve, that's for sure. More like a ten. What size shoe do you wear, Allison?"

"Seven extra narrow." I was about to ask what had happened when he shouted for Haslett again.

When Bill Armstrong came to The Sea Wall with his wife, he always seemed attentive, to her and to me; now, he was utterly preoccupied. Interesting contrast, Armstrong off duty and on.

The lieutenant told Haslett to get a cast made of the footprints, ASAP. He stared intently at the incoming surf until Haslett returned. I didn't want to break his concentration, so I just stared at the surf too. It was the same grayish green I had seen a few minutes ago, but had lost its warmth and brightness, or maybe it was just me.

Haslett began tapping a wooden form into the half-frozen sand around one of the prints. The noise made Armstrong turn his attention back to me.

"For the record, where were you this afternoon?" he asked.

"I dropped off Julie—that's my daughter, she's only six—at her grandparents' house around eight this morning, and I spent the rest of the day making deliveries and taking orders. I'm the local sales rep for Sunny Lady Cosmetics."

"The ones in the bright-yellow packages? My wife has some of those."

"Yes, I sold them to her."

"And then?"

"Then I came home, changed clothes, and left for work, walking on the beach to get there."

"Do you always walk to work on the beach?"

"Not usually. I had a few extra minutes, and it's a nice day. Or it was. Exactly what's happened, Lieutenant?"

"Someone decided to do a little carving before dinner—with that cleaver you found in the surf."

I looked at the line of footprints. He wasn't talking about Chef Louis's roast beef.

"Who?" I asked.

"We don't know yet. The evidence you found may help, if it has any fingerprints left on it between the surf and your handling of it. We'll need to take your fingerprints for comparison."

"But who was attacked?"

"The victim was Chef Louis. He was murdered."

"Oh no."

Chef Louis was the head chef and half owner of The Sea Wall. It wouldn't be much of a restaurant without him. I should have been feeling sorrow, or pity, or something, but as much as I liked Louis all I could think about was my job. If The Sea Wall closed, even for a few weeks, I'd have a heck of a time selling enough Sunny Lady to pay the rent.

"One last thing," Armstrong said, interrupting my thoughts of financial disaster. "Where's Julie's father?"

My first reaction was to say, "none of your business," but then I realized he was just trying to make all the pieces fit. Cops probably didn't like loose ends, just on principle.

"We were divorced two years ago. He lives in Chicago now."

Armstrong nodded. He turned toward the restaurant and almost tripped over Haslett, who was kneeling in the sand, waiting for the cast to set. Haslett mumbled an apology. He was kind of cute, I thought in passing. It wasn't often that you saw a cop blush.

"Okay, Allison," said Armstrong. "Why don't you go home for now.

I'm afraid you won't be working here this afternoon."

"Excuse me, Lieutenant," said Haslett. "None of the other restaurant staff are here. Maybe Ms. uh—"

"Morrison," I prompted.

"Well, maybe Ms. Morrison should take a look inside? She could tell us if anything looks out of place, or unusual."

"Good idea," said Armstrong, "if you're up to it."

"Isn't Richard D'Amico here?" I asked. "The maître d'?"

Armstrong shook his head. Richard was Louis's brother, the other half-owner, and the business end of the partnership. I knew he'd gone up the coast the night before, to meet with a potential supplier, but I thought he'd have been back by now. Some homecoming he'd have today.

None of the other waitstaff had showed up yet, so Armstrong held up the yellow tape strung across the parking lot and I ducked beneath it. At the door, he handed me a pair of blue booties to put on my feet.

"Step only where I tell you to," he instructed, while I slipped them over my boots.

Inside the restaurant, the dining room looked just like we had left it at closing the night before. The tables were set with pale-blue tablecloths and white china. Napkins of navy blue stood at attention on every dinner plate. The lobster tank bubbled away, its half-dozen inhabitants moving sluggishly across the bottom. Everything here looked as it always did. The kitchen, though, that was a mess.

Louis was still there, but already in a body bag. Seeing it made my knees feel weak. Two men in coveralls lifted him onto a stretcher and rolled him away. I was glad he couldn't see the state of his normally pristine kitchen. It looked unusual all right, wasn't that how Haslett had phrased it? And it smelled bad too—not just the blood—there was a sweet-sour undertone I recognized but couldn't quite place.

"I don't think I can be much help to you here, Lieutenant," I said.

We walked out of the kitchen and past the shelves that held extra tablecloths. As we passed them, I caught that scent again. I stopped, stepped closer, sniffed.

"What is it?" asked Armstrong.

"Lime," I said. "The scent of lime."

"Maybe Louis was making his key lime pie."

"No, that's a summer dessert. He never makes it this time of year. And it's not just lime, it's Sunny Lady Bay Lime. It's one of our new products for men. Somebody wearing Sunny Lady Bay Lime touched these tablecloths."

Armstrong sniffed the tablecloths. "You're right. I would never have noticed if you hadn't mentioned it. You sure it's not just laundry soap?"

"I sell Sunny Lady cosmetics, remember?"

"Who have you sold Bay Lime to?" asked Armstrong.

"No one yet," I said. "But I gave a sample to Richard a couple days ago. He liked it. He put some on right away. He must have been here."

I realized what I had just said. I looked at Armstrong. He looked at the tablecloths and broke into a slow smile that made the hair on the back of my neck stand up.

* * * * *

Haslett was at Louis's funeral. He took off his hat and came up to me afterward.

"Hello, Ms. Morrison," he said. "The lieutenant thought you'd like to know that Richard D'Amico confessed. He was wearing that cologne when we picked him up. And we got a partial print off the cleaver. As soon as he realized we had evidence against him, he broke down."

"Why did he do it?" I asked, as we walked toward my car.

"D'Amico said he hated the restaurant. Not just The Sea Wall, the whole business. Apparently, he wanted to get out of it for a long time and had arranged for a buyer. The buyer was really interested, but Louis refused to sell, or to buy his brother out, and D'Amico just snapped. I guess he figured he'd get out of there one way or another. People do crazy things sometimes."

"Well, he got his wish. The Sea Wall will have to be sold. But who's going to buy a restaurant where someone was murdered?"

"I know. It's too bad. The lieutenant really liked this place. So, what are you going to do?"

"I'm looking for a job in another restaurant. There aren't many around here as nice as The Sea Wall, but I'll find something. If worst comes to worst, I'll have to give up the apartment and move back in with Mom and Dad for a while. Wouldn't be my first choice, but Julie and I will manage. I still have my Sunny Lady job."

Haslett smiled. "Does Sunny Lady have any men's fragrances besides Bay Lime?"

"Two. One kind of woodsy, the other kind of spicy. Why?"

"Maybe you could bring your samples over some time. I'd like to buy some."

Now how about that, he was generous as well as cute. But he didn't seem like either the woodsy or the spicy type. "Officer Haslett, it's very kind of you to suggest that, but you don't strike me as much of a cologne wearer."

He blushed, just a little. "Well, Ms. Morrison—Allison—I don't think you know that much about me. For instance, my first name is Michael. And I *am* interested in your men's fragrances, but I would also be interested in taking you out to dinner. I think maybe it's time for someone to wait on you for a change."

I stopped walking. "You know, Officer—Michael—that's the nicest idea I've heard in a long time."

I was wrong about the cologne. He was definitely the woodsy type.

PAT VALDATA IS FICTION WRITER AND POET. HER LATEST NOVEL IS *EVE'S DAUGHTERS*, FROM MOONSHINE COVE PUBLISHING. HER OTHER NOVELS ARE *CROSSWIND* AND *THE OTHER SISTER*, WHICH WON A GOLD MEDAL FROM THE ÁRPÁD ACADEMY OF THE HUNGARIAN ASSOCIATION. HER POETRY BOOK ABOUT WOMEN AVIATION PIONEERS, *WHERE NO MAN CAN TOUCH*, WON THE 2015 DONALD JUSTICE POETRY PRIZE. HER OTHER POETRY TITLES ARE *INHERENT VICE* AND *LOOKING FOR BIVALVE*. A NATIVE OF NEW JERSEY, SHE SPENT SUMMER WEEKENDS DOWN THE SHORE. PAT HAS BEEN A MARYLANDER SINCE 1990. SHE NOW LIVES IN CRISFIELD WITH HER HUSBAND, BOB SCHREIBER.

Not Your Ordinary Thanksgiving

By Sarah Barnett

Saturday, November 23

I didn't want to go to the beach for Thanksgiving, but I didn't want to not go either. We'd always spent Thanksgiving at my home in Silver Spring, Maryland, but this year was different. When I thought about trying to prepare a festive dinner in some beach rental that was not really a home … Let's say I was going to have a hard time feeling anything, let alone thankful. Still, I wanted to spend the holiday with what was left of my family.

I had a shopping bag full of questions I didn't have answers to:

Could we prepare our usual holiday meal in an unfamiliar kitchen?

Should we bring everything we need or just wing it?

How was this going to work? *Was* it going to work?

I'd omitted the biggest mystery, which was: what was it going to be like to spend my first Thanksgiving as a divorced person with my daughter Rainey, my granddaughter Ella, and Rainey's new boyfriend and his six-year-old son? Would the kids get along? Ella was ten. What would she have in common with Jeff's son, whose name I didn't know? And what about the dogs: Lucy, my smallish black-and-white border collie who lived to chase tennis balls, and boyfriend Jeff's large, golden doodle?

Sunday, November 24

I picked up the phone on its second ring and heard, "You packed yet?" Rainey. She never bothered with the polite rituals of *hello* or *how are you?*

"Waiting 'till the last minute, as usual. You?"

"We're trying to decide whose car to take. Jeff's is bigger. We need extra room for Stanley and his dog bed."

Stanley? What kind of name is that for a dog? I censor myself and ask instead, "What's his son's name?" I hear dishes rattling, cabinet doors closing. She's emptying the dishwasher.

"Scotty."

"As in 'beam-me-up-Scotty'?"

"Mom, stop. Dad's the one who makes fun of people's names."

Right. Him. I look out at my backyard and notice the leaves of the Japanese maple have gone from red to brown overnight. "What's *he* doing for the holiday?"

"Lisa's family has a place in Fenwick."

Really? Phil hates the beach. "Too much sand," he always said whenever Rainey or I would suggest a trip to Rehoboth. He'd usually grumble and give in. Now Phil's found a new family, I think. And then I try not to think.

Monday, November 25

As I pinballed around the house—downstairs to do laundry, upstairs to hunt down a favorite sweater, and down again to rummage in the pantry for breakfast stuff to pack—I couldn't help wondering what would go wrong *this* Thanksgiving. I remembered the year Ella had a temper tantrum while my in-laws sat frozen in their seats. And the time Phil played touch football in the morning with the neighborhood dads and kids. He'd dislocated his shoulder and we spent Thanksgiving afternoon in the emergency room. Years from now when we talked about this holiday, would we remember the perfect sweet potatoes or the mystery mishap that would put its stamp on the weekend?

Probably this year's disaster would have something to do with the fact that we were an accidental grouping. Rainey waited almost four years to start dating after Greg died. She'd been seeing Jeff, also recently widowed, for about four months. They'd been to my place for dinner, but I'd never met Scotty ... or Stanley, for that matter. All of us together, like a reality show that plants random people in a house to see who survives.

Tuesday, November 26

The house lived up to the picture on the rental agent's website—inviting front porch, fenced yard, and a lived-in living room with rumpled sofa and floppy throw pillows. I was checking out the kitchen, recently painted in 1960s turquoise, when Lucy barked and ran to the front door. Rainey and Jeff had pulled into the driveway, and we went out to meet them.

Stanley bounded out of the rear of Jeff's SUV and ran straight to Lucy. The two of them circled each other, touching noses, sniffing butts. Stanley dropped down into a bow, inviting Lucy to play. We decided to take advantage of the last hour of daylight and headed to the beach a block and a half away.

The ocean that met us was a calming dusky blue. The air was crisp but not cold. Since no one was around, we released the dogs. Dashing off, they made an arresting picture, Stanley's golden curls contrasting with Lucy's silky, black-and-white coat. Ella and Scotty, both wearing jeans and sweatshirts, took off after them.

"They get along OK?" I asked, as Rainey and Jeff walked beside me, holding hands.

"Pretty much," Rainey said. "It'd be better if Ella could control her bossy streak."

I stooped to pick up a small white shell with a tiny hole at the top. "Wonder where she got that?"

Jeff laughed and put his arm around Rainey's shoulders.

As it turned out, there were zero mishaps today. Scotty's cute. His caramel-color hair almost matches Stanley's. On the beach, he kept looking back to check on Jeff. And he made me laugh with a silly knock-knock joke he heard on TV. As for Stanley … well, I never met a dog I didn't like.

Wednesday, November 27

A twelve-pound turkey, green beans, sweet potatoes, dinner rolls, day-old French bread for stuffing, celery, eggs, milk … Rainey had half of the list. We called it *tag-team shopping*.

I was picking up sausage for the stuffing when a man approached me with a package and a question in his eyes.

"Do you think I could microwave this?" He held out a plastic-wrapped chunk of meat labeled *boneless sirloin*.

I looked from the steak to him. Salt-and-pepper hair, lively hazel eyes, V-neck sweater over white shirt. "Um, people usually grill steak. Do you have an outdoor grill?" He looked surprised by the question and turned toward the ground beef in the bin near where we were standing. "You could also broil it in your oven." I wanted to explain further, but he shook his head and turned down the breakfast aisle with a quick, "Thanks, that's OK."

I considered going after him—the guy clearly needed help. But I needed poultry seasoning.

Our paths crossed in the salad dressings aisle, where he was comparing two bottles of olive oil. His shopping cart contained two containers of vanilla yogurt, three bananas, a bagged salad, and a pint of Ben & Jerry's. No steak or any other meat.

He held up the two bottles and shrugged his question.

I pointed to the brand I used. "Listen, by any chance are you on your own for the holiday?" *What was I thinking?* Maybe it was the holiday atmosphere in the store that made me feel spontaneous.

It was easier than I thought. He offered to bring wine, pie, and ice cream. I texted him the address.

"What kind of pie?" he asked.

"Your choice. See you tomorrow at two."

When I met Rainey at the checkout, I told her about our mystery guest. "His name is Stan."

"Stan?" she said. "Like Jeff's dog?"

"That's what happens when we use people names for dogs. I'm glad I don't know any Lucys." Rainey unloaded the cart while I scanned each item. "Here's what I do know: Stan's friend came down with the flu and cancelled their dinner plans. He and his wife recently separated; he teaches at Cape Henlopen High School."

Rainey grinned. "You're both teachers. Promising." She shifted her hips to give me a playful bump, something I'd seen her do with her girlfriends.

"It's just dinner. It seemed like the right thing to do. And he lives *here,* as in not even close to Silver Spring."

"But he's nice looking, age appropriate, and if he has a sense of humor, that would be most of your checklist, right?"

What could I say? I'd been telling myself to enjoy my alone time before thinking about meeting someone. Still, I couldn't deny that when I learned Phil had a girlfriend, I felt like I was in a contest I didn't know I had entered.

After putting away the groceries, we walked into town for pizza at Louie's. I'd scanned the house first for possible dog disasters. Stanley and Lucy had become quite the couple—sharing the sofa for naps and playing rowdy games of steal the other dog's squeaky toy. Oops, we'd left a bag of dinner rolls on the counter—dog magnet. I moved them to the top of the fridge.

Not Your Ordinary Thanksgiving

When we arrived home, there was an empty plastic bag on the kitchen floor. Jeff took one look and yelled, "Stanley!"

"Stanley can jump that high?" I asked.

"I'm so sorry," Jeff said. "I didn't notice the rolls up there."

I was more upset with myself than with the dog, whom I admired for his skill and determination. I'd have loved to have seen an instant replay of Stanley jumping up on the counter and then leaping to the top of the fridge to knock down the rolls. I hoped Lucy got her share of the loot.

Thursday, November 28

I was almost relieved to know today's mishap first thing this morning. Last night, after the dinner roll incident, Rainey and I prepped the Thanksgiving side dishes while Jeff and the kids worked on a jigsaw puzzle of the Cape Henlopen fire towers. I went to bed early with the uneasy feeling that we'd forgotten something. When I opened the refrigerator this morning, the neglected and solidly frozen turkey took up most of the top shelf. No way could it be defrosted and roasted in time for dinner at a reasonable hour.

Jeff, still feeling guilty over Stanley's mischief, headed to the store to hunt down a fresh turkey. Two stores had only eighteen-pounders. "Too big for that oven," he said when he returned. "I picked up two roasting chickens instead. I've got this recipe on my phone I've been meaning to try."

You gotta love a man who can cook. I left Rainey and Jeff to work on the chickens and took Ella, Scotty, and the dogs for a romp on the beach.

Scotty wandered away to study shells near the tideline. "Having a good time?" I asked Ella. When she looked up, I was struck at how much she resembled her mom—dark, curly hair, thoughtful brown eyes. She answered my question with a nod. I should know better than to ask a yes-or-no question. "What do you and Scotty usually do when you're together?" I tried.

"We play computer games. He likes me to read to him."

I had lots more questions, but I didn't want to pry. Rainey had told me she and Jeff were taking one day at time. "When we get to one month at a time, I'll let you know." is what she told me on the phone last week.

By the time Stan arrived, the house smelled like a fine French restaurant. Ella and Scotty were decorating the table with leaf silhouettes cut from construction paper (we'd vetoed turkey cutouts). "Stan, meet Stanley," I said, as the dog wandered over for a sniff.

Stan grinned. "Well, that's a first." He bent down and offered the dog his hand. "We Stanleys must stick together." Everyone laughed when the dog lifted his front paw and shook Stan's hand.

Kudos to Jeff for producing five-star roast chicken with lemon and garlic. Over dinner, we rehashed our two holiday mishaps. Stan chipped in with a Thanksgiving disaster of his own, a tale involving a malfunctioning oven and his eccentric mother, who convinced a total stranger in their apartment building to roast their turkey. By the time Stan dished out the pies (cherry and apple) and ice cream (vanilla and caramel), the six of us felt like, if not family, then good friends.

Jeff forgot to replace the dinner rolls, but nobody noticed.

Friday, November 29

Rainey and Jeff wanted to Christmas shop at the outlets, so I took Scotty and Ella into town. I was aiming for Browseabout Books, but the kids got waylaid by a souvenir shop with hermit crabs in the window. Before I knew it, we were standing around the store's aquarium watching small creatures that didn't look much like crabs. Tucked into colorful painted shells, most seemed to be sleeping.

Scotty pointed to a larger crab whose spiral-shaped shell glowed iridescent green. "I like that one."

Not Your Ordinary Thanksgiving

Uh-oh. Thanks to a girl in my English class who'd written an essay about hermit crabs, I knew they were not ideal pets. Captured from waters far from our shores, they didn't adapt well to life in cages and usually didn't live long. How to explain this to a six-year-old?

Ella jumped in and saved me. "When I was little," she said, "I had a hamster named Coco. We kept her in a cage with a wheel she could run on, but she disappeared one day. We never found her." I bent down to hug her.

"That's sad," Scotty said.

I remembered helping Rainey search the house, basement, garage, and yard for the little animal. Even after we'd given up, one of us occasionally would wonder aloud, "What do you suppose happened to Coco?"

I took Scotty's hand and Ella followed. "I bet the bookstore would have some books on hermit crabs and other interesting animals,"

Scotty chose a book about a crab seeking the perfect shell for his home by the shore. It had a happy ending. I bought Ella a book about dachshunds. She hoped the adorable cover photos would persuade her mom that their household needed a puppy.

Mishap avoided, but I think Scotty would have preferred a live crab to a book about them.

Saturday, November 30

We'd agreed to meet Stan for brunch at a restaurant near his home in Lewes. The large open space was about half full when we arrived. We'd just opened menus the size of surfboards when Ella jumped from her chair. "It's Grandpa!" We all looked across the room. Rainey and I exchanged glances. Ella was already on her way over.

Phil and a tall, dark-haired woman, who I guessed was Lisa, and an older couple, probably Lisa's parents, were seated at a nearby table.

"This only happens in movies," I said, and turned to Stan to explain,

"My former husband and his new girlfriend. Of all the gin-joints in all the towns in all the world …"

"He walks into mine," Stan finished.

I laughed. Stan was a movie buff. Then I saw that Phil and Lisa were getting up to follow Ella over to our table. Rainey went to meet them halfway. She hugged her dad and Lisa.

Stan leaned over to whisper in my ear, "Want me to play the boyfriend?"

"Thanks, but let's not make this a sitcom. We'll just be ourselves."

"I've always wanted to be Bogie," he said with a grin.

He couldn't cook, but this man was growing on me.

It was all very civil. Jeff and Phil shook hands. Phil introduced Lisa to me; I introduced Stan. I was reminded of parties I'd been to where saying goodbye was a marathon of hugs, kisses, and handshakes, and everyone was required to bid farewell to everyone else.

No more mystery about what would make this weekend memorable. This trumped the dinner roll caper and the frozen turkey fiasco.

Sunday, December 1

We'd run the dishwasher, swept the floors, and searched under the couch and beds for dog toys, crayons, and other stray stuff. Rainey and I put on jackets and walked down to the boardwalk for a last look at the ocean. It was going to be a gorgeous day at the beach—sunny and unseasonably mild. We leaned on the railing, watching the waves do their endless dance. Bicycle bells dinged behind us, and I turned to watch a quartet of riders pass.

"That'll be us in fifteen or twenty years," Rainey said.

For a moment I thought she meant the bikers, but then I saw her eyes had traveled farther down the boardwalk to a mother-daughter pair. They walked slowly, holding hands, heads bent toward each other as they talked.

"Nice picture. Something to look forward to." And then it was confession time. "You know, I had my doubts about this weekend. I thought it would be like one of those awful movies where people are stuck in a house …"

Rainey laughed. "You too? There was *so much* awkwardness potential."

"We did OK. Better than OK. Ella, Scotty, and the dogs helped. I was never bored."

"Then along came Stan."

I smiled. "That was unexpected. Turned the weekend into a much different movie."

"So …?" She looked at me, eyebrows raised, the question in her deep brown eyes that mirrored her dad's.

"It's a mystery to me. I like him, but …"

"But what?"

"I don't know if I'm ready to … date? Do people still call it that? It sounds so juvenile. And then there's the distance thing."

"Mom, it's Delaware, not Uruguay. It's a couple hours. No big deal if you really like each other."

"Easy for you to say. But we did talk about getting together in Maryland around

Christmas."

"Something to look forward to."

"Yeah," I said, a little surprised to find that this thought made me happy.

"I gotta get back and help Jeff pack the car."

"You do that. He's a keeper."

She nodded and I thought I detected a blush.

I turned back to the ocean. The tide was going out, the waves receding with every few passes, leaving a slightly wider beach. Time to finish packing and walk Lucy. *Don't forget to take that turkey from the freezer,*

Rehoboth Beach Reads

I reminded myself. In a couple of weeks, I'll cook a delayed, but more traditional, Thanksgiving meal for Rainey, Ella, Jeff, and Scotty. And Stanley, of course.

And Stan? The ending to that movie is not yet written. Still, this weekend has taught me not to think of life's interesting complications as mishaps. They're the stories my daughter and I will tell each other in fifteen or twenty years.

BEFORE RETIRING TO DELAWARE AND DISCOVERING THE JOYS OF CREATIVE WRITING, SARAH BARNETT HAD CAREERS AS TEACHER, LIBRARIAN, AND LAWYER. SHE IS VICE PRESIDENT OF THE REHOBOTH BEACH WRITERS' GUILD AND ENJOYS LEADING FREE WRITES, TEACHING WRITING CLASSES, AND DREAMING UP STORY AND ESSAY IDEAS WHILE WALKING HER DOG ON THE BEACH. SARAH ENJOYS THE PEACE AND QUIET OF OFF-SEASON REHOBOTH AND WROTE "NOT YOUR ORDINARY THANKSGIVING" AS A TRIBUTE TO A LONG-AGO HOLIDAY SPENT THERE WITH HER DAUGHTER, SON-IN-LAW, AND TWO SMALL GRANDCHILDREN. HER WORK HAS APPEARED IN DELAWARE BEACH LIFE, DELMARVA REVIEW, AND OTHER PUBLICATIONS, INCLUDING SEVERAL CAT & MOUSE PRESS BOOKS.

Beach Dreams

2020 Rehoboth Beach Reads Judges

Tyler Antoine

Tyler Antoine is the adult services librarian at the New Castle Public Library. A graduate of the English and Creative Writing undergraduate program at Temple University, Tyler spends much of his spare time reading short fiction and writing his own poems, a few of which have been published by literary magazines such as *Painted Bride Quarterly*, *bedfellows*, and *Mad House*.

Dennis Lawson

Dennis Lawson is an English instructor at Delaware Technical Community College in Wilmington. His fiction has appeared in *Philadelphia Stories*, *Fox Chase Review*, the crime anthology *Insidious Assassins*, and the Rehoboth Beach Reads anthology series. Dennis holds an MFA in Creative Writing from Rutgers-Camden, and he received an Individual Artist Fellowship from the Delaware Division of the Arts as the Emerging Artist in Fiction in 2014. He lives in Newark, Delaware, with his wife and daughter. For more information, visit www.dennislawson.net.

Rebecca Lowe

Rebecca Lowe is the adult program coordinator at the Lewes Public Library, where she is responsible for a wide range of ongoing and special library events, working with individuals and groups throughout the community to provide quality programming addressing a broad range of interests. She also is the development director and helped with the capital campaign to build the new library. Rebecca lives in Lewes with her husband, Bill, and has two children, Daniel and Hannah.

Laurel Marshfield

Laurel Marshfield is a professional writer, ghostwriter, and book coach who has helped hundreds of authors prepare their memoir, nonfiction, and fiction manuscripts for publication through her editorial services business, Blue Horizon Communications. She is also a professional intuitive and transmedium and is at work on the first of a series of novels exploring inter-species communication—from the perspective of acknowledging the sentience and sapience of all life forms.

Mary Pauer

Mary Pauer received her MFA in creative writing in 2010 from Stonecoast, at the University of Southern Maine. Pauer publishes short fiction, essays, poetry, and prose locally, nationally, and internationally. She has published in *The Delmarva Review*, *Southern Women's Review*, and *Foxchase Review*, among others. Her work can also be read in anthologies featuring Delaware writers. She judges writing nationally, as well as locally, and works with individual clients as a developmental editor. Her latest collection, *Traveling Moons*, is a compilation of nature writing. Donations from sales help the Kent County SPCA equine rescue center. Pauer was awarded the 2019 Delaware Division of the Arts Literary Fellow in Creative Nonfiction. This is her third literary fellowship from the DDoA.

Ron Sauder

Ron Sauder is the owner of Secant Publishing, LLC, an independent publishing company based in Salisbury, Maryland, that has been publishing award-winning fiction and nonfiction books with a largely regional focus since 2014. Prior to moving to Delmarva with his wife Debbie, a chemistry professor, he spent his career in newspaper journalism and university public relations in Richmond, Baltimore, and Atlanta. He is a past president of the Eastern Shore Writers Association. See www.secantpublishing.com.

Want to see *your* story in a Rehoboth Beach Reads book?

The Rehoboth Beach Reads Short Story Contest

The goal of the Rehoboth Beach Reads Short Story Contest is to showcase high-quality writing while creating a great book for summer reading. The contest seeks the kinds of short, engaging stories that help readers relax, escape, and enjoy their time at the beach.

Each story must incorporate the year's theme and have a strong connection to Rehoboth Beach (writers do not have to live in Rehoboth). The contest opens March 1 of each year and closes July 1. The cost is $10/entry. Cash prizes are awarded for the top stories and 20–25 stories are selected by the judges to be published in that year's book. Contest guidelines and entry information is available at: *catandmousepress.com/contest.*

Also from Cat & Mouse Press

Other Rehoboth Beach Reads Books

Beach Pulp

From giant creatures to ghostly specters and from heroic superheroes to hard-boiled detectives, our beaches are in for a shock. Set in Rehoboth, Bethany, Cape May, Lewes, Ocean City, and other beach towns!

Sandy Shorts

Bad men + bad dogs + bad luck = great beach reads. The characters in these stories ride the ferry, barhop in Dewey, stroll through Bethany, and run wild in Rehoboth. Now available: *More Sandy Shorts*

Children's Books

Fun with Dick and James

Follow the escapades of Dick and James (and their basset hound, Otis) as they navigate the shifting sand of Rehoboth Beach, facing one crazy conundrum after another.

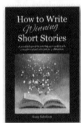

How To Write Winning Short Stories

A concise guide to writing short stories that includes preparation, theme and premise, title, characters, dialogue, setting, and more.

Online Newspaper

Jam-packed with articles on the craft of writing, editing, self-publishing, marketing, and submitting. Free. Writingisashorething.com

Come play with us!

www.catandmousepress.com
www.facebook.com/catandmousepress

Cat & Mouse Press

A Playful Publisher

When You Want a Book at the Beach

Come to Your Bookstore at the Beach

- Fiction
- Nonfiction
- Children's Books & Toys
- Local Authors
- Distinctive Gifts
- Signings/Readings

Browseabout Books
133 Rehoboth Avenue
Rehoboth Beach, DE 19971
www.browseaboutbooks.com

Made in the USA
Middletown, DE
30 June 2021

43177646R00137